SELECTED SHORTS
AND OTHER METHODS OF
TIME TRAVEL

David Goodberg

Blue World Publications
Los Angeles, CA

Selected Shorts and Other Methods of Time Travel
First Edition
© 2011 David Goodberg

Printed in the United States of America

ISBN 978-0-9827041-0-3
Library of Congress Control Number: 2010927344

Blue World Publications
5482 Wilshire Blvd.
Suite 310
Los Angeles, CA 90036
www.blueworldpublications.com

Recycled
Supporting responsible use
of forest resources
www.fsc.org Cert no. BV-COC-080310
© 1996 Forest Stewardship Council
FSC

"Once confined to fantasy and science fiction,
time travel is now simply an engineering problem."

—Dr. Michio Kaku
Theoretical Physicist

TABLE OF CONTENTS

Introduction vii

Historical Notes xi

The Doctor. 1

A Game of Golf 8

Con-Science 11

An Education for the Ages. 45

The Celebrated. 59

Staging a Scene 63

Synecdoche. 70

The Good Book 73

The Perfectionist 82

21x Watch. 89

Mercy Blow. 111

Timing of a Mad Man 115

Disabled 120

The Others. 124

An Opportunity of a Lifetime 128

Rubber Reality 133

World at War 142

A Letter from Vesta 148

The New World 152

Precautions 161
A Letter to Vesta 166
Abandoned 169
Flying Cars 172
1912 184
Frozen in Time 193
Research Methods 201
Flying Pigs 209
The Berserked 214
Selected Shorts 219
Amnesia 243
One Last Meal 248
A Familiar Face of Death 251
The Preservation Society 258
Weather Channels 261
Double 266
One for All 282
The Garbage Man 290

INTRODUCTION
FROM A DISTANCE:
AN AGENCY BEYOND TIME

I DON'T KNOW HOW IT HAPPENED. It came to me suddenly, but why my particular vision? Was there nothing else to see? Rather than a list of World Cup champions or winning lottery numbers, I saw the future of transportation. It was more linear and less mass-transit than I'd thought it would be.

Time, I've learned, is constant. There is no 'future' and there is no 'past.' Time is all happening at once. The idea of time travel, then, is not really that you're traveling forward or backward; you're traveling side to side, skipping off your current timeline and creating your own new path. Mind you, the idea of time is merely a fabrication of mankind. It's an illusion that helps us control our perceived realities and is subject to our relative position.

I believe that I experienced a hiccup, or a loop within time. I wasn't temporarily insane, I wasn't hallucinating from fatigue, and I wasn't obsessed with science-fiction scenarios or mind control or the idea of alien abductions. Those are illnesses, phenomena and wishful inklings. What I experienced was real.

It happened during an uneventful afternoon walk to the grocery store. I hadn't gone two blocks from my apartment when something struck my eye. Somethings, actually: Five strange-looking cars passed me on the road. One or two I might have shrugged off, but five?

Some people would have called them 'old-time' cars; enthusiasts might have even been able to identify their make, model, and year. I stopped to get a better look. As I stood there, a young woman wearing what had to be early 20th century attire walked past me. *What?* I thought, confused. It wasn't Halloween and five cars plus a woman in period clothing was just too odd to ignore. Something strange was happening.

I continued to walk and reached my destination: Tony's Food Store. Except it was no longer Tony's Food Store. In place of the familiar painted sign hung a fancy, brightly-lit marquee that proclaimed the building to be home to Antonio's Slaung Foods & Gifts. *Must be an international buy-out*, I thought as I stepped inside. I began to believe that I might be dislocated in time when I spotted a floating man with three eyes carrying a glowing sphere.

As I examined my surroundings more closely, I realized that everything was different. People were hovering inches off the ground, aisles were not parallel or perpendicular but rather looked like a twisted M. C. Escher sketch; and the checkout lines weren't lines at all. It appeared that people passed a tall, black pole carrying their purchases, and when it gave a reassuring ding, they were on their way.

I had no clue as to what was happening. The best thing to do, I thought, was to step outside and talk to people (or beings, as some looked to be) to try and understand where I was.

This experience is how I came to know about *From a Distance*, the world's first time travel business. Established in 2052, it quickly became the most dominant agency in its field. Many independents tried to get into commercial time travel but nearly all were unsuccessful. Some of their clients were decapitated, some suffered severe burns, some disappeared, and many died—not exactly the hallmarks of a successful enterprise.

From a Distance became not only the longest running and most powerful corporate time agency, it also became the safest, cheapest, and most reliable resource for time travelers. Secrecy, though, was its most fascinating aspect. No one knows for sure what happens after you've traveled to your destination. Nothing is guaranteed and no one returns. *From a Distance* has no liabilities. Since none of its clients return, it's hard to imagine what liability it *could* have. One thing is for sure: Unlike its competitors, *From a Distance* has shown no sign of concern.

One of their competitors gave them a run for their money, however. Ten years after *From a Distance* had established itself, *Wishful Travels* opened locations all across the globe. It started off seemingly well, but within four months, all 200 locations had been burned to the ground...and for good reason.

Wishful Travels experienced every horrid problem imaginable. Most critics and theorists believe that was because it attempted to create an impossible system: to return their explorers, as they called them (everyone else called them vacationers), to their own time. That created chaos. People returned missing limbs, lacking memories or substantial measures of their intelligence. Often, they had no remaining intelligence at all. Mikel Rainer, for example, traveled back in time to witness the creation of the pyramids. Upon his return, his memory was entirely blank. His wife filed a lawsuit against the agency. Mikel refused to go along with it, claiming that time travel was a ridiculous fairytale and he would not subject himself to such idiocy by pursuing the lawsuit.

Most businesses have their problems, of course, but what happened in 2062 changed everything. On the morning of March 14th, the citizens of Earth gazed at the night sky and made a startling discovery: The moon looked different. Instead of being grey and studded with meteor impacts, the moon had taken on red and yellow hues arranged in familiar lines.

Everyone recognized it at once, but no one knew how it had appeared overnight. How had McDonald's managed to imprint its golden arches onto *an entire half of the moon?* That wasn't the only difference. Almost every restaurant everywhere was sporting McDonald's golden arches over their entrances, whether the restaurant in question was a McDonald's or not.

Everyone was at a loss for an explanation…everyone, that is, except for Brad Jacobs, the CEO of McDonald's. A valuable lesson allowing time vacationers to return had just been learned. As a customer of *Wishful Travels*, Brad traveled back in time to the 1930s and created the McDonald's corporation before it was established by Ray Kroc. He then returned to 2060 to bask in his extraordinary business.

The end result was not a good one, to say the least. Brad Jacobs disappeared within days; rumors that he had been tortured to death by members of the Iceland Mafia widely circulated. Trillions of dollars were spent cleaning the moon and restoring it to its original state. Countless hours were lost dismantling the golden arches from unaffiliated restaurants. There were riots that led to the destruction of all *Wishful Travels'* offices and the deaths of the agency's top executives.

For this reason, we've come to know that time travel must be a one-way ticket. That way, you can change the universe as you know it, but everyone else will be oblivious to the change, accepting the world that's presented to them.

HISTORICAL NOTES:
TERMINOLOGY OF YOUR FUTURE

INTERGALACTIC PLANETARY GOVERNANCE ALLIANCE (IPGA)
1. Interplanetary science, social and military alliance
2. Established to create interplanetary peace and security
3. Promotes social and economic progress
4. Facilitates corruption amongst planetary government and provides a mechanism for international law
5. Consists of 172 member planets and 27 member solar systems

UNIFICATION OF UNIONS
1. Worldwide organization formed on Earth in 2190 to unify all countries and governments
2. Created a worldwide supranation in 2223

WORLDS WAR OF 2267
1. An 8-year war (in Earth years) between the Opus and Odieus solar systems that began in 2267
2. Combat involved 18 civilian planets in the first year and a total of 45 by the final year
3. A war credited with enabling rich networks of planets to get richer at the expense of afflicted planets

CONFIRMATORY SUCCESS
1. A policy enforced by the IPGA to promote equal opportunity within employment, education, and heath programs
2. Breakthrough policy to combat discrimination against planetary origin

JASPER (JAZZ-PER)
1. A planet in the Opus galaxy
2. Native peoples are called Jasperians
3. Frequently cited example of an afflicted planet worsened economically and socially by the Worlds War of 2267

EARTHIAN
1. Having been born beneath the Earth's ozone layer
2. Legal citizen of Earth for a minimum of five years

EXTINCT ANIMALS OF EARTH (A SHORT LIST)

Bos Taurus	Cattle (cows)
Dodo	Flightless bird (related to the pigeon and dove)
Quagga	Zebra subspecies
Tarpan	Wild horse

HISTORIC DOLLARS (HSTD)
1. Currency of the United States up to 2044
2. Currency that was deemed unreliable after the credit crack disaster in 2044

PRIEGO (PRY-E-GO)
1. Prior-self
2. An exact DNA double of one's self, encountered after traveling through time or skipping dimensions

TELEPORTVISION
1. Telecommunication medium that surpassed standard television and 3D television as the primary form of moving image entertainment
2. A television with three-dimensional depth in a two-dimensional media platform
3. A television with the ability to create a holographic, 4D environment

NOTEWORTHY TIME TRAVEL CORPORATIONS
From a Distance
Story of Life
Time and Times Again
Wishful Travels

THE DOCTOR

THE SMITH FAMILY CIRCLED THE BED of great aunt Helen. She lay silent, barely alive. She looked terrible, but at least she wasn't in any pain. The best the family could do was maintain a balance between keeping her company and giving her enough time alone.

"How are you feeling today, Aunt Helen?" Chris, her nephew, asked. All of Helen's siblings and children had passed on over the course of the past five years, making life very difficult for her to bear. In a way, it was a relief knowing it was her time to fulfill her own destiny and travel beyond her physical presence.

She was thankful to have her remaining loved ones nearby—Chris and his wife, Janice, and their two beautiful children, Jake and Melissa.

"I received an 'A' on my history test," Melissa said proudly, holding up the sheet of paper.

Helen smiled weakly. It was difficult for her to speak. Janice smiled back and spoke softly. "We have some soup simmering on the stove and it'll be done in a half hour. We'll bring you a cup once it's ready."

The Smiths walked out of the room, leaving Helen to lay in her spacious bed alone with nothing to do. Reading was a chore. It was too difficult to do on her own, and besides, being read to only occupied an hour or two at most every day. She had never been a fan of television, preferring old-fashioned entertainment instead, the kind where anyone could close their eyes and travel to any land imaginable.

As the children played video games, Janice made dinner and Chris vacuumed the living room. The doorbell rang, its sharp chime cutting through the family's accumulated noise.

Chris turned the vacuum off and shouted across the house, "You expecting anyone?"

"No, hon," Janice shouted back.

Chris propped the vacuum against the nearest wall and made his way toward the front door. When he opened it, he was surprised to see what appeared to be a 15-year-old boy, well-groomed, grinning from ear to ear, and dressed in professional attire. A thick leather handbag was tucked under his arm.

It seemed late for a young man to be out soliciting. Normally, Chris would have shut the door without saying anything, but something about this young man intrigued him, so he kept the door propped open.

The would-be solicitor didn't speak, but just continued smiling at Chris.

"Can I help you with something?" Chris finally asked.

The young man spoke, shifting his weight from one foot to the other as he answered. His tone was overly energetic, yet still professional. "In a way, sir, but the question is really if I can help *you* with something."

Another silence. Chris continued to stare at the visitor, hoping he wouldn't have to become part of his game, but he eventually gave way to curiosity. "OK," he said in a flat voice, "What can you do for me today?"

The young man jumped back into his script. "I am a medical student from the future. I understand the condition your aunt is in and I want to help."

Chris was taken aback. He tried not to let his emotions show on his face, but his mood rapidly went from hopeless wonder into utter confusion. A 15-year-old medical student was far-fetched enough. Who would believe that he was from the future? Then again, his aunt's imminent death made it impossible for Chris to logically assess the situation. He had no choice but to ask the young man in to join the family for dinner.

As she'd been doing every night, Janice brought Helen a cup of soup and sat in the chair next to her bed while the rest of her family gathered around the dinner table to enjoy what she had prepared for them. Her chair normally remained empty; tonight, though, the table was full, for the mysterious young man who called himself Mikvell was sitting in Janice's place, telling the family about what could be done to help Helen. Chris had difficulty believing all that was said to him, from the cause of terminal cancer to how it could be defeated. All of those discoveries, Mikvell said, had been made over the course of hundreds of years of research…in the distant future, of course.

Mikvell claimed that all that was needed to restore Helen's health were two simple, quick procedures, painless and unnoticeable

to the patient. The very idea defied common sanity, Chris thought…
but nevertheless, the young man intrigued him. Did he travel to
the past to find ill individuals and cure them? By Mikvell's time,
there must have been millions, if not billions of deaths from illnesses. Why spend an evening to help one person? Was this some
sick, twisted prank devised by a health company for profit?

Yet despite Chris's doubt, Mikvell was sitting at the Smith's
dinner table, thoroughly enjoying his porterhouse steak, shrimp,
tomato pepper crème soup, and cold milk.

The family finished dinner and the kids went back to their
video games. Chris and Mikvell remained at the table. Mikvell
closed his eyes slowly; a gigantic grin stretched across his face.

"That was one of the best dinners I've ever had," he said.

Chris looked at him across the table. He was growing impa-
tient. How was everything going to fall into place? Who was this
little twerp, and how did he seem to know so much about the
Smith family's lives?

"I'm glad you liked dinner," Chris replied. "Be sure to thank
my wife." He paused. He couldn't bear not knowing the motives
behind this bizarre visit, but he was unsure how to approach the
situation.

"Tell me, Mikvell," he finally said. "Why travel back through
time hundreds of years just to help one person?"

Mikvell's grin slowly faded as he opened his eyes. "Will I
really be only helping *one* person?" he asked. "*One* person, Mr.
Smith? What about the time and effort you and your family are
sacrificing? To no end, I might add. Your intentions are good, but
the means you are using are extremely archaic. There are better
ways of helping Helen."

Chris hadn't expected such an answer, especially delivered
without hesitation from a 15-year-old. He didn't know what to say.

"Do you have any other questions for me?"

Chris collected his thoughts and fired back a follow-up question. "Why travel back in time hundreds of years to focus on our small, insignificant cause? I mean, compared to helping the world and humanity? Why do you feel that our situation is more important than any other?"

Mikvell did not answer right away. Apparently, he needed a moment to gather his thoughts and reply. "Mr. Smith, it may be difficult for you to comprehend, but my presence—"

Mikvell was interrupted by Janice walking back into the dining room. Mikvell smiled. "Shall we?" he asked, a smooth smile adding ease to his words. As doubtful as Chris had become, he stood and showed Mikvell the way to Helen's room, curious about what would happen next and shamefully hopeful that what he heard was true.

The three of them entered Helen's room, and Mikvell approached the bed. "How are you feeling today, Helen?" he asked.

Helen just smiled slightly and looked attentively at him.

Mikvell put down his bag, unzipped it, and took out a shiny yellow, hand-held device. "What I have here," he said, "is an electromagnetic, thermal, neurological wave transmitter."

He held it up and began pushing buttons. One side lit up, and beeping sounds filled the room. He simply stood, holding the device.

Chris began to realize just how ridiculous the entire scenario was. Here he was, in the bedroom of his dying aunt, watching a 15-year-old boy from the future cure her terminal illness by using a handheld brain-wave transmitter. This just didn't seem right.

He took a few silent steps closer toward Mikvell, who didn't notice until it was too late. Chris snatched up the leather bag and stormed out of the room. Mikvell gasped and tried to catch him but was five steps behind. Chris burst out the front door, followed by Mikvell.

Chris grabbed the young man and pinned him against the side of the house. "Who do you think you are?" Chris yelled, tightening his fists and lifting the small boy up on his toes.

"Sir," Mikvell stuttered. "Sir, I can assure you that—"

"Just shut up!" Chris yelled back. "Not another word out of you!" He let Mikvell go.

Mikvell collapsed, quivering and whimpering slightly. Chris bent down and opened the case that was dropped during the scuffle. As he pulled the flaps to the side, he was astonished at what he saw—a deck of playing cards, a baseball-sized, soft-glowing orb, torn plastic wrappings, coaster-like plastic discs, and a small device that had some sort of depth-perception monitor on it.

"What is all this?" Chris asked.

By now, Mikvell was in tears. "Please don't hurt me, mister," he begged. "I'm sorry I lied to you. I'm not a doctor or medical student. These are all just toys and electronics from my time that I pass off as medical equipment in yours. You see, there's a lot to experience in the past that I can't get in my present. I was able to secure a meal I have never had before—beef and shrimp. Two luxuries that I must live without. And for what? Is it so terrible to give people some hope?"

In 2044, the world experienced what came to be known as the international online credit crack disaster: Hacks broke the codes of major banks and financial storage corporations and were able to then create their own lines of credit and credit cards. That led to an international halt on the use of all credit cards, which wouldn't be re-introduced for three more years.

When time travel corporations sprung up, they took advantage of this financial knowledge and sent their tourists back in time with unlimited funds for spending. So now the question remains: What came first, the credit crack hackers or time-traveling tourists?

A GAME OF GOLF

A SOUND OF THUNDER PRECEDED the sudden appearance of a well-groomed man dressed in pleated khaki shorts and a polo shirt. The two young golfers standing on the fourth-hole tee box looked on in astonishment as the man approached them.

"I am from the future," he said. "Fifteen minutes in the future, to be exact."

The two golfers looked at each other in amazement and then slowly turned their heads back to face the mystery man.

"You are probably wondering why I am here talking to you," the man continued in a calm voice. "Well, it's quite simple. I just watched you two play this hole and I am here to let you know how you did."

The man grinned and exposed bright, white teeth. He pointed to one of the golfers. "You. You will tee off first because you won the last hole. Unfortunately, you slice your drive and it lands out of bounds."

The golfer shook his head, still dumbfounded, and said, "That sucks."

The man went on. "You will then have to hit a second drive, and this one you will pull way to the left."

The golfer jerked his head back again, still disliking the news. "That totally sucks!"

The man held up a hand. "But then the ball will hit a goose in the head, veer onto the fairway, bounce along the cart path, and stop five yards in front of the green."

The golfer cheered up a bit and exclaimed, "Wow!"

The man smiled again. "Then you'll have a terrific chip, get five feet from the pin, and sink the putt for a bogey."

The golfer smiled and gave out a small snort. "Hey, I'm a lucky guy. That's awesome!"

The man's smile slowly faded as he turned to the second young man, whose curiosity to hear his fate was written all over his face. "You, my dear boy," the man said, "You will receive a bogey on the next hole."

The first golfer jerked his shoulders back and let out a sigh. "Damn!"

The Chromonzondo chocolate candy bar was introduced in Northern Sace in 2088. It was an immediate favorite among millions of Earthians and quickly became the most popular candy bar in existence. The Chromo Candy Corporation, maker of the Chromonzondo, began to buy out their candy competitors, changing their bars into variations of the Chromonzondo classic chocolate bar: The Yearbar turned into the Chromonzondo Zest, the Flight 90 turned into the Chromonzondo Air, the Soar Plenty became the Chromonzondo Fruit, and so on.

By the time 2112 rolled around, every candy bar in existence was a Chromonzondo bar. Because there was no competition, Earthians could enjoy their favorite candy bar anywhere they happened to be. The fear of the unknown had been eliminated.

CON-SCIENCE

Henry James grew up in Boscobel, Wisconsin and never traveled beyond the 20 miles it took his family to visit the Wal-Mart in Richland Center. Henry was born and raised on the family farm and there he had decided to stay.

The past 10 years had brought significant changes for Henry, which had led him to a life of solitude. His father, Edmund, had died of lung cancer 10 years prior and his mother had recently passed from complications due to Alzheimer's. He'd been devoted to taking care of her, but that life had perished along with hers.

Since her death, Henry had developed new hobbies. Sadly, however, they only served to encourage reclusive behavior—he'd taken to memorizing the TV schedule and hunting down sports memorabilia and farm equipment on QVC. One night, Henry sat on his couch and endured seven straight hours of television. Deep inside, Henry felt a pang of emptiness; he knew he should be doing something more with his life. "Then again, what could be better?" he asked himself. "My responsibilities are few, work is easy, my rewards are small but satisfying, and today I've been rained in and get to watch TV!"

Henry slouched back in his recliner and folded his hands over his small, round belly. He had always been a hard worker, strong and determined. Sometimes his belly got in the way when he needed to pick things up, but thanks to his daily farming tasks, he'd managed to stay in relatively good shape, keeping his legs strong and athletic.

Just as QVC was about to begin its segment on home and gardening (which Henry was eagerly anticipating), the antique phone shrieked its deafening tone, nearly ringing the half-rusted bells off onto the floor.

"Dang!" Henry said aloud. He hurled himself off the recliner. "Who in God's green acres is calling me, and with such terrible timing?" He ran to the phone hanging on the kitchen wall and fumbled to press it against his ear, then almost swore again when he realized that he wouldn't be able to see the television from where he was now standing.

In his habitually timid voice, Henry answered, "Yes?"

"Mr. James?" asked a professional-sounding man on the other end.

"Yes?" Henry repeated.

"My name is Mr. Stubbe, and I'm calling from IHY Investments. Are you having a good day today?"

Not used to small talk, Henry blanked for a moment. "Yes?" he finally half-answered, half-asked.

"Mr. James, I'm calling to discuss the loss on your mutual fund account."

Henry was frightened. Not only was there apparently a loss of some kind, Henry didn't know what a mutual fund was, let alone any account he had. "Sir, I, uh…I don't understand what you are talking about."

"Well, Mr. James," the man said, "the mutual fund you opened last year has been losing money recently."

Silence resonated throughout Henry's farmhouse.

The caller cleared his throat delicately. "Um, this is Henry Seymour James, isn't it?"

"Henry *Salvador* James," Henry replied slowly.

Instead of a reply, Henry heard a click. That made him a little angry—all that anticipation and confusion, and for what? Nothing. Absolutely nothing. The man must have made a simple mistake. But there was no time to analyze the situation; the QVC home and gardening segment was about to start. Henry rushed back to his TV and sprawled out on his recliner. The next hour would be nothing but bliss.

Forty-two minutes into the program, which Henry was very much enjoying, QVC brought out a large, 24" x 48" powder-coated double-deck cart with 2" side rails.

"This beautiful cart is ideal for farming or any gardening need," said the beautiful blonde who was hosting the segment. Henry was enraptured by her stunning beauty, her slender, curvaceous body, and her shimmering, flowing hair that gleamed in the light. He had never seen anyone as beautiful as her…what would it be like, he wondered, to get to know her?

Blonde hair was something Henry was not accustomed to. Somehow, all the people Henry had come across in the small area immediately surrounding his farm had been brunettes…except for

Joshua, the red-haired weasel boy who always cheated and stole. The only time Henry experienced a diverse environment of hair, skin and eye color was when he made a trip to Wal-Mart.

Everything about this woman, Ms. Rachel Outterson, captivated Henry's heart and imagination. Onscreen, she continued her description of the outdoor cart. "As you can see, there is a spacious 18" between decks, and it has 4" x 10" pneumatic tires. Direct steering, too. Best of all, it can handle approximately 1,000 pounds. It's really a beautiful cart."

Henry was sitting up straight in his recliner. "It sure is," he mumbled. "It sure is." Rachel continued to display all of its angles as it turned on a rotating platform. Everything had come together: a beautiful woman, a much-needed product, and the ability to interact with television. Henry knew he had to buy this cart.

Ms. Outterson delivered her closing comments. "We have three beautiful colors to choose from: red, silver, and green. Whether you are using your cart for light gardening or heavy farming, you will find that the dual shelves and large wheels will allow you to carry heavy equipment and manage tight turns with ease. I personally own one of these carts and use it all the time in my backyard garden. It simply works wonders!"

Henry's jaw dropped. Now he knew for certain that this was a divine product he had to own. But what color should he buy? Green would blend in with the grass and crops while red would stand out. On the other hand, silver was out. It would show signs of scrapes more readily while giving the appearance of a sterile, medical implement.

Ms. Outterson continued. "I personally would have to recommend the green cart. It blends well outdoors and doesn't show marks as much as the others."

Full of adrenaline, Henry dashed to his kitchen phone. After dialing 1-800, he realized he'd already forgotten the rest of the number, so he hopped around the corner to catch a glimpse of the television. "1-6-2-0-9-1-8."

He leapt back into the kitchen and finished dialing. The line rang twice before a woman picked up the phone.

"Thank you for calling QVC."

"Yes, ma'am!" Henry said quickly. "I'd like to place an ord—"

He was suddenly cut off. "If you would like to place an order, press 1. If you have an inquiry about an order you've already placed, press 2. For all other inquiries, please press 3."

Henry was perplexed. What was this? He pressed 1 and heard another set of rings, followed by another woman answering the phone, "Thank you for calling QVC. What product would you like to order?"

Henry waited for another series of questions followed by numbers, but there was only silence.

"Hello?" the female voice repeated.

Henry took a deep breath and blurted out, "Yes ma'am, I'd like to place an order."

"Yes, sir," the woman said promptly. "Can you give me the item number?"

Silence. Henry had no idea. All he knew was what the cart looked like and the color he wanted. "No, ma'am," he stuttered, "I don't know the number, but it's a field cart with two layered shelves and three color options." Henry became a bit nervous. Should this woman on the phone not find the number, all might be lost.

"Sir, we have an Eekman powder-coated dual-deck cart selling for $529.95. It comes in silver, red, or green."

"Green," Henry said immediately. "I want the green one."

"OK, sir," the woman replied. "Let me start this up for you."

Henry listened to the soft clicking taps of the woman typing. This was truly exciting. "Excuse me, miss," he began, slowly and hesitantly, "is there any chance I might be able to talk to Ms. Outterson?"

"Who?" asked the woman.

"Miss Outterson, the beautiful woman on the TV."

The woman took her time in replying. "Oh...I'm sorry, sir, that won't be possible. They tape the shows in New York City and our sales department is in Idaho."

Henry dropped his head. "Dang."

"I'm sorry about that, sir," came the voice on the other end. "And will you be paying by Visa or MasterCard?"

Henry was dumbfounded by the question as well as the situation. Not only had he no credit card, he had no idea how he would pay for something in a different state. It all began crashing down on him. There would be no cart, no assistance in the field, and more importantly, no connection to Rachel Outterson. "Miss, I don't know how I'm going to pay for this." There was panic in his voice, as if the fate of the world hinged on the fate of this transaction.

"Do you own a credit card, sir?" the woman asked.

"No, ma'am, I do not own one."

"You can send us a check," she said. "Do you have a checking account?"

Henry was now beginning to understand some of the terminology. Although he wasn't sure about a specific checking account, he knew he had checks. Hopefully the two were related. "I can write a check and mail it," he said.

"Great. Your total with taxes and shipping is $662.72. I'll process your order with us and it will be completed when we receive your payment. You should receive your order in six to eight weeks."

Henry was ecstatic. He got the mailing address from the kind woman on the phone and mailed the check that very night.

The next morning, Henry awakened at 5:00 a.m., well before sunrise. He walked outside to see how the ground felt after the previous day's heavy, long rains. Puddles covered the fields as far as he could see; it was clear that nothing could be done that day. That only magnified the anticipation of receiving his new cart.

Every day, Henry awakened bright and early anticipating his cart; every day, he grew more and more excited about its arrival. Each day that passed without the delivery only increased the odds of it being delivered the next day.

Coincidentally, his month of waiting was also his most farming-intensive month; every day without the cart meant lost productivity. The corn season was the most important for his farm. Locals visited every year to purchase their sweet corn for supper. Also, Wilshire Popcorn, which distributed to the northern Midwest states, bought corn from a network of independent farms, one of which was the James family farm.

One morning the temperature dropped and Henry knew that the corn was ready to be harvested. Unfortunately, though, his cart had not yet arrived. It seemed like ages since Henry had ordered it. Perhaps the check had been lost in the mail...or worse, stolen. What if the cart had been shipped to the wrong farm, a farm where someone else could enjoy its glory? Every time he heard the sound of a delivery truck in the distance, a jolt of anticipation went through Henry's body.

At least the upcoming pumpkin season wasn't especially dependent on manual labor and he wouldn't need the cart for them. Customers often preferred to hunt down their own pumpkins and tear them off the vine, anyway.

The day of the cart's arrival finally came. Two days into the start of the corn harvest, as he was managing the fields in his small tractor, Henry heard the signature squeaky brakes of a delivery truck. His head popped up above the ears of corn like a whac-a-mole.

He ran through the cornfield and around the mounds of hay faster than he had ever run in his life. Sure enough, as he rounded the corner of his house, he saw a cargo van with two men unloading a large box from it.

"Hey!" he yelled, still running toward the men, "You can put it on down there, fellas! I'll take it from there." He wanted to assemble and begin using it so badly that he didn't want to waste any time having the deliverymen carry the box to the front porch. Instead, the men lowered the box and handed Henry a form to sign. Hands shaking, he did so.

Soon, the van was gone and Henry was ripping the box apart. Twenty-seven minutes later, he had a complete cart: a stunning, large, green cart with unmarked tires and two sturdy shelves, to be exact. Henry stepped back to marvel at his accomplishment. This was truly an exciting day!

Hours passed; it was nearly dusk. Henry was still out in the fields harvesting his corn. Normally, he would be inside preparing supper and watching TV, but he was having too much fun playing with the new cart to stop…and besides, the full moon permitted him to work late. The air was chilly and silent and Henry kept hustling up and down the field, pulling off stalks of corn and stacking them in his new cart.

Henry reached the edge of the crop field, climbed up a small hill and gazed at his farm. For the first time he began to think about the future—with his new cart he could increase his productivity and increase his profit, which would enable him to buy bigger and better things.

In the light of the full moon, Henry was able to see the glimmer of the surrounding farms and houses. A light breeze rustled through the leaves and along with the crickets, created a unique symphonic backdrop to the Wisconsin nightscape. Soft hills in the distance were silhouetted against a sky filled with a myriad of sparkling stars. Henry couldn't imagine being anywhere else—this was his home.

Suddenly, in a blinding flash, daylight struck. For three seconds, the landscape turned into a bright afternoon filled with vibrant, intense colors. Just as abruptly, the colors were followed by blackness. A ball of fire erupted in the center of Henry James's cornfield. There was a great explosion—debris soared everywhere.

A strong gust of wind blew Henry over. He struggled to his feet, and seeing a small, contained fire in the distance, he peered at it. Ashes settled onto his face and hair like snowflakes. He was completely baffled. At first he contemplated running away, fearing a nuclear attack, but since he didn't see any further danger after a few moments, he decided to investigate.

Henry retreated down the hill and began to make his way through the cornfield. As he got closer the light, he noticed that the corn stalks were showing more and more signs of damage. Henry stopped. There was nothing but blackness in front of him with a dim, circular island of fire in the distance. Hesitant to take another step, Henry stopped and knelt, reaching his hand out to touch the ground in front of him. He felt nothing. Straight ahead, the small fire burned in the center of a seemingly perfect black circle of empty space, surrounded by damaged corn stalks. The center flame remained with a constant, warm glow; it seemed as though something was providing it with steady fuel. It resembled a very peculiar, giant snow globe nightlight—if there was such

a thing. It began to fade to a tiny pinhead…smaller…smaller…
smaller…

Henry felt a light tapping on his side. His eyes were shut, he
realized, and he was on the ground. Despite all the strangeness,
he'd apparently fallen asleep.

"Mr. James?" a voice said. Henry opened his eyes, but he could
not see anyone—it was still dark.

Pain shot through his head when a sudden bright light nearly
blinded him; a powerful flashlight was aimed directly at his face.

"How do you feel, Mr. James?" the voice repeated.

Henry squinted, trying to block out the light. "I'm fine, sir,"
he replied.

As three men helped Henry to his feet he was able to make
out an elderly man dressed in a black suit.

"Mr. James," the voice said, "A meteorite struck your farm, sir.
Looks like you are going to be a celebrity for a few days."

Henry was speechless.

"Let's go inside before the media show up and turn this place
into a zoo," the man urged him. Henry nodded, still at a loss for
words, and led his unexpected guests back to his house.

Once inside, Henry offered the men some home-brewed
raspberry tea. All three declined. Henry was a bit insulted and
started to lose his normally cooperative spirit.

"My name is Jack Howers," said the first man who had spoken.
He seemed to be the leader of the strange task force that had
arrived on the James farm. "Are you familiar with meteorites,
Mr. James?"

Henry felt frustrated. They had refused his tea, his cornfield had just blown up, and now he was supposed to know about meteorites?

"A meteorite, Mr. James, is an extraterrestrial object that falls to Earth. It passes through the atmosphere and hits the ground."

Henry stared blankly at Mr. Howers. The three men waited for a response but Henry didn't give one. He was still trying to understand what had blown up his cornfield.

"Mr. James," Mr. Howers continued, "a rock from space that has been flying around the sun and other stars for hundreds or possibly even thousands or millions of years has just crashed into Earth and landed on your farm."

Henry thought he was beginning to understand. "How often does this happen?" he asked.

Mr. Howers smiled. "Meteors fall toward Earth all the time but they usually burn up in the air. They don't usually impact the ground the way this one did. We are guessing that this rock is about one meter in length, although we'll be able to determine more when we have more men out here at dawn. But something like this happens about once a year. We haven't had a meteorite of this size hit our country for eight years, though, so this is quite a finding."

Henry didn't care about the rarity or the scientific importance of the meteorite. All he cared about was the large amount of corn that had been destroyed.

"Now, Mr. James," Mr. Howers continued, "were you able to witness the crash?"

In truth, Henry didn't care to discuss the matter any further unless it dealt with replacing his corn. But he figured he would cooperate—that would be best for everyone. Besides, cooperation might be the only way to get reimbursement for his corn.

"Yes, I saw it land," he began. "I was sitting on the eastern hill when I saw the explosion..."

Memories began flashing back. He hadn't questioned why or how he'd fallen down or why he'd been sleeping, but Henry distinctly remembered watching the small, controlled flame. It had grown brighter and he noticed a metallic clicking noise coming from the flames at a soft, steady pace. The clicking intensified in beat and volume. Henry was ready to cover his ears from the sharp, raspy clanking. Suddenly, a single ball of light had shot straight up into the sky and disappeared into space, followed by a second, which like a rocket had blasted into the heavens and also disappeared. The bright fire dimmed...but then a third light escaped. Instead of flying far off into space, though, it shot upward and then immediately fell and hovered inches above the ground before flying directly at Henry and striking him.

"How does it feel to witness such a marvel of science? A marvel that most people will never get to see?" Mr. Howers asked.

Henry was growing tired of the conversation; he wished everyone would leave so that he could get some sleep.

"Isn't it mystical how the night glows before impact?" Mr. Howers asked.

What was Henry supposed to say?

TELL THEM NOTHING, he suddenly heard. THEY ARE LEECHES. THEY WANT FAME AND FORTUNE THROUGH YOUR DISCOVERY. TELL THEM THEY CAN RESEARCH ALL THEY WANT BUT THE ROCK IS YOURS AND YOU NEED TO GET SOME SLEEP.

Henry was confused—where was that voice coming from? He was looking at the men in suits but none of them was talking. The voice was an unrecognizable one, too soft for a man's and too deep for a woman's.

"Mr. James," said one of the men, "you look confused. Are you all right?"

Shaken, Henry slowly replied, "I am quite tired. I need to get some sleep. You can do research in my fields, but the rock…well, the rock is mine and I need to sleep now."

Mr. Howers smiled and responded, "Sure thing. Thank you for your time and I'll speak with you tomorrow. I suggest that if you'd like to get some sleep, leave your phone off the hook for the night—you will be receiving a mess of calls."

The three men stood. Mr. Howers held out his hand, which Henry shook. He left, taking his two followers with him.

Henry locked the door behind them. It was the first time he had locked the door since he had thought the boogey man was breaking into the house 22 years earlier.

Hours later, Henry awakened to the same mysterious voice he'd heard the day before. TODAY IS AN IMPORTANT DAY, HENRY. WAKE UP, GET DRESSED, AND GO OUTSIDE TO SPEAK TO THE WOMAN IN THE YELLOW DRESS.

He rolled onto his back and gazed at the ceiling above him. Someone invisible was talking to him. Not just talking to him—telling him what to do. What would happen if he didn't wake up, didn't get dressed, and didn't go outside to find a woman in a yellow dress? WAKE UP NOW, HENRY. THIS IS IMPORTANT. YOUR FARM IS AT STAKE.

Without further ado, Henry leapt out of bed, threw on his overalls, and headed down the stairs and out the door.

There was a massive crowd of people milling around outside: news crews, men dressed in suits, and scientists carrying electronic devices. As he walked closer to the scar the meteorite had left on his fields, Henry was able to get a better look at what happened the night before.

Everyone was crowded around a circular crater in the middle of his cornfield. It was as if a giant ice cream scoop had come down and hollowed out a chunk of his farm and then left a strange object protruding upward from the center. Across the crater, he noticed a woman in a yellow dress. She was standing beside two men in suits.

Henry's thoughts about the hole in his field quickly dissipated— now he was worried about the voice in his head and what it had demanded from him. It was time to talk with the woman in yellow.

The woman was quick to notice that Henry was approaching. She greeted him with a friendly smile. "Mr. James," she asked excitedly, "how do you feel?"

Henry was puzzled. Was he supposed to be grateful for such an event? "Half my cornfield is destroyed, ma'am," he said timidly. "There is a gigantic hole here and the rest of the crops have been smothered in dirt. They'll probably die."

DON'T BE NEGATIVE, the voice admonished him. THIS IS THE ONE WOMAN WHO CAN HELP YOU. SHE IS A REPORTER FOR THE *MILWAUKEE-JOURNAL SENTINEL*. AVOID ALL TV INTERVIEWS. THEY WILL ONLY HURT YOU.

"I'm sorry," said the reporter lady. "I did notice that...but thankfully, you and your house were not damaged. Besides, the amount of money you are going to make selling this meteorite will more than compensate for any crop losses."

TELL HER YOU DON'T PLAN ON SELLING THE ROCK, urged the voice.

Silence. The woman in yellow gave a little twitch as if to prompt a response from Henry. He just stood, staring, too confused to answer.

IF YOU SELL THE ROCK, IT WILL GET YOU THOUSANDS OF DOLLARS, the voice told him. IF YOU KEEP IT, IT WILL GET YOU MILLIONS.

Henry finally spoke. "I don't want to sell the rock, ma'am. It is important that I keep it."

The woman looked astonished. "But then what are your plans for it? Are you laying low to increase the bids?"

Henry didn't respond. That was a good question—why was he keeping it?

"Oh, I'm sorry!" the woman said hastily. "My name is Claire Winters. I'm a reporter for the *Milwaukee Journal-Sentinel*." She extended her hand toward Henry and they shook.

"Nice to meet you, ma'am." Another awkward silence. Claire probably thought that she was dealing with an idiot, but the simple truth was that Henry was stuck in a situation he did not understand.

TELL HER THAT YOU WANT TO KEEP THE ROCK FOR YOUR PERSONAL COLLECTION AND STUDIES. The voice sounded calm and reasonable.

Despite the reassuring voice, Henry still couldn't comprehend what he was getting himself into. He somehow knew, though, that he should not ignore the voice's instructions.

"Ma'am, I want to keep this rock for my own studies."

Claire's countenance changed to one of befuddlement. "Your studies?" she slowly asked.

I HAVE BEEN EARNING AN ASTROBIOLOGICAL DEGREE ONLINE AND WANT TO KEEP THE ROCK FOR MY STUDIES.

Henry had no concept of astrobiology but nonetheless, he took the voice's cue. "I'm an abiology…" he started, trying to remember what he was told. "I'm...ah...an online student and want to keep this rock for myself."

Claire smiled as if she was looking at a baby that had just giggled, then said, "But, Mr. James, many people will want to offer you large sums of money for this rock! Others will want it to be in a museum."

YOU NEED IT FOR YOUR STUDIES, the voice reminded him. IN TIME, IT WILL BE IN A MUSEUM, BUT FOR NOW, IT'S YOURS.

Henry felt compelled to repeat what the voice was saying. "It's my rock, ma'am. I need it for my degree—when the time comes, I'll put it in a museum."

WALK AWAY QUICKLY, the voice instructed. DON'T SAY ANYTHING ELSE OR ALLOW HER TO SAY ANYTHING.

Henry stood, doubtful of which way he was supposed to walk. TURN AROUND AND WALK AWAY NOW.

Henry did as he was told and went back into his humble home.

The day passed. Henry stayed put, obeying the voice that told him not to leave or talk to anyone. From time to time there would be a knock on his door, but he refused to answer. His phone was still off the hook and no one was able to reach him. Because there was little corn left in his field, there wasn't much to attend to, anyway.

Time passed more easily by watching TV. Usually, he never had time to fully experience it, aside from rainy days and a few hours in the evening when he used to take breaks from caring for his mother.

By 8:00 p.m., his farm was empty. It was quiet again...until the voice started to speak.

THEY WILL BE BACK TOMORROW MORNING, BUT THEY ARE GONE FOR THE NIGHT.

Not having heard the mysterious voice for hours, he had begun to think it was gone, but now he realized it wasn't.

WOULD YOU LIKE SOME COMPANY TONIGHT?

Henry froze. He had always been lonely, even when his parents were around. It seemed like he'd never had anyone to play with as a child or anyone his age to relate to while growing up. And now he was feeling more alone than ever. But what on Earth was this voice suggesting? That they stay up all night talking to each other?

Henry spoke aloud in an uncharacteristically direct way. "Just who are you, sir? I need some explanation here! I don't know *where* you are, either."

The voice answered without hesitation. I AM AN ASSISTANCE PROGRAM ENTITY FROM A DISTANT PLANET. IT IS LIKE EARTH, BUT IT IS VERY FAR AWAY. TRAVELERS FROM MY HOMEWORLD CRASHED ON YOUR FARM IN THE METEORITE AND WERE ABLE TO ESCAPE INTO SPACE. SIGNS OF THEIR EXISTENCE WERE BURNED AWAY BEFORE ANYONE INSPECTED THE SCENE. I AM NOW HERE TO BE YOUR SERVANT, GUIDE, AND PROTECTOR.

Henry sat down heavily on his couch. He couldn't help but utter his thoughts out loud. "A guardian angel…"

There was silence for quite some time. Henry just sat, contemplating the reality of having his own spiritual guide.

YOU WILL HAVE SOME COMPANY IN TWO HOURS. IN THE MEANTIME, RELAX AND WATCH SOME TELEVISION.

Henry grinned, leaned back, put his feet up, and gazed at the TV.

Precisely two hours later, the voice conveniently returned after the end credits of the local news. YOU ARE A CELEBRITY

NOW, HENRY. AFTER TONIGHT, YOU WILL BE A HERO AS WELL. GO OUTSIDE AND START WALKING TOWARD THE HENDERSON HOUSE.

"A hero?" Henry asked aloud. "That sounds good." Henry stood, turned off the TV, and walked out the front door.

Night had befallen Boscobel. The crickets were chirping and the leaves were rustling in the light breeze. With no interference from artificial lights, the full moon lit the landscape almost as though it were daytime.

The Henderson house was about a forty-minute walk away. "I'm not goin' all the way to the Henderson's', am I? That's a long way to walk."

YES YOU ARE. THIS IS VERY IMPORTANT. MAKE SURE YOU STAY ON THE RIGHT SIDE OF THE ROAD. ALL THE WAY TO THE RIGHT. WALK ON THE GRASS IF YOU CAN.

That was fine by Henry. He preferred the grass to the rocky dirt road, especially at night; there were fewer items to cause him to slide and trip.

Henry was very curious about what was going to happen. 'A hero,' he thought. 'Maybe the Henderson's cat has been trapped in a tree and I can bring him down. That would get me a night's company and two dozen cupcakes for sure.'

Henry spoke aloud, "Sir, is there anything I need to do now? How do I become a hero? Is there danger involved? Why am I walking on the right side of the road? Who will I meet tonight?"

THERE IS NO NEED TO QUESTION MY DIRECTIONS OR JUDGEMENT. I AM AN ALL-EMPOWERING, ALL-KNOWING BEING. I ENJOY YOUR CURIOSITY; IT IS HEALTHY AND SHOWS SIGNS OF YOUR

INTELLIGENCE. FOR NOW, THOUGH, JUST FOLLOW MY DIRECTIONS.

Henry continued to walk and keep his thoughts to himself. The silent night offered clues for how Henry would become a hero. He was still under the assumption that it must have something to do with the Henderson's cat.

Henry approached the home of Blake, a no-good, do-nothing farmer. Henry's ma and pa had always insisted that Henry avoid Blake's house because he most likely earned a living by selling illegal plants. Henry had done as he was told without ever fully understanding how or why a plant would be illegal. Maybe it had been stolen off someone else's property. Either way, he knew very little about Blake and his background. He just knew enough to avoid him.

Henry slowed down as he passed the house. He rarely walked this far and had surely never visited these parts. The moon shone softly on the house, illuminating the southern-style porch that wrapped around to the side. A single window was lit.

Henry stopped to wonder what was happening inside; he was always curious about other peoples' lives and activities. He stood and stared at the window, curious about how his neighbor was entertaining himself for the night.

A loud crash jolted Henry back a few steps. A lamp shattered the lit window and fell onto the porch, breaking apart. The front door flew open and a young woman bolted down the porch steps. She tripped, tumbling onto the pavement. Behind her came Blake with his right hand clenched in a fist and his left gripping a torn piece of fabric. The woman stood and faced Blake; he continued his relentless rush toward her.

BLAKE IS GOING TO PUNCH THAT WOMAN SO HARD HE'LL KILL HER INSTANTLY. GRAB THAT SHOVEL AND STOP HIM NOW!

Henry looked down and saw a shovel jammed in the ground. He pulled it out and without hesitation, swung it as hard as he could, cracking it against Blake's face. He fell with a thump.

Henry looked over at the woman and realized that she was utterly beautiful. Never had he met a woman as beautiful as she— he couldn't help but lose himself in her luminous eyes.

SHE'S TALKING TO YOU, the voice cut in.

Henry snapped to attention. "What?" he asked, slightly out of breath.

The woman didn't repeat herself; instead, she threw her arms around Henry and started kissing him wildly. Henry was hesitant and nervous. He wanted to explain his presence, but with her lips wrapped tightly around his, he found that rather difficult. Her passionate persuasion pushed Henry back a few steps onto the front lawn.

The two toppled onto the grass. Blake remained motionless on the ground as Henry and the woman enjoyed a passionate moment. When they eventually separated, they were both out of breath.

Henry was at a loss for words. He gazed upward at the glowing stars and wondered what was going on with this woman. "Excuse me, miss, but I was just a'-wonderin—"

He was cut off by the woman putting her index finger over Henry's lips. "I have to get going now, my dear hero," she said. "I have no means to pay you for saving my life and ridding me of my problems, but I hope the last few minutes were a repayment of sorts."

The woman stood, smoothed out her skirt, and walked over to Blake's motionless body. She knelt and touched his face, then quickly stood back up with the shovel in hand. She slowly lifted it above her head, thin arms straining, and slammed the shovel down onto Blake's forehead.

Henry flinched and turned his head. He slowly took in a deep breath of air to calm himself and gain his composure. Henry had never acted in such a violent way and never experienced such a violent death, let alone murder. Not wanting any further involvement, and figuring that his playtime with the mystery woman would surely not continue, Henry headed onward to the Henderson's house.

WALK BACK HOME.

Henry stopped in his tracks.

YOU ACCOMPLISHED YOUR JOURNEY FOR THE NIGHT. THERE'S NOTHING FOR YOU TO DO AT THE HENDERSON'S. WALK HOME.

Henry paused to contemplate what had just happened. There was no doubt that the woman would have been beaten, if not killed, had he not intervened. On the other hand, Blake could be dead, murdered. He hadn't killed Blake directly, but perhaps by saving the woman he had opened the door for her to finish him off.

Henry was very confused and disturbed. His mind was swimming. He couldn't stop thinking of this woman with whom he just had an intimate encounter.

THIS IS AN IMPORTANT WEEK FOR YOU, HENRY, the voice calmly interrupted. YOU ARE GOING TO BECOME RICH AND FAMOUS AND HELP EVERYONE ON THIS PLANET WITH SEVERAL INVENTIONS YOU WILL BE INTRODUCING TO THE WORLD.

Despite what the voice was telling him, Henry still couldn't tear his thoughts away from the woman and his recent experience.

Henry heard rapidly-approaching footsteps behind him and turned to see the woman racing toward him.

"Hey!" she shouted, "you left before I could get your name!" She ran up to him, smiled, and threw her arms around his lanky body. "I'm Jess."

Henry looked deep into her eyes, obsessed with her beauty.

"I am Henry," he replied.

"Henry? Would you mind some company tonight? I need to leave for Chicago tomorrow and I wouldn't feel right staying at Blake's, with the condition he's in and all."

Henry smiled, gazing at Jess's flowing hair, curvaceous body and astonishingly white teeth. He couldn't concentrate on anything but her glowing eyes. "I sure do reckon I'd like that," he replied.

Henry awoke the next morning much later than he usually did. He was alone in the bed; his guest had left without a word.

SOME MEN ARE GOING TO KNOCK ON YOUR DOOR IN A FEW MOMENTS, the voice said. THEY ARE GOING TO INQUIRE IF YOU KNOW ANYTHING ABOUT BLAKE. NEVER SAY ANYTHING ABOUT WHAT YOU DID LAST NIGHT. AS FAR AS ANYONE IS CONCERNED, YOU WORKED IN YOUR FIELDS.

Henry heard a knock. He sat up in bed with his body shaking, nervous about the impending interrogation. He stood, but had trouble walking a straight line.

DO NOT WORRY. BLAKE IS PERFECTLY FINE, BUT HE WAS CAUGHT SMUGGLING HIS ILLEGAL PLANTS THIS MORNING AND THESE MEN ONLY WANT TO KNOW WHAT YOU KNOW ABOUT IT.

Henry perked up, relieved in thinking that Blake wasn't dead. He walked to the front door in his wrinkled pajamas, opened it, and found two men in suits staring at him.

"Henry James?" the man on the right asked. "May we come in?" Without waiting for Henry to respond, the two men walked in.

"Something terrible happened to your neighbor down the street. A Mr. Blake Wilhelm," the man continued. "May I ask where you were last night, Henry? How good are you with a shovel?"

Henry was waiting to hear what happened with the illegal plants. "I was in my field farming all evening, sir," he replied. "I don't do illegal farming."

Both men stood staring at Henry, waiting for him to continue, but he didn't.

One of the men smiled and said, "How's that huge rock in the back doing? Better off here than in a museum to be studied and shared by everyone?"

Henry didn't like the man's tone; he found himself feeling a hint of anger.

DON'T LET HIM BOTHER YOU, the voice warned. TELL THEM YOU ARE ABOUT TO FARM YOUR LAND AND THEY CAN STAY AS LONG AS THEY WANT.

"I have to tend to my crops, sirs," Henry said. "If you'd like, you can stay here and wait around to have lunch in a few hours."

The two men just stared at him. "Thanks for all your cooperation," one of the men said. They both walked out and slammed the door behind them.

Henry didn't think anything of it; he turned around and put on his big rubber boots that stood by the doorway.

DON'T PUT THOSE ON.

"But you said—"

The voice cut Henry off. I TOLD YOU WHAT TO SAY, THAT IS ALL. WE ARE GOING ON A TRIP TO CHICAGO. PACK YOUR BAGS FOR A FIVE-DAY TRIP.

Henry slowly removed his right rubber boot. He had never been to Chicago…or anywhere else outside Boscobel or Richland Center, for that matter. He had no idea what to pack, let alone what bags to take.

THERE IS A MEDIUM-SIZED SUITCASE IN YOUR PARENTS' CLOSET. USE THAT.

Henry made his way into his parents' bedroom, grabbed the suitcase, and filled it with clothes. Soon, he was on his way to the Amtrak train station, following the precise directions given to him.

Henry arrived safely in Chicago. Within four weeks, he was transformed from a poor farmer into an international celebrity. He even wound up reuniting with Jess at the penthouse suite in the Peninsula Hotel.

His fame began when Henry, with his newfound guardian's help, 'invented' Teleportvision the third day he was in Chicago. The voice gave Henry precise instructions for every detail, down to the supply sources and wiring. All Henry had to do was to follow the given instructions. The voice told him everything: which line was the fastest at the store, how to use body gestures, which specific product he should buy off the shelf, even which items on restaurant menus were the tastiest based on both the chef's skill and the freshness of the ingredients. There was no reason to think, no need to doubt or worry. Everything he needed to say was told to him. All of his concerns and questions were taken care of before he knew he had them.

The voice always provided him with the best possible solution. Whom to talk to, which publicist to call, where to walk, whose hands to shake, where to go…everything was arranged before Henry had to make any decisions. Most importantly, the decisions made for him were always correct.

The voice proved its loyalty by providing Henry with fame, fortune, and the companionship of Jess. While the functionality of Teleportvision was a mystery around the globe, within months, the majority of households across Earth would own one. It didn't matter that no one could understand the technology behind three-dimensional depth in two-dimensional media. Henry didn't have any clue, either—he only obeyed the voice inside his head. He was, in short, a complete dependent. But it didn't matter. What mattered was that the almighty being was supporting him throughout the journey, and Henry even enjoyed the constant company. Experiencing a big city was something he'd always fantasized about when watching television, and now he was a part of it.

YOU ARE DOING A FANTASTIC JOB, HENRY, the voice said one morning.

Henry sat upright in the king-sized bed of his penthouse suite. Jess was taking a shower in the luxurious bathroom, getting ready for another big day of photographs and encounters with the rich and famous.

I HAVE SOMETHING NEW FOR YOU TO INVENT. THIS NEXT ONE IS WHY WE CAME TO CHICAGO.

"What are we going to invent this time?" Henry asked.

YOU, HENRY. YOU ARE GOING TO INVENT A DEVICE THAT WILL HEAL ALL AILMENTS.

"A what, sir?" Henry asked.

I'LL LET YOU KNOW WHAT TO DO WHEN THE TIME COMES. YOU HAVE A DINNER RESERVATION

TONIGHT AT MEEKAS AS PART OF THE ANNUAL
SCIENCE MAGAZINE'S AWARDS BANQUET FOR THE
YEAR'S BEST ACHIEVEMENTS. I'LL LET YOU KNOW
WHAT TO DO THEN.

Jess walked out in her towel, still wet from the shower. Henry
stared at her, his mouth agape.

"Yes?" she asked when she saw him.

TELL HER SHE LOOKS PRETTY.

"You are lookin' very pretty, Jess," Henry said.

Jess just smiled and chuckled playfully.

The *Science Magazine* party was kicked off amidst a media
frenzy that Henry had become accustomed to over the course of
the past few weeks. Everyone was eager to talk to him and ask
about the secret behind his technology.

JUST GIVE THE SAME ANSWER AS ALWAYS,
HENRY.

"Well sir," he told one questioner, "if I go on and tell you,
you'll create my next invention before I can." The man laughed;
so did a nearby woman.

The entire room was filled with people dressed to impress.
Henry was wearing one of three tuxedos that he now owned. He
had never worn formal clothing before and despite his awkward
posture, his appearance was rather impressive.

He looked around to see if he'd recognize anyone in the room
from a previous function, but he didn't. He did notice the stage
towering over the crowd at one end of the room. It was to be used
for introductions, he decided.

Had Henry not been told whom to talk to or where to stand,
he would have surely made a fool of himself. Without the voice he
would be totally lost. He had become so accustomed and dependent

on it that he had forgotten how to function without it. Henry was filled with gratitude for his guiding spirit.

DON'T WORRY HENRY. EVERYTHING IS GOING TO WORK PERFECTLY TONIGHT. THE MAN YOU WANT TO TALK TO IS CHARLES RICHARDSON. NO NEED TO GO LOOKING FOR HIM. HE WILL FIND YOU WITHIN THE NEXT FEW MINUTES. JUST MAKE SURE YOU ARE ALONE.

Henry turned to Jess, "Jess, dear, there is a man I need to speak with right now, so I'll have to excuse myself for a moment."

Jess smiled and walked away, enjoying every second that she could show off her diamond-encrusted dress as it glittered under the lights.

"Mr. James!" a voice exclaimed from behind Henry. "Or should I say, the man of the millennium!"

Henry turned to see a well-groomed man in a pinstriped suit.

THIS IS MR. RICHARDSON.

"Hello Mr. Richardson," Henry said, extending his hand.

Mr. Richardson shook hands and furrowed his eyebrows in curiosity. "You know who I am?"

HE IS THE FOUNDER OF REATEN GROUP AND VICE PRESIDENT OF *SCIENCE MAGAZINE*.

"You founded Reaten and are the vice president of *Science*," Henry said.

Mr. Richardson smiled. "It's an honor to meet you, Henry."

TELL HIM YOU WANT HIM TO INVEST IN YOUR NEXT INVENTION. IT WILL BE A LARGER BREAKTHROUGH THAN TELEPORTVISION.

"Mr. Richardson, I have a new invention in mind, and I want you to invest in it."

Mr. Richardson perked up. "Oh?" he asked.

"Yes," Henry continued. "This one will have twice the impact of my Teleportvision device."

I HAVE A PROPOSAL I WOULD LIKE TO SHARE WITH EVERYONE AT THE BANQUET, IF I MAY, the voice prompted him.

"I have a proposal I would like to share with everyone," Henry continued.

Mr. Richardson smiled. "I'll be giving a toast in 10 minutes," he said. "I'd love to introduce you and let you say a few words."

Mr. Richardson soon took the stage and stood in front of the microphones at the podium. "Ladies and gentlemen," he began. "Before I toast this evening and begin our annual awards ceremony, I would like to introduce a very special guest who is with us tonight. Many of us are familiar with his recent work—soon, I'm sure, we will all be inspired and touched by what he has given to all of us."

"Mr. Henry James, inventor of the Teleportvision, please come up."

The crowd began applauding enthusiastically. Henry stepped onto the stage and behind the microphones. He stood and listened as the voice began to speak; he repeated everything it said line by line, more or less. The audience sat motionless, thoroughly engrossed.

TOMORROW I AM MEETING WITH MR. RICHARDSON ABOUT A NEW INVENTION THAT WILL COST TENS OF BILLIONS OF DOLLARS. THE RESULT, HOWEVER, WILL BE STUNNING. LET'S JUST SAY THAT PHYSICAL AILMENTS WILL BE THE FOCUS OF MY NEURAL HI-WAVE DEVICE.

CANCER WILL BE A THING OF THE PAST, AND THAT'S JUST THE BEGINNING. WE ALL KNOW

ABOUT MY TELEPORTVISION AND WHAT IT WILL BRING TO OUR CULTURE. THIS NEW MACHINE WILL REVOLUTIONIZE MORE THAN JUST OUR TECHNOLOGY. IT WILL REVOLUTIONIZE THE HUMAN RACE AS WE KNOW IT.

Henry finished his speech; the crowd roared with excitement. Mr. Richardson walked to the podium, patted Henry on the back and shook his hand once more. "You better hope my assistant can make room for you tomorrow," he whispered into his ear. He drew back and looked at Henry with a smile on his face. Henry looked at him in shock.

HE IS KIDDING. SMILE BACK AND WALK OFF THE STAGE. YOU ARE DONE FOR THE NIGHT.

The following day, Henry and his lawyers (who had worked with his Teleportvision options and contracts) went to meet with Mr. Richardson. He was more than eager to agree to every request that was made: use of his production facilities, scientists, engineers, and resources of Reaten Group, all in exchange for 50% of the profits from the Neural Hi-Wave Device.

"I trust in what you will create, Henry, even though you won't fully disclose the details of your project. That is why I want to do business with you," Mr. Richardson said enthusiastically. "The Teleportvision has revolutionized the entertainment industry. I can't imagine what this new invention will do for the health industry. If it does half of what you say, we will have a smashing success on our hands."

After the meeting, papers were signed and the lawyers took over. Henry was free to leave.

GOOD WORK, HENRY, the voice congratulated him. YOU ARE DOING AN EXCELLENT JOB. NOW JUST ANSWER SOME BASIC QUESTIONS FOR THE NEWS

MEDIA THAT ARE OUTSIDE AND YOU'LL BE DONE FOR THE DAY. TOMORROW YOU'LL START BUILDING YOUR NEW INVENTION. SOON, HUMANITY WILL STOP ITS DECLINE AND BEGIN ASCENDING TO ITS PROPER PLACE WITHIN THE UNIVERSE.

Henry smiled, knowing that his actions would help nearly everyone on the planet.

A barrage of camera flashes hit Henry when he exited the Chicago skyscraper. The media had set up a small podium for him to answer questions, which he did, and as instructed, he kept his comments vague and cheery.

Two weeks passed as Henry set up production on what the media was calling 'The Magical Brain Machine.' Now that his new invention had hit the headlines and there were Teleportvision demos being held across the globe, Henry became a celebrity superstar. His personal life became the major news story each day: where he ate, who he talked to, and where he was spotted; the media was in a frenzy over Henry. As more details about the Teleportvision release became public, everyone wanted to know more and more about him: who he was, what he liked, and how a genius with no formal education had emerged out of the middle of nowhere, Wisconsin.

Over 30 billion dollars were invested in Henry's Brain Machine. Most of the money was spent on a limited, rare resource that was virtually unknown to mankind. Found miles below the surface in the Chersky mountain range (which was located in what had been Siberia), scientists were perplexed as to what Henry was requesting—they didn't know how the substance should be categorized or used. This, combined with *substance x*, as Henry referred to it, created unprecedented amounts of energy. Unbeknown to the scientists, *substance x* was extracted from a piece of the meteorite that had fallen on Henry's farm. Henry was given strict instruction to never reveal the source to anyone.

Many scientific advances were made through the production of the Brain Machine: new strategic uses of lasers, previously unknown elements (some unstable), and bizarre methods of synching mechanical movements with the rotation of the Earth and alignment of constellations. The scientists who worked on Henry's invention were astonished, but remained true to their agreement of secrecy. They told the media only a few words: "This is unlike anything we have ever seen."

At a press conference, Henry announced that the first test of the Brain Machine would be a public demonstration. Still not knowing exactly what it would do, he finished the final touches on the machine just moments before he unveiled it.

Thousands attended the demonstration. It was also set to broadcast live on television and, for the lucky ones, Teleportvision.

Henry stood in front of the euphoric crowd and prepared to unveil his highly-anticipated Brain Machine. The crowd was eager to see it; it had been 15 months in the making.

NEARLY EVERYONE IN THE WORLD IS WATCHING YOU RIGHT NOW, HENRY. JUST RELAX AND REPEAT AFTER ME. REMEMBER THAT TODAY YOU ARE MAKING EARTH HISTORY.

Despite the voice's calm certainty, Henry was nervous. Nothing that had happened since his move to Chicago had prepared him for what was about to happen; he was about to speak to hundreds of thousands of people, if not millions or even billions. For well over a year, nothing had been required of Henry except to obey. No independent thought was necessary, yet he knew that everything would work out in the end. Now he was center stage in front of a massive crowd and countless cameras. Body shaking and voice trembling, he was having trouble controlling his emotions.

CLOSE YOUR EYES AND THINK OF YOUR MOTHER, HENRY.

Henry dutifully envisioned his life back in Wisconsin, enjoying a home-cooked meal with his parents.

YOU NEED TO TALK TO THESE PEOPLE. THEY NEED YOU. NO NEED TO BE NERVOUS—THERE IS NOTHING TO BE NERVOUS ABOUT.

Henry began to get over his stage fright—he did, after all, need to introduce an important scientific discovery to the world. He concentrated on repeating what the voice told him. "Today, I am unveiling my new invention, the Gatsby!" he shouted.

The crowd roared as Henry tugged on a thick rope, pulling down the large sheets that covered the giant Brain Machine. It was the height of a small building and consisted of large cylindrical objects. A clear tube stood in the center of the machine, sized to fit an average human.

He continued with his speech as the crowd began to settle down. "What I have created here is something that will benefit all humankind, something that will help us focus on the issues of tomorrow and stop wallowing in the problems of the past. All cancers, viruses, and syndromes will become no more problematic than a common cold!"

The crowd cheered again as Henry shuffled his feet somewhat nervously. He waited for the crowd to calm down before continuing. "Today, at 2:27 p.m., I shall be the first human to test the Gatsby. In only a matter of seconds, my physical condition will be preserved and I will no longer be susceptible to disease."

The crowd increased its applause and roared as Henry stepped inside the small entrance to the tall, clear cylinder.

Henry signaled for an assistant to start the machine and begin the test.

A low rumble turned into a soothing hum. The entrance to the cylinder closed; all eyes were on Henry. Vibrations that could only be produced by heavy objects rotating at unimaginable speeds spread into the crowd as the clear tube slowly began glowing a dim blue.

As the vibrations intensified, the light became more concentrated…then, in an instant, the vibrations stopped and the blue light disappeared. The crowd grew silent as Henry's body went limp and fell, leaning against the interior wall of the cylinder. The masses grasped their heads and covered their ears when a short succession of intensely splintering metallic-sounding cracks emanated from the machine. A ball of fiery light shot out from Henry's motionless body and rocketed upward through the cylinder, racing into the sky.

An assistant ran and pried the entrance open, placing his hand on Henry's shoulder. Henry slowly opened his eyes, for a moment almost forgetting where he was.

He stood and, after gazing back at the crowd, remembered what he was doing: introducing to the world an invention that was beyond his knowledge, and through that, becoming a hero. But something was different, something that he couldn't cope with—his internal guide was gone, leaving him alone with his own thoughts, ideas and actions.

Thousands of awestruck citizens stared at him. Billions more were watching from their homes, all waiting to hear an explanation from a man who knew nothing.

ESQVVUT:	No, Damon! You can't eat that!
Damon:	What—this? Why?
ESQVVUT:	Your kind is not allowed to eat the sacred seeds of the maerr flower.
Damon:	Why?
ESQVVUT:	Because the consumption of maerr seeds is strictly for Slaungs, not humans.
Damon:	Come on, nothing will happen. Let me try it.
ESQVVUT:	NO! They are not for humans!
Damon:	That's crazy. You eat them all day long and you're getting fat off them. It's quite clear that you are abusing the sacredness of the maerr seeds.

An Education for the Ages

B ETHANY FELT THE VIBRATIONS of the garage door opening as they gently shook the house. She leapt into the air, raced across the kitchen, and impatiently waited. This was the day she had been waiting for.

Her older brother Richard worked in the educational research department at *From a Distance*, and he'd promised to bring a special guest home for the night. No one knew who this special guest might be, but it was certain that this 'educator,' would probably be from 50 to 100 years in the future.

She wondered if he would be bearing gifts. Probably not, she reasoned. At the very least, he would possess the most fantastic stories and more knowledge than anyone could wish to hear, and Bethany was going to be in his company all day and night.

Bethany's excitement grew as she heard the main door being unlocked…but then fizzled away when Richard walked into the kitchen alone. 'No man of the future?' she thought.

"There has been a slight change in plans, Beth," Richard said slowly, placing his bag on the counter and his hand on Bethany's thin, delicate shoulder. He looked at her with confident eyes and smiled.

Bethany watched, disappointed, as her older brother walked back to the garage and shut the door behind him. 'Change in plans? Great,' she thought. 'No one from the future, tonight or ever. Just great!'

Pouting, she retreated to the Teleportvision room, stomping her feet loudly against the floor as she went to express her displeasure. She sighed and went back to feeding Darno, her semi-transparent half-man, half-monkey virtual pet creation.

Bethany had always been fascinated by the future and the wonders it might hold. As a small child, in fact, she had been forbidden to venture off on her own because her desire to explore had a tendency to leave her disoriented and lost, which in turn meant that her embarrassed parents often had to publicly announce that they'd misplaced their child and ask for help in finding her.

As she got older, Bethany developed an avid interest in urban planning and the development of parks and buildings. She loved to experience a time and place prior to construction and then visit it periodically as it was developed, always envisioning what the end result would look like.

Since the day *From a Distance* opened its doors, she had dearly wanted to travel though time, but into the future, not the past.

The past did not interest her. To experience future inventions, music and art—some of which may not have been even thought of yet—was her greatest wish. Seeing the fate of organizations, structures, disease, planning, and products would be an excitement beyond her comprehension. Being only a teenager, she knew that she had ample time to fulfill her dreams and change the world for the better.

Darno was her newest creation, a new breed of life that she had single-handedly strung together. His level of intelligence was increasing, she'd noticed, and she'd vowed to spend more time making sure that he received a proper diet and plenty of attention.

Richard quietly made his way to the Teleportvision room. He leaned against the doorframe and watched his little sister care for Darno, who was currently misbehaving. He kept climbing trees and jumping from branch to branch as Bethany attempted unsuccessfully to calm him down with a plastic wand.

When she noticed Richard, she put the environment on hold, limiting Darno's actions, and looked at her brother.

"Plans may have changed a bit, but there are still plans, Bethany," Richard said.

Bethany shrugged. "I knew this would happen," she said. "What did you bring me instead of a person? A blueberry pie that I'll make when I become a grandmother?"

A young woman dressed in a tattered black dress peeked out from behind Richard and made eye contact with Bethany.

Bethany was shocked. 'He really did bring someone back from the future!' she thought. 'But by the looks of that dirty dress, she is probably not an architect or scientist. That's still okay...'

Richard smiled as he saw the delight on his sister's face. "This is Sarah," Richard said, gesturing toward the woman. "Bethany, Sarah. Sarah, Bethany."

Bethany put aside her prejudices against the woman; she was obviously poor and possibly uneducated as well. No point in being rude to her...besides, she was still from the future.

"Sarah is from the year 1936, Bethany," Richard said happily.

Bethany's enthusiastic grin immediately vanished. "What?"

Richard kept smiling. "Sarah is from the year 1936. She lives about 500 kilometers east of us, near what was the city of Chicago in her time."

Sarah was confused. "Does Chicago change its name in the future?"

Richard gave a hesitant reply. "Chicago was destroyed in a very large war. A very, very, very...big war."

Sarah's confusion changed to shock. "You don't—" she paused in an obvious effort to clarify her thoughts. "You don't think the Great War will continue then? Or does it?"

Now it was Richard's turn to be confused. "I have no idea what war you're talking about, but the war that destroys Chicago didn't happen for hundreds of years after your time."

Sarah was so completely confused by Richard's words that she didn't reply.

"Sarah," Richard said. "Why don't you have a seat with Bethany here? She can explain this game of hers to you and maybe give you a tour of the house."

Sarah took a hesitant step into the room and sat on the empty sofa behind Bethany.

"I'll be back in two hours at most," Richard said. "I have some very special ingredients to pick up for dinner tonight. See you soon." The door shut, and Richard was gone.

Sarah thought that she was handling the situation she now found herself in quite well. She knew it was best to carefully consider her surroundings before coming to any conclusions—after all, she was hundreds of years in the future. By the looks of Richard's house, though, and its size and amenities, she guessed he and Bethany were some kind of royalty.

She sat quietly and watched Bethany wave a wand around a small, transparent animal who was bouncing wildly throughout the room. She found the scene a bit terrifying. She didn't even know what a television was, never mind Teleportvision reality. So she closed her eyes and sat.

Bethany wasn't paying any attention to her time-traveling guest. She was irritated that her brother had deserted her, forcing her to babysit for an insignificant, antique woman.

Bethany kept waving her motion wand back and forth in an attempt to calm Darno down, but he wouldn't respond to her attempts. After a few more minutes, she gave up. Darno only continued to run around, destroying the layout of the room, toppling virtual trees and random solid objects Bethany had created. His antics had lasted far too long, so she decided to turn everything off and return to Darno after dinner.

Only when the Teleportvision was off did Bethany realize that she had ignored her guest for a full half hour. "Sarah?"

Sarah slowly opened her eyes and struggled to smile. She was relieved not to see the strange creature bouncing around the room.

"C'mon," Bethany said. "I'll give you a tour of the house." Sarah dutifully got up and followed her.

First, Bethany brought Sarah into the kitchen. "This is the kitchen," Bethany said, although without enthusiasm. There was nothing more she felt she needed to say.

Sarah looked around and tried to fathom the use of each appliance. To her, the house kitchen seemed like a kitchen made for a restaurant. She was most attracted to a shiny box with a window on it that was hanging above the large stove. "What is that?" Sarah asked, pointing to the mysterious box.

Bethany rolled her eyes. "That's the hi-wave. It cooks food."

Sarah was confused and couldn't help asking more questions. "But how does it do that? Isn't this a stove below it?"

Bethany rolled her eyes again. "It's a hi-wave oven. It cooks food quickly. You just put food inside, close the door, and push that button. The oven sends out hi-waves through the food to heat it up. That stove has burners; they cook food through direct heat."

Sarah stood, staring back at Bethany. She had no idea what the girl had just said. "But I don't understand why it's here," she said hesitantly. "If it heats food, why do you need the stove, too?"

Bethany reluctantly answered. "The hi-wave cooks food more quickly, but depending on what you're cooking, it might taste better if you cooked it on the stove and vice versa. Don't you know what a hi-wave is?"

Sarah didn't know what to say. There was so much that she wanted to know but was now afraid to ask. "No, I don't," she replied. "What are hi-waves?"

Bethany paused, never having thought to ask that question herself. "Um…" she began. "It's like a frequency, I guess."

"What are frequencies?"

Bethany looked away, not knowing how to deal with this flurry of questions. She took a breath and faced Sarah again. "I don't know."

"You don't know how this works?" Sarah tapped her finger lightly on the front of the hi-wave oven.

"No, I guess not!" Bethany replied a bit rudely.

"Well, then," Sarah paused, trying to comprehend the issue at hand. "What do you do if it needs repair?"

"Repair?" Bethany said in a tone that suggested Sarah had made a joke. "Nothing. Throw it out and buy a new one."

Sarah decided to stop bothering Bethany with her questions. She would have more luck with Richard when he returned. "I'm sorry, Bethany," she said. "This is all so overwhelming for me."

Sarah nervously walked back into the room where she had been sitting, worried that the unexplainable, bouncing animal might come back.

In one sense, Bethany felt relieved, but on the other hand, she felt badly about the situation. Richard would be home soon and wouldn't appreciate negative feelings around the dinner table. But what a disappointment! She and Sarah were hundreds of years apart, and there was nothing to gain from the other woman. Why on Earth did Richard not only fail to bring someone back from the future but then go out of his way to dig someone up from the past?

Bethany peeked her head into the Teleportvision room and found Sarah reading a book on the sofa. "I see you found a book," Bethany said in a much more polite manner.

Sarah looked up from the page and smiled.

Bethany walked over and sat next to Sarah on the sofa. She figured she would hide her disinterest in the woman by answering all of Sarah's questions, thereby redeeming herself. Richard would be home soon. "Ah, *The Adventures of Raymond Elaister Mahoney*," she said in a friendly tone. "Why did you pick that one?"

"Well," Sarah said. "There is quite a collection on the shelf. It was a quick decision. Adventures of the 22nd century sound like they'd be interesting and educational."

Bethany smiled. "Well, I'm sure it's entertaining, but I'm sorry to say that it's a work of fiction. It's not real."

Sarah shrugged and closed the book gently. "That's okay. I'm sure there are better ways to spend my limited time here than reading a book I won't finish."

Bethany suddenly realized that she wouldn't have to sit and answer questions all afternoon. She actually did have some questions of her own. "How did you meet Richard?" she asked.

Sarah's answer was slow in coming. "I don't really know. It's hard to explain, but I can't recall much about how I got here."

Bethany's spark of eagerness to chat with Sarah vanished; she had no reason to talk to her after all.

Sarah held the book up against her chest and smiled. "This is so interesting," she said. "I don't know what anything in here does, but it's all interesting. And look how clean everything is!"

Bethany didn't bother to look around. "Yup."

Sarah went on. "And that wave machine that heats food, how does it work again?"

Bethany slouched back against the corner of the sofa. "It creates hi-waves and cooks the food," she replied.

"Yes, you said that before. But what are hi-waves?"

Bethany rolled her eyes and began tapping her fingers against the sofa. "I don't know."

"Is it safe to use?"

Bethany couldn't believe what she was hearing. "Yeah, of course it's safe."

Sarah decided to give up on the hi-wave machine and direct her questions toward something else. "What is that animal that hops around the room?"

Bethany's heart sank as she realized that all of Sarah's questions would be repetitive 'what's.' "The animal is a video game," she replied. "He's a virtual pet."

Despite Bethany's obvious impatience with her questions, Sarah couldn't help asking them. "But what is it? How does it work? How does an animal just appear and walk around you?"

Bethany nearly lost it. She couldn't fathom that Sarah not only couldn't understand what a video game was but that she also wanted to know how it worked. "Why don't we go upstairs? I can show you the bedroom, workroom, and bathrooms," Bethany suggested. She hoped that would fend off further questions.

Before Richard returned, Bethany gave Sarah a brief but thorough tour of the second floor of the house. She tried to skip over any household appliance that would result in further questioning, although that proved difficult.

In the first room, Sarah pointed to a long bar sitting by itself on Richard's desk. "What is that?" she asked.

Bethany shrugged. "It's a computer. I really don't think you are going to understand it, so just accept that it's beyond your reach." After dismissing a few of her other questions, Bethany went back downstairs. Sarah, on the other hand, stayed upstairs and explored the rest of the rooms, mystified at all there was to see.

Bethany went back to trying to calm Darno, who was still running around uncontrollably. "Darno! Stop it and learn to clean up your mess!" she yelled.

Darno stopped instantly, halted his wild screaming, and looked over at Bethany. She had never shouted at him like that before, and clearly he didn't quite know what to make of it.

Bethany calmed down. "You need to learn how to take responsibility, young man. You can't just go around doing whatever it is that you're doing without a care in the world. Your actions have consequences, mister!"

Darno kept staring at Bethany, but then a moment later, he leapt into the air and resumed his shenanigans, hollering and screaming and jumping around.

"Darno! CALM DOWN!" she yelled. She grabbed her wand and tapped the bottom of it against her leg, which instantly put a virtual wand into Darno's environment.

"Come to the wand," she said.

Darno continued with his antics.

"Come to the wand, Darno," Bethany said, this time with a sterner tone. "COME TO THE WAND!" She began swinging her wand wildly, an action mimicked by the virtual wand.

Darno turned around just in time to see the virtual wand racing toward him, but it was too late. It struck him with such incredible force that he fell to the ground, motionless.

Bethany began to quiver. "No…" she mumbled, her wide eyes fixed on his lifeless body. "No!…NO!" She leaned over his limp, virtual-hologram body. "No…"

His body faded into nothingness, and a voice echoed throughout the room. "Creation deceased."

Bethany put her face in her hands and began to weep.

A loud crash startled Bethany from her tears. It came from upstairs and was followed by the sound of water pouring on to the floor.

"What is it?" Bethany yelled as she rushed upstairs.

She found Sarah standing inside the bathroom. "What did you do?" Bethany shouted.

Sarah didn't know what to say; the only sound was the water pouring out of a floorboard and the top of a mirror that was hung on the wall. "What were you doing in here?" Bethany shouted again.

Sarah stood silent, confused.

Bethany rushed over to the far wall and reached behind the wastebasket, trying to turn something on or off. It worked. Within seconds, the water stopped streaming out of the wall and floor. Without a word, Bethany walked out and returned with a handful of large towels. "Here," she said, handing them to Sarah. "Make sure this room is drip-dry. You know what that means, I'm sure." Bethany stormed out of the bathroom and left Sarah behind.

As Bethany made her way down the steps, she felt vibrations coming from the garage door. Richard was home. 'Oh no,' she thought. She ran back upstairs and into the bathroom, where Sarah was on her hands and knees soaking up the water.

"Get up!" Bethany yelled. "Up! Up! Out! Out!"

Sarah quickly stood up and backed out of the bathroom. Bethany grabbed the towels and threw them into a cabinet, then pressed a button on the wall. A low, rustling sound was immediately heard; the water that remained on the floor evaporated into thin air in a matter of seconds. Bethany released the button and walked out of the now-spotless room. "Come on," she said. "Richard is home with dinner."

As Bethany went down the stairs, she heard two voices—one was Richard's, and the other belonged to a man she didn't know. Rounding the corner to the kitchen, Bethany saw a stranger standing there wearing a bright light-blue suit that almost seemed to glow.

The man noticed her and smiled. "Hi," he said. "My name is James."

Richard looked up from unpacking groceries and smiled. "Bethany," Richard said. "James is from 300 years in the future. We brought back some cuisine for us all to try."

Bethany's jaw dropped wide open. What she had always dreamed of had come true—being able to talk with someone from the future. There were so many things to learn and so many wonders to discover!

Sarah walked up behind her, and James turned his smile to her. "You must be Sarah," he said. "You're from a long time ago! I'm very excited to talk to you and learn about your cultural norms."

Bethany rolled her eyes and blurted out, "She's from, like, the Stone Age."

"There, there, Bethany," Richard said. "We all have a lot to learn from each other."

Bethany perked up when she noticed all of the bags that were lying on the counter. "What did you bring?" she asked with rising excitement.

James picked up one of the bags. "Well," he said. "We can go through most of these after dinner, but for now... um, I think I'll show you ladies one token item from the future." He pulled out a small, circular device. It was light green and looked almost transparent, as if it was a soft liquid.

"Wow, what is that?" Bethany barely breathed.

"Just watch," he said, and he waved two fingers over the object.

"What's it doing?" she asked.

"Just watch," he replied again, but was interrupted by Bethany and her rapid-fire questions.

"What's it going to do? Is it harmless? Does it cure type-L cancers? Can we—"

"Enough," James said, cutting her off. He lightly touched the object, sending a soft ripple across its skin as it gently swayed back and forth.

"How cool!" Bethany shouted. In her excitement, she reached out to touch the object. Just as her fingers made contact...

…blackness. The lights, the Teleportvision, the stove lamps, the hi-wave clock, and the electric candles on the dinner table all turned off with a *POP* that made everyone jump.

Bethany looked out the back windows, but nothing could be seen, not even the electric lamps that were never supposed to turn off. Bethany pulled her phone from her pocket, but it wasn't on, either, nor would it turn on no matter how many times she tried.

"What just happened?" Bethany asked, almost hysterical.

Richard's voice came out of the darkness. "I've never seen something like this. The candles are out, and even the emergency lights aren't responding. Let me find a match and some of those collectible candles I got from work."

The room was silent except for the scurrying sounds of Richard opening cabinets. Bethany, Sarah, and James stood waiting, motionless in the dark.

"The match doesn't work," Richard said after a moment. "Not having heat might make it hard to cook dinner, let alone see what we are eating."

"The food is all raw," James said. "It has to be cooked, or we'll all get sick. Your preservatives are a thing of the past."

The group stood in the kitchen in darkness and silence, no one knowing what to say or do.

James chuckled. "Well, we probably just have a conflict of electronic signals here. Anyone have any idea how to make some food?"

We have developed a life form incapable of independent thought, a life form whose sole purpose is to produce exports for our corporation.

THE CELEBRATED

"LEAVE ME ALONE to enjoy my dinner," Brandon Jean-Luke said pointedly to a fan that approached his table at the Burro Loco while he tried to take a bite out of his burrito.

Ted, never one to take rejection lightly, became enraged by Brandon's unwillingness to engage in conversation. "Just because you are a big movie star," Ted began, "doesn't give you the right to be a complete jerk to everyone!"

Brandon, whose attention had already returned to his burrito, realized that this random stranger was not going away easily. He slowly placed the burrito back into the basket and looked up at the man who was towering over him.

"We are strangers, good sir," Brandon calmly said. "I get hassled multiple times a day from people like you wanting something from me, treating me like nothing more than an elephant at the zoo, just so they can boast to their friends that they met and talked to a famous person. They seem to think that, if a public figure acknowledges their existence, it gives them purpose. However, aside from the fact that you know my name and my profession, we have nothing in common. So please, do us both a favor and let me be."

That response only fueled Ted's rage. "Well, I'm *so sorry* that you got into the entertainment field where you make millions of dollars, and everyone knows who you are because you are a celebrity. What a rough life you must live, never having to worry about anything!" he hammered back.

Brandon just stared in disbelief. "So you're saying that because I'm an actor," he replied, "I should have to spend all my free time talking to ignorant people like you? Does the fact that I make more money than you mean I have no problems? Do you think that happiness and well-being only revolves around money and *not* around family, friends, accomplishments, and passions? What about privacy?"

Ted was at a loss for a response.

Brandon continued to stare. "You Earthian?" he finally asked Ted.

"Yes."

"Well, then," Brandon replied, "I'm sure your life is just riddled with problems then, isn't it? What a shame it is to live on one of the richest planet in our galaxy. Why don't you move to Edggat where you will become an instant celebrity simply because of your Earthian citizenship? On Edggat, your finances would make you one of the richest citizens on the planet. Then *you'd* know what it's like to have no private life. Everyone you will come into contact with will either beg for money or demand that you mingle with them. Why don't you do us both a favor and stop embarrassing yourself and leave me alone?"

Look at her over there. She's so happy despite her life being a complete misery. Someone should really take that ball out of her hands and explain to her how dreadful her life is. Adolescence. If only she could comprehend what she is and how much assistance she needs. Just imagine what will happen when she hits puberty. Try explaining hormones to her. God, what a damn waste. Stuck in a wheelchair because her legs don't work and stuck with constant supervision because her brain doesn't work. If only she knew what she truly was, maybe she wouldn't be happy with her life, especially so excited over something as stupid as a rubber ball. What a shame.

STAGING A SCENE

IN 2023, ONE THOUSAND RESIDENTS of Arland County arrived at Arland Field to build a stage for their annual Arland Concert. Considering that Arland only has twelve hundred citizens, this was an amazing feat. They brought their tools with them. They were determined to build a stage large enough to attract the biggest and best musical acts to represent their county and celebrate their culture. Truckloads of spare lumber, enough to build the entire stage, were donated by two companies who were known for their generous community donations. Architect-residents brought the designs; local college administrators organized everyone into groups and coordinated construction agendas. Everything was in place, and everything was a collective effort. Surely, this year's concert would be even more popular than it was last year. Seeing as nearly everyone in the county would have a hand in making it happen, everyone could take pride in it.

But something happened that summer day in 2023 that hadn't occurred in past years—the heat index hit an all-time high, and additional water and breaks became necessary. Soon, many of the residents began to complain. Team Butterfly—the college administrators were to thank for that name—was the first to crack.

It all began when several members complained about their duties. Nick, a 30-year-old businessman who worked in sales, threw down his shovel and looked up at his team. "This is terrible. It's too hot out for this. And what am I digging a hole for? Secondary garbage back-up? That's only if the primary garbage fills up. This probably won't even be needed! And why are there 10 of us doing this when we only have six shovels between us?"

The other members of Team Butterfly quietly gazed at Nick, waiting to see what he would say next.

"There are 10 of us doing something that is pretty much useless," he plowed on. "There are one thousand people here working. I'm leaving. There is no point in me being here."

Nick climbed up and over the dirt pile that lay next to the freshly dug hole. The team members turned their heads and followed him with their eyes as he walked off the field and toward the parking lot.

"There goes the strongest, youngest member of our team," Roger said, sounding upset. He was a 58-year-old piano teacher with a thin, gangly body who was standing in the bottom of the small hole they'd dug. "Wow."

The other eight remaining members of the team, figuring there was no point in losing their tempers over one man leaving, didn't say a word.

"I can't believe this guy!" Roger exclaimed, starting to sound more strident than upset. "Who does he think he is, anyway?" Roger slammed his shovel into the earth, catching more dirt than he could lift. He pulled and struggled and pulled again, his face getting more and more red.

Eventually, he let go, and the shovel fell. His breaths came in deep gasps. Struggling with his footsteps, he finally managed to climb out of the hole. "I'm leaving, everybody!" he yelled. "Best of luck with the back-up hole. You know it's not going to make any difference if I leave. I'm only one person, and besides, I'm an old fart." He brushed by the remaining eight team members and walked toward the parking lot.

Roger let out a loud sigh of relief. He fumbled around in his pockets, pulled out his keys, and stopped to look around. Hundreds of cars filled the lot. If only he remembered where he'd parked. The searing heat was making the situation worse.

Among the remaining eight members of Team Butterfly, the six members with shovels continued to dig their hole, while the other two walked away. "We'll bring back some water," one said.

The six in the hole kept digging. Ed, a 46-year-old man, stopping to catch his breath, looked up and around the field. Several hundred people were all working on their various projects. Not far off in the distance, he could see a team working on digging the primary garbage back-up. Beyond them was the pile of lumber and steel bars, surrounded by men and women in hard hats. Across the field, other teams were working on an assortment of tasks, from setting up temporary fences and garbage cans to constructing concession stands.

Ed looked back at the stage, which at the moment consisted of just a few poles and support beams. "Tell me something," he began, directing his words in the general direction of the woman working next to him. "Why do we build a magnificent new stage every year and then tear it down and build a new one the year after?"

The woman stopped digging and glanced over toward the stage. "I don't know," she said. "It does seem rather silly."

Ed continued. "This is our one and only field. Maybe it takes up too much space to use it for anything else during the year." He paused to take in the actions of all the volunteers diligently working around him. "But it still doesn't make any sense. Why the repetition? Why the expenses? I mean, we do this every year, and for what? For it all to be torn down again? Surely there is a better way to utilize our resources. How much does this stage cost to build every year?"

The woman, Gail, who was 27 and had blonde pigtails, kept looking at the stage. "I'm not sure. All I know is the workers are all volunteers, and the supplies are donated."

Ed's stare hardened. "Donations or not, this costs tens of thousands of dollars, if not more. Wouldn't that money be better utilized for our health or educational systems? Couldn't those hours and planning be better devoted toward more meaningful things? I mean, we are building the same thing every year and tearing it down again. It makes no sense." Ed looked over to see that Gail had started digging again. His audience lost, Ed grabbed his shovel and resumed moving earth.

Hours passed. Ed was in dire need of a break, if not a nap. He looked around for the two non-shoveling members of the team, but no one was standing at the base of the hole. "Where are the free men in this group?" he asked.

Gail looked over and responded, "They're still here, but they are digging on the other side of this wall. The two people they relieved probably just went home."

"Great!" Ed grumbled again. "Well, I still need a break." He grabbed hold of the edge of the hole and pulled himself up, sprawling out on the hard ground. He rolled over on his back and closed his eyes.

The nap that ensued was pleasant but short. An administrator with a misshaped and oversized ball cap and clipboard soon awakened him.

"You sleeping?" the administrator asked.

"Yeah, we don't have any relief in this so-called team here. I can't dig for three hours straight without a 15-minute breather," Ed replied.

The administrator, Adam, as his nametag said, looked like he didn't take kindly to people leaving their duties. He looked at Team Butterfly and the hole they'd dug so far. "We wanted this hole done by 3:00 p.m. today, team. It's 3:20 right now, and you're not anywhere near completion. I also noticed that you are now only a team of six when you started out as a team of 10. Where are your four other team members?" Adam asked.

Ed sat up. "They were sick of doing this, so they left. It doesn't really matter, though. What's one or two people, really? Besides, we still have a shovel for each person. We may be moving slowly, but we'll get there."

Now it was Adam's turn to grumble. "I appreciate all of your help, but without the completion of this secondary garbage unit, your efforts toward completing the stage won't be worth anything. According to the schedule, you are already supposed to be working on the stage itself. Other teams are losing volunteers, too, one by one. Every minute you go past schedule is another minute lost in the completion of the stage. The sun sets in two hours, so please try and finish soon."

Adam walked away to give the same speech to the next team.

Four hours later, Arland Field was empty. The stage, whose completion had been scheduled for a half-hour before sunset, still was not finished. Too many volunteers had left their teams, causing their tasks to be delayed or incomplete. That meant the team that was working on the completion of the stage had far fewer volunteers by the time evening rolled around. The stage, fences, gardens, and pedestrian markings were not finished, and because everything was taking place on a Sunday, the work couldn't be completed. Nearly all of the volunteers had jobs the following day, and there were no available funds to hire professionals to finish the stage.

The annual Arland Concert was a disaster. Word of the poor construction and faulty landscaping spread quickly, and attendance was poor. The musicians and artists who played Arland weren't very motivated to participate in future events.

The following year, knowing that interest in attending the concert had dropped, fewer volunteers donated time and supplies to the construction of the stage and landscaping of new gardens and walkways. As the years passed, the town of Arland struggled to secure decent bands for their annual concert. Soon enough, the concert had become nothing but a distant memory of a time when all of the citizens had come together to represent their community.

What did you have for dinner a week ago from today? Do you remember anything? What did you do that day? What did you do today that you will remember a week from now?

SYNECDOCHE

BILLY, DANNY, AND MICHAEL, all students in Mr. Yeard's third grade class, sat outside for lunch on the far picnic table in the courtyard, where they were approached by an out-of-solar-system guest, Yarou, who asked to join them. The kids kindly accepted his request and offered to share their lunches. Yarou graciously took half of the sandwich that Billy was straining to hold up above his head.

"Thank you very much. You are very kind," he said. His voice was light in delivery and high in pitch but easily understandable. Yarou took a bite and a single chew. He suddenly froze and immediately spit the food out of his mouth and onto the table. "What is in that food you gave me!?" Yarou yelled, raising his voice.

Billy, having brought his sandwich up to his open mouth, slowly lowered it and placed it on the table. He looked up at Yarou's glaring eyes, which had begun to glow. "That is a turkey sandwich," Billy replied, starting to shake.

"What is turkey?" Yarou yelled again. Billy stared back, not knowing how to answer the question. Steam began to emerge from the pores on Yarou's face. "Is it a plant? A tree? A species? A seed?" Yarou's voice became louder and more threatening. The three boys were staring at the table, trying not to make eye contact.

"It's a bird," Billy said, almost crying.

Yarou walked over behind Billy, who still refused to look up. Yarou's eyes were now bright red and steam flew from his face at a staggering rate. He raised his right arm and violently came down on Billy's head with a thundering crack. In an instant, Billy's body went limp and fell to the ground, after which Yarou proceeded to step on him. After several powerful kicks and stomps, Yarou looked up at Danny and Michael. His eyes dimmed in color, and the steam lessened. Then he spoke.

"Killing is wrong, especially for food. Let this be a lesson to you."

Danny and Michael began to cry.

The rocket began to rumble. Randle turned his head and looked toward Pherty. Only two men were in the cabin.

The countdown reached 20 seconds; thundering vibrations shook the rocket. An asteroid was racing toward the planet, and Randle and Pherty were Earth's last chance to save all life from complete destruction. All other missions had failed.

"Pherty?" Randle shouted from across the cabin.

Pherty turned his head to listen.

"Do you believe in extraterrestrial civilizations?" The rumbling became louder and louder, and Pherty's face became an abstract blur.

"Because if they exist," Randle yelled, "they should have done something for us by now. They would have shown their faces and helped us. Why would they allow this to happen?"

THE GOOD BOOK

THE MEDFORD FAMILY packed themselves into their rusted compact and hit the road to Flippy's Land of Enlightenment, an international theme park with cutting-edge technological attractions and futuristic rides.

Big Mama sat in the passenger seat while Pappy drove the 15-year-old rusted compact. The two offspring sat in the back, shaking with excitement. Ten-year-old Mary impatiently tilted her head back and forth, letting her blonde ponytails lightly hit the sides of her face. Her older brother Joshua sat quietly, already having read through a pamphlet of the park's attractions. He felt he was an expert on what it had to offer.

"Mary," Joshua began, "I think you'll like the floating bumper cars the most."

"Floating bumper cars?" she asked.

"Yes," Joshua said. "They're like regular bumper cars, but the cars aren't stuck to the ground. You can go up, down, left, right… any angle you want."

"I don't believe you—stop lying!" Mary shouted.

"Now, now," came a deep, calm voice from the front of the car. "There will be none of that." Pappy felt relaxed whenever he drove the family compact. "Mary, darling, what your brother is saying is true. Flippy's Land of Enlightenment is a wonderful place with many extraordinary rides, rides you can only dream of! In fact, it's probably the most important attraction land in existence. Big Mama and I had to apply to get invitations for us to vacation here, which took years to get. Not everyone experiences Flippy's."

Flippy's Land of Enlightenment truly did contain some of the most advanced attractions in the world. Flying bumper cars was only one highlight for young people. There was also the mega merry-go-round, over twice as wide as any other on Earth and with 11 stories, as well as the mega Ferris wheel, which stood 450 feet tall. There was even the Eternal Sunshine Roller Coaster, the longest roller coaster in the world—the ride lasted a full 13 minutes.

Aside from larger and longer attractions, there were plenty of other extraordinary sightings and rides to be found only at Flippy's. The exotic zoo contained new breeds of all walks of life, including the polka-dotted hippo, the five-horned owl, and the singing rhinoceros. Roller coasters were designed with multiple loops, flips and twists guaranteed not to make riders sick. There were anti-gravity arenas with trampolines and virtual reality rubberized rooms that were so real no one could tell the difference between what went on in the rooms and actual reality. On top of all of that, there was a 3,000-foot-tall sky deck, the tallest known structure in the world. It was so high up that people descending from it often said they'd thought they were in heaven.

For Mary and Joshua, their years of waiting had finally come down to this last day of driving. "Big Mama?" asked Mary, "how much longer until we get there?"

Big Mama reached into her purse and pulled out *The Good Book: A Citizen's Guide to Flippy's Land of Enlightenment.* It was a leather-bound, hardcover book several inches thick. It was so heavy that it made you wonder how much information was really needed to understand Flippy's.

Big Mama began paging through and soon reached a section that caught her eye. "It says here," Big Mama began, "that once we reach the Jefferson Store of Convenience, we have about seven hours to go."

Mary could hardly contain herself. "Seven hours! Yippee!" she yelled.

"Shut up, stupid!" Joshua blurted out. "We could be four hours from the convenience store."

Big Mama turned around with a disappointed look on her face. "Joshua, you know we aren't four hours from the convenience store. I told you this morning when we all looked at *The Good Book* in our hotel room that we were five hours from the convenience store. Seeing that we have been on the road for about five hours, that would put us in the vicinity of the store right now, wouldn't it?"

Mary looked over at Joshua, stuck out her tongue and went *pphhhbt.*

Joshua pushed her against the side of the car. "What about all the traffic we hit in Burlander?" he asked. "Do you think that set us back?"

Big Mama glared at Joshua. "Don't get smart with me, boy. We'll get there when we get there." Big Mama turned her attention back to the road.

Mary stuck her tongue out again and crossed her eyes at her brother to spite him.

"Shut up!" Joshua shouted and pushed her again to the side. The sibling battle continued.

An hour later, the Medford family passed the Jefferson Store of Convenience. "Now we're seven hours away," Joshua proclaimed and lightly nudged Mary on her shoulder. Joshua was normally a thoughtful boy, but his increasing excitement was making him behave in a rash manner. "Man, I can't wait to hit up some of Flippy's cotton candy," he exclaimed.

"Big Mama is not gonna let you eat any cotton candy!" said Mary.

"No, you don't get it," he replied. "Their cotton candy not only doesn't have any sugar in it, but it is also designed to clean your teeth! And supposedly it even tastes better than regular cotton candy!"

Big Mama opened *The Good Book* again. "It says here that Flippy's cotton candy took 20 years to develop and an extra 10 years to disguise the ingredients so that no one could steal the secret recipe. And you can only buy the cotton candy in the park despite huge corporate offers to market it."

Big Mama flipped to another chapter titled "Day 1." The page was filled with statistics about crowd control in the park and date, time of day, and weather conditions. Every single possible detail was accounted for. She took out a scrap piece of paper and began making notes.

Mary and Joshua sat impatiently in the back. Joshua's hand moved over slowly, inch by inch, toward Mary. It was barely a hair away from her leg when she noticed.

"Big Mama!" she yelled, "Joshua is not staying on his side of the car!"

"I'm not even near your side!" Joshua yelled back.

"Uh-huh!" Mary screamed. "You're just doing this to make me angry!"

"I don't know what you are talking about," said Joshua stoutly. Mary responded with another scream. The two started to squabble and push each other until—

"KNOCK IT OFF!" yelled Pappy. The kids had never heard him be that loud before. His voice quickly returned to his soothing calmness, "We are on our way to Flippy's Land of Enlightenment, kids. This is an experience of a lifetime. Stop bickering."

The trip continued in complete silence. Both Joshua and Mary sat staring forward, not knowing if it was okay to talk.

Big Mama broke the uncomfortable silence. "How about we go over the park itinerary plans that I am creating?"

That boosted their spirits. They started bobbing up and down and moving uncontrollably.

"Yeah!" exclaimed Mary.

"Definitely!" said Joshua.

"Okay. Tomorrow morning we will wake up at 6 a.m. so we can get to the park when they open and be one of the first ones in," said Big Mama, "and it's important that—"

"Which section of the park are we going to tomorrow?" interrupted Joshua.

"The Roaring Future," she replied.

"Why? Can't we go to Artnoir first? Joshua asked impatiently

"No."

"Why not?"

"Because *The Good Book* recommends it. Not only will the crowd levels be lower since it will be a Sunday, but Artnoir has specials that can only be redeemed on a Tuesday, so that's when we'll go.

"Tomorrow, we'll be at the gate by 8 a.m., which will put us in the front of the crowd when they open and we'll make a dash for The Enchanted. We have to make sure to line up by the east entrance. That way, we can take the shortcut to The Enchanted by cutting over the Watershed bridge."

"Which ride is The Enchanted?" asked Joshua.

Big Mama flipped through some pages and found the ride description, "The Enchanted is an interactive theater experience that simulates the act of flying a kite."

"That's stupid," Joshua blurted out.

"Excuse me?" Big Mama sounded shocked.

"That's a stupid ride…if you can even call it a ride. What about the Tumbler or the R is for Rocket rides? Those sound like the best!"

"Joshua, this is the guide for Flippy's. The people who wrote this designed the rides and tested everything years and years before you were even born, and then other people updated and enhanced the guide over generations. If they say that The Enchanted is a top attraction, then we must see it as one of our first rides. I think they know what they are talking about."

"But it's a stupid ride!" he shouted.

"Joshua, I've had just about enough!" said Big Mama sternly. "We are on vacation, and damn it, we are going to have fun as a family! *The Good Book* can tell us how to do that!"

"But it sounds so stupid!" Joshua cried out.

"You are going to stop your bickering this instant or else!"

"Can't I just run over to Battle Wars and meet up with you, Pappy, and Mary later?"

"Absolutely not! We can't ride that ride until after 3 p.m., when the line levels are lower. You may think that there won't be a line at 8 a.m., but that is where everyone is going to go, which means you'll get stuck in the oblivious crowd that just meanders around not knowing what is best. We're better than them—we have *The Good Book* and we are going to stick to it word for word. You think you can just wander off and find your way through Flippy's Land of Enlightenment by yourself? Well, you're wrong, mister! The truth is, you may think you are having a good time, but without guidance from those who know and who have built this great land, you would be completely lost."

Big Mama took a deep breath and turned around to face the front.

Joshua sat in his seat, dumbfounded.

Mary looked over and smiled at Joshua. He noticed her from the corner of his eye, but he didn't dare react at a time like this. How could he have managed to anger both his parents before experiencing the first day at Flippy's?

The Medford vehicle exited the freeway and stopped at the ramp light. Both Joshua and Mary, who had fallen asleep, were awakened by the halt in motion. Their hearts began to beat like a hummingbird as they realized how close they were to Flippy's.

Up ahead, a sign read "Flippy's Land of Enlightenment: Only 10 More Minutes." Joshua and Mary let out screams. Even Big Mama and Pappy were smiling.

The light turned green and the family continued on their way. Soon enough, large gates could be seen in the distance.

"You got the tickets, Big Mama?" Mary asked.

"Sure do, kiddo," she replied. Big Mama held four bronze tickets, each bearing one of their names.

The gates grew taller and taller as the car approached. Joshua began to shake. It seemed like he'd been looking forward to this his entire life.

A well-groomed man sat in a booth in front of the gate. The car slowly came to a stop.

"Welcome, welcome," the man greeted them.

Pappy took the bronze tickets from Big Mama and handed them over to the man. "Four of us for Flippy's Land of Enlightenment," Pappy said cheerfully.

There was a long pause. Joshua squirmed from left to right, trying to see inside the booth, but it was no use. His smile quickly vanished; had something gone terribly wrong?

Seconds turned to minutes…minutes seemed to turn into hours. All Medford family members sat silently, waiting and waiting. Joshua and Mary made eye contact and could see their confusion mirrored on each other's faces.

"Your tickets are not valid," said the voice. "We are full for this week."

Another gap of silence. Pappy began to stammer. "But we applied for these tickets over 10 years ago and they are only valid this week!"

The man replied, "The Land of Enlightenment is full. Had you arrived earlier, or if you had silver or gold tickets, you would have access, but unfortunately, you don't."

Another long pause. Pappy looked over at Big Mama, who looked as shocked as he felt. "This isn't fair," he said.

"What can I say?" replied the man. "You didn't follow exact protocol. If you had been more precise in your planning and choices, maybe you would not be in this situation." He stopped, then added, "It's fortunate that you can re-apply, try again, and learn from your mistakes."

If I didn't know about it, I wouldn't care.

THE PERFECTIONIST

JANE SWANSON SOUGHT A BETTER LIFE: Everywhere she looked, she recognized problems and opportunities for improvement. That urge to change everything for the better is why she booked a trip with *Story of Life*. Although she didn't know their policy regarding changing her own time path, Jane applied for a trip on the grounds of wanting to travel eight years back to watch the first date between herself and the man who had become her husband.

For the past five years, her life had been miserable. Taking care of two children and struggling financially had made Jane constantly question her professional goals and social choices. Had she been able to afford a nanny, she would have been able to finish culinary school, she'd realized.

Her husband, stuck in a low-salary desk job, made just enough to ensure that the family could survive. The dreams and goals Jane had established and *not* pursued over the last few years had been plaguing her self-esteem and spawning doubt about the path her life had taken.

Jane sat in the *Story of Life* waiting room with a letter folded in her back pocket, a letter that held all the information she would need to achieve riches and success. Only one thing was necessary: being certain that the letter made its way to her prior self during that first date. Should she need to change clothes or strip down prior to travel, she would surely have to leave it behind. But nervousness was really the only danger—Jane had the letter memorized. Her life was full of many regrets and disappointments, and the letter was a collection of all her wishes and desires for a new life. Those could hardly be erased from her memory.

It was a quiet morning at *Story of Life* and Jane was the only client in the waiting room. Twenty minutes before her appointment, the receptionist let her know that the scientists were ready to see her. Jane gracefully stood up, thanked the man behind the desk, and walked into the back room. She had no idea what to expect now. All the guidebooks and underground information, including ways to 'cheat' and information that was supposedly secret, couldn't reveal what happened after travelers were called back.

A female scientist met Jane in the hallway and handed her a stack of papers. "This is your test," the scientist said. "Please step into Room 6, fill it out, remove all of your clothes, and step into Room A." The scientist left her to find her way into Room 6.

Jane walked in to find a small room with a small table. There were no windows, just one other door labeled 'Room A.'

Jane broke into a cold sweat when she realized that her note would not be safe left behind in her pants. She hastily took out the small piece of paper and stuffed it into her mouth, chewing quickly and hoping it would soften enough to swallow.

She chewed hard and long on that piece of paper through-out the simple exam that she proceeded to take. The questions asked the specifics about Jane's travels, about the regulations that restricted her, and about her actions in the past. Having read through many manuals, Jane knew she had all the right answers. She filled in her last circle and gulped down the soft pulp of a note that remained in her mouth. She stood up, undressed, placed her clothes on the table, and entered Room A.

The entire trip didn't turn out to be more than just a vague memory, prompting her to wonder if *Story of Life* had drugged her to limit her actions in the past and ensure she wouldn't do anything against policy. Or it was quite possible that she was able to experience the distant memory as a dream and not create a static point of view from an outsider's position.

Either way, she followed her prior self and eventual husband throughout their date, from the coffee shop to the park and then onto their embarrassing goodbye at the end of the night. (She had tried to lure him up to her apartment, but he had left because he didn't want to come off as being too interested.)

At the park, Jane had found a scrap piece of paper in the trash and managed to write her notes down with a dirty stick. She expressed her disappointment with what her life had/would become and scribbled down a few pieces of information to help her on her life journey: the February 11, 2063 winning giga-funds lottery numbers, the names of two corporations to invest in, the job that her future husband should not accept.

That had been it, except for one thing—how should she present this information to her prior self? She gazed at her priego, sitting peacefully under a tree in the park and contemplated how to approach the situation. Surely, placing a note in her pocket or purse would not have been convincing, so when her husband left for a minute to urinate in the bushes, Jane had caught up to her priego, made eye contact, and quickly said, "I'm unhappy with my life. I wrote this note for you to better yourself." Then she'd darted off before any kind of conversation could take place.

Jane had spent the rest of the evening gazing at her prior self with a warm satisfaction. This was the best day of her life: She was discovering the best person imaginable and knowing that the future had endless possibilities. And now that would be truer that ever!

Jane returned to *Story of Life* without having had problems or having made any mistakes. She paid the remainder of her bill, changed back into her original clothing, and left.

Things were already looking better. When she paid, she noticed that her credit card was now a premiere elite series rather than regular silver. Outside, she found her car to be a shiny new BMW, quite a step up from the 12-year-old Honda she was used to. Before driving home, she checked her license to locate her address; sure enough, it too had changed.

Jane pulled into the driveway of her new home and immediately began noticing all the differences: Her old home was made of dirty wood panels and cracked brick, but now she saw a house made of marble and stone, with a towering third floor sporting enormous windows that overlooked the elaborate landscaping surrounding the house. There was also a separate guesthouse in the backyard...maybe to house the maids?

Jane ran upstairs and found her husband sitting at a computer. "Bobby!" she yelled, rushing over to him and wrapping her arms tightly around his chest.

"Not now, honey!" he said sharply, shoving her arms away. "This report is due in Japan in five hours. I can't be disturbed.

Make sure I have some food to eat by then, and shut the doors behind you."

Bobby continued tinkering with the computer and didn't bother to make eye contact. Bemused, Jane backed out of the room and gently closed the double doors behind her, then walked down the hallway to explore her new unfamiliar territory. She was bubbling with excitement and joy to be living in such an upscale house with so much room. And talk about organization! Everything was immaculately clean and shining; it all seemed to sing to her.

After looking in every room, Jane noticed that her children were nowhere in sight. She walked across the back lawn and knocked on the guesthouse door.

A young woman in a black uniform answered the door. "Yes, Ms. Swanson?" the woman asked with a demure nod.

"Where are the kids?" Jane asked.

The woman glanced up, looking somewhat confused. "They are with Jessica, as they are every afternoon before supper."

Jane was dumbfounded. She now had people taking care of her kids, too? "Oh, okay," she responded. "Dinner will be a little later tonight. Bobby has to work for another five hours, so I'll start preparing dinner in a few. Thanks."

Jane turned and headed toward the house.

"Wait!" the woman called out.

Jane turned.

"I'll take care of dinner tonight, Ms. Swanson. You don't need to worry about it."

Jane stood in a daze, not knowing how to digest the information. Finally, she nodded slightly and headed back into the house.

With her husband busy at work, her kids being watched over by someone else, her house in pristine condition, and dinner provided, Jane sat back on the living room couch and pondered what to do. Everything was now taken care of for her; she would never need to worry about finances ever again. Her dreams and goals were all accounted for. It felt uncomfortable not having things to do—no kids running around, no mess to clean up. She no longer needed to worry and stress over what she wouldn't be able to do. Finally, she could truly be happy.

Charles huffed and puffed as he jumped into Jim's SUV and slammed the door behind him. Jim floored it. The vehicle flew ahead, dodging falling buildings and open chasms in the road.

The raptures had started, and those left on Earth were without a doubt paying the price.

"Thank you, Jim," Charles gasped, trying to catch his breath. "I can't believe this is really happening. Sorry for making fun of you all these years for owning an SUV, it surely saved my life. Now I see why they are so important."

21x WATCH

I DON'T KNOW WHERE TO START. No, wait, I do, I just don't know how to come off as a sane individual. Perhaps mentioning that I am 26 and still living with my parents would be a poor decision; you probably wouldn't quite give me the respect I deserve.

My name is Ben Bucksley, as you know. I graduated from Idaho State a few years back with a degree in philosophy and haven't amounted to anything yet. I'm hoping there's still a chance for me, but I don't think you'd believe that. You're probably wondering how I got this black eye. You might also be wondering if there's something wrong with me...I don't blame you. But I assure you that I can explain everything in plain and simple terms.

Actually, I think we might be getting off on the wrong foot. I am a responsible person, I assure you. I have good morals and intentions and would never have made a conscious decision to put myself in the situation I find myself in now.

The two parking tickets I got last month were the only reason I got caught. You might call what I did fraud; I call it pure genius. Those two parking tickets amounted to $168.73. I could barely afford the fines, let alone an increase in my car insurance. The trick, I figured, is to pay parking tickets with a check—a check that's written out for a couple dollars more than what's due. Then the city sends a refund check, and even though the violations are accounted for, the fine isn't filed and completed until I cash the refund, which of course I would never do. My insurance company would therefore be none the wiser. But as I've said, things didn't turn out the way I'd planned.

It all started last Tuesday afternoon. It was a typical Tuesday, and I was at work filing and organizing insurance policies and claims at Howard and Murphy. (Yes, I'm a file clerk. Keep in mind that I majored in philosophy. Not a big market out there for philosophers...)

As he often does, Officer Harding came into the office with a bag of items. Between the police and insurance investigators, many items are confiscated. If the rightful owner doesn't claim the property, most likely because it was stolen in the first place, the items are handed over for police auctions. Anything not worth auctioning off is brought to us. We only see worthless sentimental items. I never care about them. They're mostly boring things, like fancy bookmarks, CDs, USB electronics, or other useless antiques. But this time was different.

This time, Officer Harding brought an item for each of us in the office. He told us to pick out something special. Being the lowly paper sorter, I hung back. I didn't want to step in front of anyone in the office who did actual work.

After a few minutes, I approached the bag to find the remaining item—stolen, illegal, confiscated, and now mine—a plastic watch. It was completely useless, like something a kid would receive from a quarter machine at a grocery store. I looked around the room. Antonio had gotten a music player, still working, albeit severely damaged, and Janice a straw hat. Michael, who's the dim-minded child of well-off parents and a person with no concept of accomplishment or self-worth, got a set of headphones. I observed my newly inherited piece of crap in silence. Okay, yes, it was free, but it was pure crap compared to the items the others had gotten. I went back to my file cabinet.

I soon realized that the watch didn't even tell time. The only characters on it were 21x. I figured it was completely broken.

Soon enough, the final 30-minutes-of-the-day countdown began. It's the slowest yet most exciting time of day because every time you look at the clock, it's that much closer to leaving. I'm always packed up and ready to go with 10 minutes left. It's somehow comforting to know that I don't have to do anything for 10 minutes. I can simply sit and zone out. I basically think about how to improve my life, how I could get a different job so that my intelligence and determination could actually cause a positive change in this world we live in.

Janice walked by in her new straw hat and stopped to chat, ruining my time to relax. "You like my new hat, cowboy?" she asked, tugging at it.

I told her that the hat made her look like one of the animals from the farm she came from. Don't worry, though, I said it in a cute way. She let out an annoyed grunt and walked away.

With nothing better to do, I thought I'd try to fix my watch. There was only one button on the side, so I pressed it. Nothing happened. I gave up. I didn't care much about it, really. It was just something I'd throw out sooner or later. I crossed my arms and closed my eyes.

The next thing I knew, Janice was poking me in the arm. I must have fallen asleep. Her poke wasn't a gentle poke, though. It was a mean, hard kind of poke.

"Hey there, cowboy," she said. "Fall asleep on the job?" She grinned, expecting me to laugh.

I just stared back at her. There were probably bruises on my arm.

She smiled and asked if I liked her new hat again.

I didn't know what she was trying to get out of repeating her earlier question, so I just replied bluntly, "No, I hate it. Go away."

She gave me a dirty look and left. I peered at the clock and noticed that there were still 10 minutes left of work. That didn't make any sense. I stared at the wall clock for another moment and convinced myself that I must have misread it earlier. Makes sense, wanting the day to finish up sooner. What other explanation was there? Little did I know what I was getting myself into.

It's interesting how we experience events out of the ordinary and never piece them together. We just accept the irregularities and brush them off as if they weren't out of place. We are used to our routines; after all, the familiar feels safe and comforting. Maybe that's why I never moved far from home. Actually, maybe that's why I'm still living at home, looking for an apartment near home.

Life can be odd…and it was even more peculiar that day. It took several bizarre occurrences before I put it together, and when I did, I could barely make sense of it.

At 5:00, I immediately left work. That's the happiest time of the day for me. I know that hours of enjoyment lie ahead before I'll have to wake up and start everything all over.

I called my friend Ryan, but he wasn't in. When he isn't around to hang out with, I'm out of luck. Not much of a social life for me. No young professionals live in this town. I wound up just going home, watching some pointless prime time Teleportvision, ordering some Austrech take-out, and socializing on the IPGA network.

That night, as I lay in bed pondering late-night thoughts, I noticed the watch, which was still on my wrist. It was glimmering with unusual patterns of mixed greens, reds, and purples in the dim light of my bedside lamp. I held the watch close up to my eye and noticed the fine details on its digital screen.

Nine hours later, I was sitting at my desk again, wishing for the end of the day. Oh, what endless joy it would be to skip to 5:00. There was a stack of papers to my right and uncountable folders to be filed. Luckily, the big bad boss man doesn't show up till 10:00 a.m., so needless to say, I don't do much till then. I understand the importance of pretending to work—office morale is key, after all—but for the most part, I just don't care. It would be one thing if I categorized, labeled, and filed important paperwork, paperwork that helped people and made a difference, but what I handle are merely leftovers that have to be stored for legal reasons.

Once I did an impromptu investigation and found that only .0274% of the paperwork I file is actually used. That means that over 99% of the work I do is useless. Over 99% of my professional life, which takes precedence over my social life, is wasted. It is true, though, that the .0274% of paperwork that *is* later utilized creates revenue and prevents catastrophic liabilities for the company; in other words, the work that I do is worth thousands, if not millions of dollars a year. Should these files not be stored properly, Howard and Murphy would be in big trouble. It's a good thing I know what I'm doing and am good at what I do. Problem is, even though I save the firm scads of money every year, I have the lowest paid and most boring job. Some things in life are just not fair.

Our boss can show up anytime between 9:00 and 10:00 a.m. That's usually when I sit and think, walk around pretending to do something, trim my nails, and read print-outs of novels that I bring from home to make it appear as if I'm looking over paperwork.

I sit at my desk, bored as can be, staring at the wall clock, watching the way the second hand clicks from one notch to the next. Some second hands move at a continuous pace, circling endlessly in a spiral. The one at the office clicked, which was entertaining to some degree because it was not consistent. It would wobble back and forth after it jolted from mark to mark. Sometimes it would get stuck; then suddenly, it would be shoot over violently with a *sproing!* sound. Okay, maybe it's not that exciting, but if you catch it at the right time, it can be fascinating.

I looked around for something to occupy my time and noticed that my plastic watch was still on my wrist. I got excited. Now I had something to do. I felt like I was on a mission to fix it.

The display still read 21x. I held the side button down, hoping that the display would change. Nothing. A couple more quick presses—nothing. In various angles of light, the clear plastic that protected the display reflected strange metallic colors...probably due to the manufacturer's inability to afford high-quality plastic.

I tinkered with it for a while longer and gave up. It had had a good run; I'd worn it for a successful day, give or take a few hours, and now it was time to say goodbye. I took the watch off, stood up from my desk, eyed the trash bin at the far corner of the room, and flipped the watch in its direction. The watch flew magnificently through the air, slammed into the back edge of the trash can, and dropped with a satisfying thud.

You probably want to know when the truly strange part happened. This was it. I walked over to the trash and saw my watch sitting at the bottom of the metal basket. I had a change of heart, picked it up, and put it back on. I couldn't let this bizarre gizmo, functioning or not, be thrown out just yet.

Just then, I noticed that the office was unusually quiet. I had thought that somebody else was already there, but when I looked around, I didn't see anyone. That was very odd. It was at least 8:30 a.m.....at least I thought it was until I glanced up at the clock. It read 6:44 a.m.

What was I doing at work? Had I been there since 6:00? I backtracked my steps in my mind. Who had I seen on my way in? The janitor probably. Not surprising he was at work so early, but what was I doing there?

I quickly calculated how much more sleep I would be able to sneak in if I went home. By the time I'd driven home and come back, I would be able to grab approximately 20 minutes of sleep...or I could get an hour of sleep if I slept on the sofa in the lounge. I thought about how humiliating it would be to get caught sleeping at work and then realized I didn't care. I went to the sofa.

I was brutally awakened by a cold sensation running down my leg. My eyes snapped open; I jumped up and realized Michael had just finished pouring stale, cold coffee all over my lap.

The stubby facial hair sticking out beyond the pudgy folds in his oddly proportioned face was even more disgusting than usual...not to mention his rancid breath. "Wake up, file boy," he announced, then threw the empty cup at me before walking off.

Aside from having to put up with another encounter with Michael, a large stain on my pants, and my wet, cold underwear, I felt great.

I sat down at my desk and realized that it was only 8:00 a.m. What a lousy day—and really, it hadn't even started. To make things worse, I was already getting hungry for lunch.

10:00 a.m. rolled around; I was starving. So I did what anyone else would do—I left for 'lunch,' a.k.a. my brilliant excuse to leave the office for an hour. I only do it twice a month. I just tell my supervisor that I have to retrieve original copies of documents. Doesn't really matter what they are, but should files be misplaced and then be needed in the future, all would be lost, so they trust me. Good thing.

I left at 10:00 knowing that I wouldn't be needed until 1:00 p.m. I slowly walked to my car, but it was gone. I had no idea where it was. You'd think I'd have pieced this together by now, but no. In my stained pants and soggy underwear, I walked home, stopping off for tacos on the way.

I decided to give fixing my watch another try as I waited in line at the Taco Grande. Anything was better than listening to the old man in front of me slowly mispronounce Mexican food names.

"Tortelows?" the man asked. Ugh...unbearable.

My watch still looked the same. The digital display read 21x, and the front screen shone like the cheap plastic protective panel that it was. Maybe there is a method to the button, I thought. Pressing and holding in conjunction with a simple tap, perhaps? I held the button down and let go. Nothing happened. I held it in again, this time for several seconds, then followed with a quick press. Nothing. I pressed it again. Still nothing, but at least the old man had stopped talking.

I stepped up to the counter and noticed no one was there. It was, in fact, dead silent. The employee taking orders and the confused old man had both vanished. The lights were off, too. I turned and looked around the restaurant. It was empty. I could have sworn there had been at least a few people in there when I entered. I gazed back into the kitchen and felt a chill; from what I could see, it was empty.

I debated what to do next. I needed to eat, but it seemed like there was no point in staying in an empty restaurant. All I wanted was some food, and quickly.

But there it was, something that could maybe shed light on what was happening to me. A clock above the unlit menu read 8:24. There'd been a man in front of me seconds ago, of that I had no doubt. And where had the employee gone?

I shouted into the kitchen asking for anyone, but there was no response. It's funny how it took me so long to put the pieces together. I went to leave and found the door locked. My body continued moving after my arm failed to open the door. I collided with the glass and banged my head, causing me to take a step backwards and clutch my forehead with my hand.

I heard rapid footsteps approaching. "Sir?"

I turned around and beheld a middle-aged man in a much-too-tight shirt and tie. He was giving me the oddest look. "Can I help you, sir?" he asked.

Pain shot through my head; I squinted in discomfort. "Can I just order something to eat?" I asked.

It was as though I'd told a bad joke; the guy was not amused. "How did you get in here?" he demanded.

"Through this door," I answered shortly, countering his curt tone with one of my own. "How do you think?"

"That door is locked," he blasted back. "You shooting up in the bathroom? Who let you in here? Miguel?"

"What?" I said, annoyed. Rage was starting to creep into my voice. "I just want to order some food."

The guy stepped forward and grabbed my arm.

"Ow!" I yelled. He didn't respond to my shout; instead, he fumbled through his keys with his free hand, opened the door, and threw me out, locking the door behind me.

I bent over as the pain shot through my head and went into my arm. After a moment, I'd recovered enough to look inside. I saw no movement, just darkness. A sticker on the window stated the hours: *M–F: 10 a.m. to 8 p.m.*

Made sense, except for the fact I'd just been thrown out of the place, and it was apparently 8:00 a.m. I took a seat on the curb and thought through the possibilities until I'd narrowed them down to three. One: Existentialism is reality (although I can't remember how I came up with that). Two: I'd traveled back in time. Three: I was crazy. Crazy or not, I still needed to get home. I started walking.

Three blocks later, I noticed DeeGee's Donuts. I was still really hungry, so I went in and made extra sure to maintain a normal, calm, and cohesive demeanor.

I was the only customer in the place; I could hear workers in the back moving things around. I put my elbows on the counter and leaned forward to check out the menu.

A woman came out from the back. She looked Latina, so I decided to give my admittedly minimal Spanish skills from high school a whirl. I don't know why I thought to do that. I've never been one to make chitchat with random people, but after the morning I'd had, I felt the need to talk to someone.

"Hola, cómo estás?" I asked.

She smiled and in a somewhat flirtatious way replied, "Bien."

I'd noticed that her nametag read *Michelle.* "Michelle, voy a tomar un jamon bocadillo con queso y tres rosquillas: chocolate, coco, y un Boston créma. Nada más."

Still smiling, she grabbed a few protective wax papers.

I thought to myself that if I were crazy, I would surely hear voices, which I hadn't. If I were crazy, I would have lost control of myself at some point, which I hadn't. And if I were truly crazy, I would be thinking irrational thoughts, another check on the 'no' list. It's always funny that being crazy is more often than not defined by hearing voices. I'd say it's more of an issue when people obey what the voices tell them to do. Now that's insanity!

I looked at my watch and contemplated my sanity. Was this cheap, plastic teller of time my gateway to time travel? I pressed the button in hopes of proving myself wrong.

Michelle, who'd just been putting my donuts into a bag, suddenly disappeared. Nothing clears your mind like a person in front of you vanishing into thin air.

I hopped over the counter and grabbed a coconut donut, then calmly stood and ate it. Delicious. Nothing is better than a donut, especially a reappearing donut.

Just as I took my last bite, Michele came around the corner. Upon seeing me, she halted, gave a little scream, and put her hand over her chest.

"Get out!" she yelled. "Get out, get out, get out!" She was furiously shooing me toward the door. I didn't think she was going to attack me. Twenty-four-hour donut shops get crazies on a daily basis and are accustomed to dealing with them.

I slowly reached under the counter and grabbed my own bag and sheet of wax paper. I opened the bag with a quick shake and grabbed a chocolate donut and a Boston crème. When they were in the bag, I smiled.

Michelle was anything but delighted. "Get out of here," she demanded again.

I hopped the counter and headed toward the door. Before exiting, though, I turned around and looked back. Had I just robbed DeeGee's Donut shop? What had gotten into me? I noticed a clock next to the hanging menu and decided to do a final test to see what the watch would do.

I pressed the button. The minute hand immediately twirled backwards 20 minutes...or was it 21 minutes? Now it all made sense: 21x!

Michelle had disappeared again, probably in the back. I put the donut bag on the ground and walked back to the counter to check the results of my new discovery. "Michelle?" I shouted.

Sure enough, out came Michelle from the back with a very puzzled look on her face. "Can...I...help you?" she asked, confused.

"No, not really," I replied. "Just checking to see if you were working today. Thanks!" I turned around, picked up my bag of donuts, and left.

The two donuts satisfied me during my walk home. As I put the key in the front lock, I realized that if I didn't return to work immediately, I would be playing hooky. Real hooky, not original-documents-needed, 'legit' hooky, since technically I haven't arrived to work yet.

I ran to the nearest clock to find it was 8:50. That meant I needed to be at work in 10 minutes to ensure I was there when the workday started. I ran back outside, and sure enough, there was my car, sitting in the driveway. I jumped in the car, ready to speed away to work, when I reached for my watch, intending to press it, then reconsidered.

It wasn't even 9:00 in the morning, yet it felt like bedtime. My body clock was in shock, and I was exhausted. If I pushed it again and again to be at work on time, it would only dig me into a deeper hole, and I'd have to relive the day all over again. Why not show up to work late, and if confronted by the boss, then push the button? Why push it before there is a potential problem? If I get caught, it's just a simple fix—an amazing contraption to avoid all consequences. Brilliant!

I entered work late, and before I could sit down, Michael approached my desk.

"Welcome to work, buddy. You seem to be running a little late there." He stopped to size me up and down. "Ben," he continued slowly and with mock concern. "Did you wet yourself on your way to work?"

I looked down. Displayed prominently on my crotch was the coffee stain. Then Michael squinted at the redness on my forehead from having run into the door at Taco Grande. "You know, we really value everything you do here, champ. No one could possibly replace you without years of training. And even if someone tried, he wouldn't compare to the way you look after pissing your pants and banging your head after falling off your tricycle."

I put my hand to the aching bump on my head and had a stroke of brilliance. "Oh, this little bump? I didn't fall off my tricycle, Michael. I think your father whacked me with a baseball bat."

Michael didn't take kindly to my words. He sucker punched me in the arm. "What was that?" Michael whispered.

I hesitantly answered, "Nothing."

He smiled in an unsmiling way and took a step back.

I had to do something. Michael stood there, enjoying seeing me in agony. I could feel my heart pounding through my chest, and I knew I couldn't let him just walk away. A month earlier, I copied and filed all the paperwork concerning Michael's divorcing parents. Knowing I'd find some juicy statements, I'd been sure to make copies so that I could someday wreak havoc on his warped little mind. That day had come. Michael's father, victim of his mother's wild affairs, had beaten three different men in the head with a baseball bat...only to discover that not one had had any relations with his then-wife. "You know, Michael," I began. "It's a shame what happened with your mother and father. And think of how terrible it would be if there were something your mother had not told you about the entire ordeal."

Michael's expression immediately changed from leering into panic, frustration, and anger. Although he remained silent, the way the individual sweat beads trickled down his face made his feelings clear. I almost felt bad for him.

As soon as I'd begun my speech, I had picked up my metal folding chair, ready for action, but he never charged me; I think my words had hit him hard enough.

I stepped around the desk, chair in hand, ready to defend myself. He took a slow step toward me with both hands clenched into fists. A vein was popping out from his forehead, and his unblinking eyes were dead set on mine. He looked like a wild predator following its prey. That's when I raised my metal chair and struck him across the face, sending him to the ground.

I could feel everyone in the office staring at me and had to struggle to come to grips with what I'd just done. Even though I hated him, violence is never the answer. It sure made me feel better, though.

I watched him squirm on the ground, trying to maintain his composure if not his consciousness. He had been picking on me since my first week at the job. Week after week, month after month, he would harass me and pull mindless pranks for his own amusement. I had ignored him, hoping he would stop, but he never did. He'd been born into a rich family of doctors and lawyers and was an up-and-coming player in the insurance firm. Everything was given to him, yet he spent his time belittling others, mainly me. If I'd been in his shoes, I would have found something more useful and noble to do with my time. Think about it; he is in a position of power, yet he spends his time doing petty things for his own benefit. It totally boggles my mind.

The office was silent; all eyes were on me. Michael still was on the ground, and I was still exploding with energy. I had never felt more alive in my life. I briefly pondered Michael's point of view. Maybe he didn't know how miserable he made others. Even without the watch, I had the power to change the course of both our lives forever. A wake-up call for him, possibly, but a certain life of misery for me.

I decided it would be best to take care of the situation before it got any worse, so I reached over and pressed the button on my watch. The environment suddenly popped back into place, 21 minutes prior, and I sat back down at my desk. It felt like a tremendous load had been lifted off my chest. I had just done what I'd wanted to do ever since my first day on the job and yet would never have to endure any of the consequences for it.

I couldn't help but smile, knowing how torn Michael had been over my comments. He had a true weakness. And wouldn't you know it, just then, he walked by my desk.

"When did you get here?" he asked.

I looked up, kept a smile on my lips, and replied, "Not too long ago. It takes time for my tricycle to pick up speed, you know."

He kept on walking. A much more positive interaction than I had previously had, but without the adrenaline rush.

I began to ponder how I could use the watch to my advantage. Money came to mind. How much could I get, and how could I get it? Robbing a bank didn't seem to make sense, but I could always grab money out of a cash register and then run away, traveling back through time during my escape. Or maybe take money out of the ATM and max it out, only to travel back and do it over and over again. That seemed simple enough. Provided I had to relive 21 minutes a day, I could get a free $500 a day, no questions asked. How simple. With $500 a day, I wouldn't need my job. Should I decide to make thousands of dollars a day, I wouldn't need *any* job.

I got up and walked out. I had a plan. I left Howard and Murphy feeling giddier than I ever had in my entire life.

I practically skipped two blocks to one of my bank's ATMs. I took out my maximum withdrawal: $300. Not quite the sum I'd envisioned, but hey, $300 is not bad. I put the money in my pocket and pressed the watch button and then had an initial flash of panic that the money would disappear. It didn't. I had to check my balance to ensure that everything was working according to plan. It was. I took out another $300, put it in my pocket, and walked away while pressing the button.

And that's when it came to me—so perfect, so ingenious. The giga-funds lottery. It was all over the news—the drawing that night that was worth $234 million. Two hundred and thirty four million dollars! Lump-sum option and that's at least $100 million in the bank. No need to bother with the ATM again—here was the one sure way to make a living and never have to worry about money again.

I quickly researched the matter on my phone. I needed to know how long before the drawing they stopped selling tickets. It turned out to be an hour prior. Perfect. Three pushes would give me a minute or three to memorize the winning numbers, travel back in time, and then purchase a winning ticket.

I'd have to spend the rest of the afternoon ensuring my winnings. The drawing was always held at 9:35 p.m. I had to find a way to know what the numbers would be while inside a store so that I could immediately travel back in time and purchase a ticket.

Starting tomorrow, I could buy anything I ever wanted. I could win jackpot after jackpot and become the richest person ever to have lived. I could build my own buildings, businesses, and even colonies on the moon. No…on Mars! Nothing but good thoughts.

I headed home and napped for a few hours. When I woke up, I had about eight hours to kill before I needed to be in place for my moneymaking opportunity. I celebrated in advance with video games, pizza, and loud music. It's the only way to go!

9:00 p.m. rolled around, and I knew I had to head out and find a local mart with a TV. I knew just the place: Max's Mart. I strolled in at 9:25; I was the only customer in the store. The TV above the counter was showing the news. Perfect.

I looked at the guy at the counter. "The lotto going to be on soon?"

"Yeah," he replied. "In 10 minutes or so."

Perfect. With paper and pen in hand, I was ready to make some money.

I waited impatiently, ready to jot down the numbers. The minutes slowly ticked by, and finally the news anchor announced the giga-funds numbers: 10-12-17-31-52, with the giga number being 22. I wrote them all down, stuffed the paper in my pocket, and pressed my watch three times.

I quickly threw a dollar at the same guy behind the counter and asked for a giga-funds ticket.

He stared back at me blankly. "Ticket sales end an hour before the drawing. It's an hour before the drawing."

I looked in shock at the clock on the wall and sure enough, it read 8:35. I should have had three more minutes! Had I miscalculated? Well, no emergency.

I pressed the watch button once more and secured my fortune.

Again, I smiled at the man at the counter and asked for a giga-funds ticket.

"Your numbers or random ones?" he asked.

I couldn't help but chuckle. "Mine: 10-12-17-31-52 and the giga number of 22."

He printed the ticket. I triple-checked it and left. In just over an hour, I would be a millionaire! I went back home to my pizza and video games and awaited the 9:35 drawing.

Sure enough, I won the lottery. I began to think of all the wonderful things I could do—vacations, homes, hotels, casinos, women…not to mention worthy charitable causes.

I had to celebrate, so I immediately called Ryan. He picked up on the first ring.

"I am taking us out for a night on the town, man!" I yelled into the phone.

There was a pause, and then he slowly replied, "I've got a lot of work to do. It's Tuesday."

I couldn't contain myself. "C'mon on, I'll buy you that solid oak pool table you've always wanted!"

Silence.

"I won the lottery!" I shouted. It took him a moment to believe me, but eventually he agreed to let me take him out. I told him to meet me at the Tiki Lounge, a fancy, trendy, and, of course, expensive, club to start out the evening. "Be there in an hour or else," I said in a joking-threatening tone before I hung up the phone.

After taking a hot shower and applying some unnecessary musk, cologne, and hair gel, I leapt in my car and drove off to the Tiki Lounge. I felt indestructible. $234 million under my belt! No need to worry about a job, money, anything. I could even move out of my parents' place and build my own mansion or two! With a moat. And underground secret passages! There were so many things to think about.

Everything that happened after I stepped out of my car and into the Tiki Lounge is a blur. I can't help but wonder what is racing through your heads right now. Probably doubt and disbelief. But I mean, seriously, how else could I have won the lottery in one try? I'd never even bought a ticket before that night. Wasn't my style. I think the lottery is nothing but an exploitation of the poor and ignorant.

I remember that Ryan and I played pool, and I talked to some women for a while. I do remember driving a girl to another club, but I'm pretty sure that wasn't Clarita. Clarita was a real party girl. I don't know how I wound up with her. I've never been good with the ladies, but somehow we were headed back to my place at the end of the night. I have no recollection of leaving the bar. I have no recollection of even driving, really.

While I was behind the wheel and trying to focus on the intersection of Alsace and Randolph, from out of nowhere, a red sports car came bursting from the opposite direction. This part I remember clearly. I saw the oncoming headlights and had only a split second to brace myself. It crashed into the side of my car with unimaginable brute force, and before I knew it, my car was spinning around, and bits of glass were sticking into my face.

When the car stopped moving, I looked over and saw Clarita's body smashed onto the windshield. There was blood all over everything. I felt okay, but then again, I knew I was too intoxicated to know if I was injured.

Through the broken windshield of my car, I saw another automobile in front of me, the front of it totaled. It was the red sports car. A man stumbled out of it and mumbled garbled dialogue.

I reacted with a gut instinct. I started my car up and ran him over.

His body toppled onto my hood, his torso twisting. He slid off my car, and his head cracked against the pavement. I knew I needed to use my watch.

I frantically pushed the button…but nothing happened. I pressed the watch again and again. I was still covered in blood, and Clarita's body was still splayed across the hood of the car. Her legs were dangling inside the passenger window.

I must have pressed that watch button 100 times before I decided to flee. The car still worked, so I kept my foot shoved down on the gas all the way home.

Imagine my surprise to see you two guys waiting for me when I got there. The sun was starting to rise, yet mere minutes after the accident, I had two suits at my door. And you thought you were coming to chide me over some petty insurance fraud! I guess you know the rest. Be thankful I was in control enough to park the car and not drive the both of you over.

I've been thinking about that watch and why it didn't work that night. Was it because alcohol was involved? Did I somehow deserve to have all of that happen? Probably not.

Probably the simple truth is that the watch was only going to work 21 times for 20 minutes each press. But I'll never know for sure.

The watch face went blank that night. No one believes my story. I doubt anyone ever will. But does that really matter now? I'm a multimillionaire. I'll buy this city while I'm still in prison. I'll be the most popular, insane, time-traveling inmate in the country. Think about what awaits me—reality shows, books, novels, big-time Hollywood movies.

Two deaths, and I might only be responsible for one of them. Think about that. It doesn't matter what I did. I have more money than I know what to do with. I have the best lawyers in the world helping me. The public is interested in me now. I'm their new star.

Ben Bucksley, the narrator of the story you just heard, sat patiently at his interrogation table across from two men wearing suits. They hadn't said a word for the last hour. They'd just sat, staring at Ben as he spun out his tale of time travel as an excuse for running down a drunk driver without remorse. Turned out the drunk driver had been at the Tiki Lounge with Ben earlier that night and was encouraged to put as many drinks as he wanted on the growing tab. It also turned out that Ben's intoxication had had nothing to do with the traffic accident, only the murder that followed.

Ben had finished talking; everyone sat in silence. Eventually, the detectives stood and walked out the door of the bare interrogation room, shutting it behind them.

Ben sat alone, chained to the chair he sat in. The suits gazed at Ben through the small glass pane in the door. One of them spoke.

"I'll meet you in the conference room in 10 minutes." The suit walked away; the other stood alone in the hallway, examining Ben, who, despite the fact that he was sitting in shackles, didn't seem to be disturbed by any of the events of the day.

The detective reached into his pocket, pulled out the cheap plastic watch, and hastily slapped it onto his wrist. He pressed the side button.

Behind him, through the glass panel of the door, the two suits could be seen listening to the end of Ben's story all over again.

The detective looked down at the watch, which now read 22x. He took a deep breath and walked away.

Explain to a family living without electricity in a country you never heard of how all of your hard work in life is responsible for your wealth.

MERCY BLOW

SOME SAY THAT OUTSIDERS in any given society have a better understanding of the world they live in. Others think of them as being a magnet for discrimination and a way to fight social injustice.

When I was 13, I stood out. It wasn't so much because of my appearance or the first impression I made; it was what everyone knew about me that made me different. I couldn't make friends, no one would talk to me in school, and I was never asked to play sports during recess.

High school wasn't much better. While I was able to socialize, lingering rumors haunted me through graduation. What am I supposed to say when everyone asks if it is true? Is it something

I do often? Did I take pleasure in it? No one cared to hear me out. No one has ever wanted me to explain why I did it. It was all bad timing.

Kimberly and Amanda, the two popular girls in seventh grade, had been walking home from school on a sunny spring afternoon and had just happened to see me bash in a rabbit's head with a stick. Not once, but three times, in fact. That day changed my life in ways I could have never imagined. If the two girls had been walking home 30 seconds earlier, my life would have been different. But as it was, I'd had to learn to live with my actions.

After that, the next day at school had been a nightmare. If only that incident had happened on a Friday afternoon. But it had happened on a Tuesday, which meant three whole days of intimidation before the weekend.

When I woke up that Wednesday, I felt sick. I knew others would know what I'd done, that they'd be asking about what I'd done, that they'd ridicule me. And that's exactly what happened. I didn't have a class with Kimberly or Amanda, but I might as well have. Everyone gave me horrible looks that day and all the days that followed.

Josh Campins, the class tough kid, came up to me during lunch that day. "Is what I'm hearing true?" he asked.

I looked up, not knowing what to say.

"You bash in a bunny's head with a stick in the park for kicks?" he continued.

I still had no idea what to say.

"You're sick," he blurted out, and gave me a threatening glare. And that was when I knew that my life as I knew it was over.

I only lived five minutes from my middle school, so it was convenient to ride my bike when the weather was nice. I even often beat the bus home. My path took me through a busy intersection, and to avoid that, I always cut through the city park. On my way home on that eventful day, I'd been cycling through the park when a rabbit had skipped out of a nearby bush and dashed in front of my bike. I didn't have any time to react. The event was over before I knew it. My front tire was suddenly twisted over the poor guy, and I'd been thrown onto the ground.

I stood up to find the rabbit lying next to my bicycle with its eyes wide open. It seemed as if he was staring right at me, blaming me for what had happened. His jaw opened, and his feet began to flail, and he screamed like a small child.

I stood, motionless, watching death creep slowly and painfully over the innocent creature. Life is a cruel thing. He kept twitching and grunting, shaking back and forth.

Nearby was a thick branch. I could either stand and watch the rabbit suffer in pain until his eventual death, or I could end it all immediately. It wasn't a difficult decision to make.

I quickly grabbed the stick, knelt down beside him, and, with a powerful swing, bashed in his head.

The noises stopped, but his body continued to convulse. My mental capacity to handle such a situation had long ended. My eyes hadn't blinked in minutes, and my heart was pounding so loudly that it was all I could hear.

I raised my hand again. Before I could consciously register what I was doing, I'd swung and cracked open the rabbit's head with two strong blows. It was all over now for the poor creature.

That was when I heard girls whispering. I turned to see Amanda and Kimberly not 10 feet away from me. As my mind slowly began to clear, I wondered what they had seen.

That's all well and good, but I'm not Edggatin-Jasperian; I'm Rhet. I'm not Edggatin and I'm not from planet Jasper, so stop defining my appearance and identity by location. I know plenty of individuals who are both Edggatin and from Jasper who are not Rhets, in fact, and you don't define them as such. Why are you so concerned with what a person is instead of who they are?

Timing of a Mad Man

DAMN! WOULD YOU LOOK at this woman? How can anyone not know what to order after standing in line for 10 minutes? It's not like there are many choices. This is McDonald's! Did she just ask for a medium-rare burger? And for breakfast? Who the hell is this woman? Well, she is on the older side, so that's a bit of an excuse.

Oh God, she just asked to use a check. Come on! Okay, you have your food now. Don't stand there wasting counter space when I could be ordering! Move to the side, and *then* worry about the extra pennies in your 1890s-style change purse, okay? Okay?? OKAY??? Move over, move over…move just a little bit. GOD! Thank you. About time!

"Hi. Number four with an orange drink, no ice. No ice in the drink."

Man, I feel bad repeating things sometimes. Especially to this kid. He seems like he has things together. But dammit, don't put ice in the drink if I asked for no ice. Is he putting ice in? Wait, yes. He's doing it. He's doing it! He just put ice in my drink! What the hell!

"I asked for no ice in my drink."

That's right, turn around, dump it out. What? He's pouring it into another cup and using the lid to keep the ice back. Why do you think I asked for no ice? It's already watered down. NO! Dammit!

"Okay, thanks…"

I can't believe it. Then again, it's McDonald's. This is what I get—ridiculous minimum-wage workers. If they could be paid less, they would. But it's not their fault. As soon as I start making a decent wage, I can upgrade to Dunkin' Donuts. Then maybe I can move up to Starbucks. That would be nice, but not today. Four months from now, maybe.

Can you get out of the doorway? Seriously, what the hell. Out of all places to stop and turn your back against society, why pick a doorway, let alone a McDonald's doorway? Get out of the doorway!

Listen, you fat tub of lard, I know you have very little to do before you head off to the Mayo Clinic, but let's think about other people, not just the extra 125 pounds hanging from your front side.

"Hi, excuse me, please, could I get by? Thank you." Yeah, that's right. God. Can't believe people like that. Someone should put her to sleep immediately.

Ah, my red beauty. How I always will have faith in you, my loyal Toyota. What's this? Did someone key me? This is deep!

What the hell! Goddamn it! But that's what I get for going to McDonald's.

DAMN! ARRGGHHH! Anyone looking at me? Any potential suspects? Pricks. God. I should go back inside. NO—I'm already running late as is. This is ridiculous. All right, off I go.

No. No. No! NO! Not a standstill on the freeway! Damn! I'M LATE! I have six minutes to get to work. SIX! I'll be lucky to get there in forty. It's that cheap, crappy alarm clock I have. It skips out on the snooze and makes me late.

Damn that paperboy who knocks over my porch light. Damn that long line at McDonald's, those Neanderthal employees, those old and fat customers, and the prick who keyed my car. And damn whoever created this mess on the freeway.

Jacob Lutt—those were his thoughts—was indeed late for work that morning. Of the possible obstructions that could have popped up to interfere with his routine, nearly all of them got in his way and made him late. His alarm clock snooze was delayed, so he got out of bed 40 seconds later than normal. His toaster snagged when it should have released, so not only did it burn the toast, it dinged 20 seconds after it should have. The line at McDonald's was on par for a weekday morning, but the old woman in front of him, the dimwitted employee, and the ignorant, fat woman at the door all contributed to Jacob's tardiness by an additional 26 seconds, not to mention the eight seconds wasted in the parking lot when he saw that his car had been keyed.

Jacob was running 1 minute and 34 seconds late, and that's all it took. Had he been on time, his car would have been flattened by a moving van that had twisted and turned over on the freeway when its tire blew out. He would have been killed instantly. Had he gotten onto the freeway any sooner, he would have been involved in a hundred-car-long pile-up.

Instead, Jacob was just mad as hell for being over two hours late for work.

Tommy awoke in a cold sweat and saw four of his closet friends sitting by his side. He jerked his head back and forth and blurted out, "We have to take care of little Missy! Frank needs $50,000 for a new heart! Quick, we need to build new roads in the East to improve conditions for those who live there!"

One of the four friends put his hand on Tommy's chest and calmly said, "Tommy, the last 60 years was just a five-second memory implant. None of that actually exists."

Tommy looked around the room and realized he was in a laboratory; suddenly, his pre-implant memories rushed back to him. He raised his eyebrows and asked, "So…Missy, Frank, and those in the East don't exist? I don't need to do anything?"

Another friend replied, "No, Tommy, they're just a figment of your imagination."

Tommy leaned back and let out a sigh. "What a relief!"

Disabled

JESSICA FEALB SAT IN THE BACK, alone and talking to no one, on her first day of high school. She had spent all summer dreaming about the possibilities of attending a new school filled with new teachers, new students, new opportunities, and new friends. Unfortunately, however, nothing was going the way she had hoped.

Ever since her early years, Jessica had been picked on and left out. She could still remember her first day of kindergarten, when all the children kept staring at her, pointing and asking what was wrong with her and why she was missing arms. True, things had changed over the years, but not by much. Instead of giving her dirty looks, now no one looked at her at all. Callous comments and vicious name-calling had been replaced by silence. If only she looked like everyone else, she could have been treated like everyone else. All she had ever wanted in life was to be normal.

Over time, Jessica learned to cope with her disability; with the advances that had been made in medical science, she had even been able to receive prosthetic limbs and engage in day-to-day activities like everyone else. But it wasn't the same. She could never hide her mechanical attachments or compete athletically like the other girls and boys. At first, she'd been placed in a special classroom setting for the 'disabled.' After proving that hers was only a physical deformity and not a mental handicap, though, she'd been moved back into a normal classroom with everyone else.

She had hoped that her days of ridicule were over, but strangers still avoided her. She was beginning to doubt that high school would be any different, that it would be a time to make friends and enjoy life and to finally be happy with who she was.

By the end of that first day, her high hopes and dreams had been completely crushed. She decided to walk home and avoid the bus filled with students' awkward stares and their blatant laughing.

In short, for a day that was supposed to be filled with joy and hopes for the future, Jessica's 15th birthday offered no signs of happiness. She was the same as she'd been the day she was born; her surroundings hadn't improved or changed in any positive way. She was an outcast, a freak, and a loner.

Jessica reached the front door to her house. Somehow, despite feeling alone and shut out from the rest of the world, she felt safe and comfortable when she was at home; there, with her stepmother, she felt like a complete individual.

"Mom?" Jessica called. She didn't see her stepmother in the kitchen or lounge, which was where she usually spent her afternoon.

After taking a brief walk around the house, Jessica heard voices coming from the back porch. She walked over to the sliding door and stepped out onto the back deck. Her stepmother was talking to a woman Jessica didn't know.

The woman looked over at Jessica, and her eyes instantly filled up with tears. She covered her mouth in shock.

Jessica didn't know how to react; was the woman another counselor sent to help her cope with life as a disabled person?

The woman quickly walked over and wrapped her arms around Jessica before she had time to react. Something was wrong, though…through the woman's irregular breathing and tears, Jessica sensed something different. There were two hands locked around her back, not four. "It's so good to see you again, Jessica," the woman cried out.

Jessica reached out with her two hands and additional two mechanical prosthetics to return the hug. She hugged the woman tightly and immediately noticed that this woman, like her, only had two arms.

"Jessica, this is your biological mother," her stepmother said. "We met during the Worlds War when she was pregnant with you. She was injured, so rather than send you back to Earth and perhaps never see you again, I adopted you in hopes that she would find us here. I'm sorry I kept her identity from you for so long, but I didn't find out until this morning that she had survived. You two have a lot of catching up to do!"

Twenty-five years after the Worlds War of 2267 ended, large populations of Earth were left mired in poverty. Nowadays, extra-terrestrial civilizations take vacations in the area to view the ancient landmarks and historical sites. They photograph the poverty-stricken conditions and don't lift a finger to do anything about it even though they come from a civilization that's far more advanced and has the means to help.

THE OTHERS

ON A NOT-TOO-DISTANT PLANET, we visit a schoolyard. What makes this planet and schoolyard unique is that everything is harmonized: The sky is always blue, the grass is always green, and the people are always orange. Everyone always wears the same purple outfit and trims the fur on their long ears in the same way. The children have learned the same textbook material for the last 1,500 years. There has never been reason to change.

Why should anyone think anything should change? Everyone is happy. The words 'question' and 'concern' aren't in their vocabulary. 'Consistency' and 'familiarity' are, and those concepts limit disputes, irregularities, and, best of all, concern about the unknown.

This is how life on Draxel has existed since language developed. The occasional individual has spoken out and tested social norms, yes, but overall, doing things like that has never caught on. Counter-culture and freakish outbursts have always been deemed dangerous. The rare occurrences of them have been handled in a discrete manner: The Insufficient Neurological Society isolates the individual until they are fully diagnosed and put out of their misery, a process that usually takes 1–5 days (12–60 Earth hours). Hence, nothing in the Draxelian mindset has prepared them for something outside of the daily routine.

On the sunny, fateful day that something finally *did* happen, the schoolyard was filled with children, all playing the same game in the same way. A giant shadow covered the field.

All the children stopped and looked up in awe. This was unlike anything any of them had ever seen. They soon realized that the moon-like object was a craft with people inside.

The interstellar explorers landed, carefully stepped out of their ship, and walked to the front of the gathered crowd of schoolchildren and a few adults. They had been studying life on Draxel for nearly 20 of their planets' days and had decided it was safe to land and interact with the Draxelians. Various conduct codes of the Intergalactic Planetary Governance Alliance prohibited such a non-educational, unprepared visit and first contact, but Draxel was outside registered territories, which meant that it was an uncharted planet inhabited by an 'unintelligent' species, one incapable of universal wave communication and prolonged interplanetary relocation.

The four explorers took off their helmets and greeted the crowd with smiles. Of course, they didn't understand each other's language; speaking would be of little use to them. Still, they knew it was important to express themselves, their differences, and exhibit their native traditions. "Eaiiiou uiooea eeeeuiooa," one of them said.

The children all stared blankly, looking almost fearful. After gifts of toys and food had been brought out, however, the children embraced their newly-discovered friends. The adults welcomed the four visitors inside the schoolhouse and ushered them into an empty classroom.

After approximately one Earth hour had passed, the explorers collectively decided that there was a problem. They were unaccustomed to fear and hostility and had a suspicion that the Draxelians held such feelings toward them—they had been sitting alone in the locked room for far too long. The explorers discussed the possibility of waiting to consult with high authorities on the matter, but after another Earth hour passed, they broke the door down and carefully stepped out into the hallway, being sure to stay together and not separate.

No Draxelians were in sight; the hallways were empty. Bemused, the explorers found their way outside to the empty schoolyard and back to their landing site. The four carefully walked around the schoolyard and found nothing and no one; everything was silent. After careful discussion, they decided it would be best to travel to their second destination on Draxel. It was surely too soon for the locals to have communicated any fears they might have had to the rest of the population.

The group walked up to their ship and found a small box lying on the ground in front of the door. It was a small, shiny metal box that could fit snugly into the palm of their hand. Three explorers looked on while one picked it up.

It beeped, then gave a sudden, harsh ring tone...and exploded. The explorers, and their spaceship and the school, were immediately destroyed.

I wouldn't mind snow if it were warm.

An Opportunity of a Lifetime

Ms. Tanner's eighth-grade students sat patiently at their desks at 7:59 a.m. and waited for the day to begin. Ms. Tanner, a skeletal 40-year-old woman wearing an old-fashioned blue floral dress, walked up to the front podium.

As always, she smiled to start the day. "Today we have a very special guest," she said. "Mr. Slueess is here from Divine Visions and will be talking to us this morning. Divine Visions is a relatively new concept that has been criticized publicly by many groups, but he is here to explain what he does and give us some demonstrations.

"Mr. Slueess?" Ms. Tanner looked expectantly toward the back of the room.

All of the students turned to see an odd-looking man sitting in the back. He wore a light brown suit that seemed too small for his irregularly-shaped, chubby body; his bald head and thick glasses only served to further emphasize his unusual appearance.

He stood up, walked to the front of the room, and took the podium. "Thank you very much," he said. In contrast to his startling looks, his voice was soothing. "Today I am going to give a demonstration that would normally be available only to the rich and famous. You will all have an opportunity to experience what few people today have experienced: a vision of your future."

A tough-looking kid raised his hand.

Mr. Slueess stopped and looked at him. "Yes?"

"My dad told me that seeing what the future holds only hinders our ability to reason for ourselves," the boy said bluntly.

Mr. Slueess chuckled. "Yes, lad, that is correct. That is why we run Divine Visions the way we do; you're able to experience a vision and come away with only its important, life-impacting moments rather than the outcome. After all, when people look at life and events, they only choose to remember the extremes.

"I went to Hong Kong II, for example. I remember one meal that was terrible, for example, and I remember the whole day I spent buying a Teleportvision. We tend to remember only the landmarks of life rather than life itself and everything that comprises it. Today, however, you will all have the chance to witness something very important. Today, we will witness an event that will affect us all in our lifetimes."

Mr. Slueess reached into his jacket pocket and pulled out a small box. "This is a DVI, a Divine Visions Identifier. There is a small scanner on the side that you will each press to have it calculate particular events in your life. We're all about to view a presentation of our deaths. The DVI will send a series of images to the classroom's projector, and we will view how each of us will die."

The same tough-looking boy raised his hand, but this time he did not wait for approval to speak. "If we see ourselves and how we die, why can't we just avoid it?"

Mr. Slueess gave a dry cough-snicker and tightened his tie with his swollen hands. "My dear boy, life is too complex for things like that. As I was saying before, we as a species are only concerned with the big picture. With Divine Visions, you will take away the essential moments that make up who you are and what you do. This morning, then, we are going to witness each of your deaths. Some take place a long time from now—some will be sooner than we would like. But after we complete the viewing, you will all forget what you have seen thanks to a memory sensor beam I will administer.

"We can't allow you to retain your full memories. You will each be able to see exactly how you will look and act when you die, yes, whether it's due to disease, old age, abuse, drugs, or a number of other misfortunes, but in the end, you will not remember what you have seen. What you *will* be allowed to take away is three words that you feel will help guide your life. They cannot be related to anything concerning your death and final moments. After we watch everyone's vision, you will write down your three words and I will approve or disapprove them in accordance with Divine Visions policy."

Mr. Slueess stopped and looked around the room at the faces of the students.

As expected, there were several alarmed and frightened ones.

Ms. Tanner spoke from the back of the room. "Those who do not wish to participate will be allowed to step outside and join a different classroom for the remainder of the morning."

The room was silent. One girl, dressed in pink, slowly stood up; all eyes quickly settled upon her. She looked around, moved away from her desk, and made her way out the door, quietly closing it behind her.

"Anyone else?" Mr. Slueess asked. "Very good. We will start at the right side of the room and work our way over to the left. Each vision will last approximately three minutes and will vary in detail and imagery."

Ms. Tanner's students thoroughly enjoyed witnessing visions of their deaths. They watched with anticipation, fear, and shock as they discovered how their lives would end. As promised, their memories were cleared of these visions shortly afterwards. They were left with just three words of wisdom to guide their lives.

Why go out when it costs so much money? Besides, tomorrow we'll be right back here without our money and with only our memories of the day before, and then those will slowly fade away. I say we juice up on the electromagno, watch some Teleportvision, and then apply the mind beam so we forget about the night. If we only remember static images and ideas, why experience them? We'll take some goofy pictures and pretend we did something enjoyable to remember tomorrow and for years to come. That way we'll have proof that we had a blast and we'll feel good about ourselves.

RUBBER REALITY

"**N**OW, REMEMBER, JEREMY," Mr. Sedpath whispered, "try not to worry about what happened today. I can't quite explain it, but I'm sure it's nothing to worry about. You just concentrate on giving the best performance of the night."

Jeremy continued to stare out of the stagecoach, not saying a word.

Mr. Sedpath put his hand on Jeremy's shoulder. "You have nothing to worry about, my dear boy; that is, of course, if you don't include the wonderful compliments and applause you will receive." Mr. Sedpath couldn't help but feel unwanted as he continued to talk to the back of the young man's head. Jeremy's career had been his dream come true; Mr. Sedpath had spent the last 12 years, ever since Jeremy's infancy, being his tutor, mentor and teacher.

"You know Jeremy," Mr. Sedpath pointed out, "your father might just make it to tonight's performance."

Jeremy's head quickly swung around. "Really?"

"Yes," Mr. Sedpath replied. "You see, because the king has taken such a liking to your music, he has made it possible for your father to attend one of your concerts."

Jeremy's eyes watered as his head lowered. He turned back toward the window. "I want nothing more than to see my father," he murmured.

"Ah, yes," said Mr. Sedpath, "and the more you practice and create, the better you will become. The better you become, the more attention and acclaim you receive. The more acclaim you receive, the better the chances are that the king will allow you to see your father. After all, it is not only for the betterment of mankind that you create such beautiful music and share it for the world to enjoy; you do it for your own well-being, too." He paused. "There's something I've been hoping to be able to tell you for some time, Jeremy, but the news has only come to my attention this week."

The coach passed Seelte Street and the front entrance to the Vienna Theater. There, an eager crowd had gathered, dressed in shades of grays and browns, many with elaborate white wigs atop their heads.

Jeremy had never understood why so many people devoutly followed his work. He had always had a passion for music, but why did his talents stand out among the more notable contemporary composers?

The coach turned the corner to the back entrance of the theater and came to a stop.

Mr. Sedpath opened the door and escorted Jeremy down the stairs and into the performer's room backstage. "You wait here, Jeremy," said Mr. Sedpath. "I'll come back and get you in about an hour. Use the time to practice; the piano here is the same as the one that's on the stage."

Mr. Sedpath left the room and shut the metal door behind him. Jeremy stood in the center of the room, contemplating what to do next. The piano would serve him well for any last-minute preparations before his performance, but practicing was the least of Jeremy's concerns. The silence overwhelmed any inclination to practice.

Something about the silence was odd, too—Jeremy's senses were tingling. Typically, he was comfortable with silence…except that now he stood in what seemed to be a mute container. Never before had he felt the desire to escape, but he did now.

No noise from outside could be heard, nor could he feel any resonances.

The piano sat in the corner, gleaming under the elaborate chandelier. Too many candles to count lit the room, projecting a variety of glowing dots across the walls and floor.

A crack along the wall captured Jeremy's attention. It ran deep and narrow, all the way up to the ceiling where an air vent was mounted. There was something about the vent that made him curious. If there was no sound, there should be no air moving through the vent, yet a string that was attached to the grate was fluttering.

Jeremy stepped on the piano bench and then up onto the piano itself. His wooden shoes clanked along the top of the piano as he made his way toward the corner of the room. Jeremy reached his right arm up as high as he could and pressed the tips of two fingers against the vent. Although his balance wasn't steady and his shoes were barely touching the edge of the piano, Jeremy reached up higher and felt a cool breeze coming from the vent. Strange...

The silence continued to bother him. He pressed his two fingers together and felt something he could not explain—it was as if he had grasped an invisible object. It felt like an air current, but he was holding it, squeezing it, and pressing it together with his fingers.

He held it tightly and pulled his hand back just a little bit. The feeling stayed between his fingers, as if it was being pulled and stretched. Jeremy reached up with his other hand and felt for the object. He quickly found it and closed his hand around it.

"Jeremy!" a voice yelled from behind him.

Jeremy jerked his head around to see Mr. Sedpath standing on the floor in the middle of the room. Before he could comprehend what Mr. Sedpath wanted, he lost his balance and fell backward onto the floor, landing on his head.

Soreness overcame Jeremy; his eyelids were too heavy to lift. He tried to move his hands but felt too weak to do much more than twitch his fingers. It felt like he was in a bed, a bed with sheets made out of the softest material he had ever touched. Even the air was cleaner than it had been before.

Jeremy tried opening his eyes again, but to no avail.

"Jeremy?" a sweet female voice asked. "Are you awake?"

Jeremy murmured and tried to speak, but all that came out were garbled words. He felt a hand on his chest as the female voice spoke again. "Everything will be okay, Jeremy. You are safe now. You had a nasty fall and are recovering in a hospital with those who love and care about you."

Instead of trying to speak, Jeremy relaxed his head, gave up trying to move, and fell back asleep.

Jeremy awoke once again to feel the same soft hand on his chest.

"Jeremy? Are you awake?" Jeremy still felt too weak to move or even open his eyes, but he managed to let out a faint grunt.

"Mr. Sedpath is on the Teleportvision and is making a public statement." Well and good, but Jeremy didn't know what a Teleportvision was or why Mr. Sedpath was making a public statement, though he did hear the voice of Mr. Sedpath; it sounded as if he was in the very same room.

"No, I can't take any questions at this time," he heard Mr. Sedpath say over the sound of mumbling. "Please let me finish my statement."

There was a short pause before Mr. Sedpath continued speaking. "I gave Jeremy Winchester a false reality and false hope. He believed the year was 1624 and that his father was very much alive...although admittedly in prison. Instead of presenting the world as it exists, I created an alternative environment for Jeremy, a world where he lived and wrote his music, always believing that there was nothing else to life. Of course, everything ran perfectly until the glitches that started last week resulted in Jeremy's concussion and spinal cord injury. I can only hope that he makes a full recovery, which doctors say he will.

"The Rab Boy 2.0 worked like a charm until the problem we recently encountered. For those of you not familiar with Rubber Realities, the Rab Boy is a large rubber-like sphere that simulates reality; the subject is inside of it. It molds to form shapes both hard and soft, and because it uses liquid display crystals, it can project any environment imaginable. The problem arose when the predictability timeline began to deteriorate. You see, the Rab Boy plans out objects, weather, and scenarios three hours in advance, so when that timeline started to wane, we began experiencing problems. Those problems ultimately led to Jeremy's injury."

Jeremy lay in his bed with his eyes closed. Since he understood very little of what Mr. Sedpath was saying and nothing of the concept of Teleportvision, Jeremy's greatest confusion laid with why Mr. Sedpath was not speaking directly to him.

The crowd began mumbling again; Mr. Sedpath told them to keep quiet. "Yes, I am quite aware that this is the top news story on Earth. Everyone I encounter and every newspaper I read all ask the same thing: How could I do this? How could I let this happen? These questions are reasonable, and I understand the hostility directed toward me. Keep in mind that I rescued Jeremy when he was just an infant; in fact, I rescued him just before his parents were deported to Rigel Four and executed for acts against the government. If not for my actions, Jeremy would not have reached his first birthday. I have given Jeremy a fulfilling childhood.

"Although he's fully immersed in work and performances, Jeremy has learned important work ethics for his adult life. His childhood was like any other; it was filled with excitement, anticipation, hard work, fear, struggle, and a desire to fit in. My first idea of this project came to me 20 years ago when the Rab Boy beta was introduced into the market for fellow scientists. What if? I thought. What if I could pull a child from an alternate reality and make him believe that the year was 1600. What if I could educate him in classical music and encourage him to become a composer? Without the influences of poorly-conceived modern music, the electronic flat world, and the media always reporting on a declining social society, I could produce a modern classical-era composer.

"Little Jeremy is just beginning his voyage to become our last great Earthian composer. He has already written two operas and three symphonies, plus a number of piano concertos, string quartets, and duets for a variety of instruments. To deny my work and Jeremy's accomplishments would be to deny the world and galaxy of the music he has created." He paused again; the crowd's muttering increased. "I'm due back at the hearing, so I must be leaving. Thank you for your time."

Jeremy heard the ruckus of the crowd following the words of Mr. Sedpath...and then there was a faint click before all of the voices fell silent.

Jeremy felt the female's hand on his chest again. "I don't understand," he said.

"What don't you understand?" asked the female voice.

Jeremy managed to open his eyes, but could only see light, not objects. "I don't understand why Mr. Sedpath didn't come here to talk to me. What is happening?"

"He should be here soon, Jeremy. What you were listening to was a news conference he was giving outside this building. You are a celebrity, Jeremy. Everyone in the world is curious about your music." That confused Jeremy even more.

"Jeremy?" a voice rang out. It was Mr. Sedpath. Jeremy heard footsteps approach him and stop next to his bed.

"What is happening, Mr. Sedpath?" Jeremy asked, almost in tears. "I don't understand what you said earlier. I'm so confused!"

Mr. Sedpath placed a hand on Jeremy's shoulder. "I raised you, Jeremy," Mr. Sedpath began, "but I lied to you. I could control what you saw and things that happened to you. I created a false world for you, one that you believed was true.

"The year is actually 2356, not 1624. We live in an electronically-dominated world where classical music is no longer composed...but I created a world for you that mimicked life in the 1600s and exposed you to all classical music created before and after the 1600s.

"I love you, Jeremy. I never meant for you to be hurt or to feel that your abilities in life were limited."

Jeremy lay in silence, still not fully understanding what Mr. Sedpath was explaining.

"It's like when you read a sheet of music, Jeremy," Mr. Sedpath continued. "When I gave you Mozart's Piano Concerto Number 19, you became totally immersed in what you were reading. You were so oblivious to the world around you that you couldn't even hear me call your name. You focused all your attention on that music and didn't comprehend that it was merely an idea and not music itself.

"I have to go now, Jeremy. Please don't let others make you believe that I am evil for having done what I did. You had a wonderful childhood, and although it was controlled and not a natural one, I believe you are a stronger individual for having grown up the way you did. Continue with your music despite what others will advise. I lived in the 1600s with you, Jeremy. Don't let the inspiration you sought be the means to the end. Let it be the beginning."

Mr. Sedpath let go of Jeremy's hand and walked away. Jeremy was left alone in his bed, blind to the world around him, too weak and injured to understand what his new life had in store for him.

Do you speak any languages other than English?

No, why would I need to?

WORLD AT WAR

PRIOR TO THE UNIFICATION OF UNIONS in 2190, which proceeded to create a worldwide supranation in 2223, Earth was in bad shape. Poor countries were in desperate need of financial and economic support, while the greater nations had problems of their own—illegal immigration, the initiation of and involvement in costly wars, and internal corruption.

Despite all this, in 2215, Earth rejoiced and came together to celebrate the first commercial rocket travel to Mars. Ever since the first non-research mission in 2138, when a group of forty astronauts landed on the red surface to start a permanent colony, Earthians had taken great joy and pride in their species' accomplishment.

Soon, they knew, they could leave their dying planet and begin anew on Mars.

On the morning of January 5, 2215, citizens came together to experience one of the most important world events in their lifetimes. Two thousand selected citizens from all regions of Earth, including full families, couples, and singles, had been randomly selected from a list of billions to have the first opportunity to move to Mars.

At 7:04 a.m., the ESF54P rocket blasted off and broke away from Earth's surface. During the few seconds the land-bound citizens had to view the ship for the last time, they couldn't help but feel relief. Relief because no matter how badly they had messed up Earth by continuing to promote misplaced agendas, there would now be a new generation of humans out there still living in Earth's solar system. Earthians, they all thought, might completely destroy their native homeland over the next few millennia, but at least humans would still have the opportunity to develop their methods of education and thinking and to organize their resources to make a fresh start on a world not so far away.

The ESF54P shot upward like lightning, soaring into distant space, but just before it was to be a mere memory in the minds of every citizen on Earth, an unfamiliar sound echoed through the atmosphere.

A giant ball of blue light came flashing down and intercepted the starship; the two collided in an unbelievable explosion. It was obvious that everyone on board had surely died an instant death.

The ball of flames and smoke hung in the atmosphere even as the sky filled with blue rain. It was as though giant flames were descending from the heavens. As the balls of light impacted the Earth, everything within a mile of its center of contact was instantly destroyed.

Earth was under attack. The millions of citizens that had gathered outside to view the rocket blast off scurried for shelter, but there was little hope for anyone on the planet. Blue rain continued to pour down, destroying everything in its path. It wasn't long after that that the battleships arrived.

Earth was given a challenging test of her ability to defend herself. The outlook appeared grim. Smaller countries were zapped in a matter of seconds, while the superpowers struggled to maintain an effective defense. The United States had the strongest military forces, but those had been scattered across the globe, serving unsuccessfully as peacekeepers within unstable countries.

Even with well-positioned heavy artillery, nothing could bring down the blue battleships that came along with the rain. No one knew were they came from or what they wanted. All the Earthians knew was that the invaders wanted to destroy the human race.

Every country felt the impact of the colossal death toll. Damages to roads, businesses, homes, and priceless monuments and art instantly climbed into the trillions of dollars.

After two days of worldwide panic, Earth fell silent. Citizens carefully stepped out of their houses and shelters to find that the horrific bombings, blue rains, and blue ships had ceased their attack. The ships, in fact, were nowhere to be found.

It was a miraculous day for Earth and all its citizens. The world came together in a way it never had before. World leaders were praised for their cooperation and leadership in defeating the extraterrestrial attack. The large industrialized nations had utilized their military equipment, the secondary nations had developed attack plans and defense routes, and the poorer nations became safety zones and hospitals. All Earthian resources were utilized to their highest potential.

The world lost interest in its previous petty wars and the hierarchy of nations. Everyone was now equal and united. In the years to come, the Unification of Unions had no difficulties uniting the planet. A supranation was formed eight years later without violence or contention.

In 2237, a variety of theories regarding the attack on Earth in 2215 (which came to be called The Rains of 2215) became commonly held beliefs. The cultural assertions began as underground conspiracy theories and were later accepted as most likely being true.

What first caught the attention of the conspiracy theorists was the damage and death toll across the planet. The extraterrestrials had attacked the strongest military bases, which were conveniently located in the most unstable countries on the planet. All five of them, in fact, had been occupied by never-ending civil wars. The rich countries had experienced much less destruction than what one might expect from an invading army—although large cities lost significant skylines and even city blocks, the damage wasn't nearly as devastating as it would have been had the attacks been initiated during regular business hours.

The reported death toll of The Rain of 2215 was 87,673,339 citizens. That, of course, was the number given by the government. Independent polling suggested that the actual number was less than a third of the government's report.

Too many critical, historical structures and foundations of the United States had been conveniently left intact, critics said. Too many troubled countries had been obliterated, and the world had been too quick to come together in peace and unify into a single government. How could an alien species more advanced than us be defeated by a relatively primitive culture in a matter of days? Why would an advanced culture need to attack us in the first place?

If the extraterrestrials had perfected space travel, they surely had solved problems with food development and storage and interplanetary travel. Surely they had eliminated conflicts within their own species. There was no reason for an attack, no logical foresight to their attack patterns, and realistically no possibility for Earth to have been able to defend herself. The powerful nations on Earth may have carried out The Rains of 2215 in an effort to unify the planet. Considering the enormous benefits The Rains had brought, however, no opposition to the unification had ever developed.

She works to sell and lives to buy. She consumes for pleasure and exists to be bought. She pursues advertising and hobbies consumerism. She fears being misplaced in the masses and values her accessories. She seeks the best, then strives for the better. It is because of this that she will never realize what happiness is.

A Letter from Vesta

Intergalactic Planetary Governance Alliance
4958 N. Woodland
Chicago, IL W-0021
West World 1
Earth

Chancellor Gaurudo Mousen
3326 N. 15B
Ovalarium
South Krate
Vesta

February 11, 2353

Intergalactic Planetary Governance Alliance,

I am writing with unease and frustration concerning your "confirmatory success" hiring policy. For the past 20 years, my fellow residents on Vesta have been continuously ignored and discriminated against.

Confirmatory success supports discrimination by discriminating against others. It was created to end discrimination based on hair color and thickness and planet of origin, but rather than excluding these factors, confirmatory success policies force hiring administrators to base their judgments solely on these issues.

Both maroon-haired and Vesta-born individuals are being ignored. Since the end of the Worlds War in 2267, we have been at a disadvantage. Having had all of our resources depleted due to warfare, as well as having had our strongest youth conscripted into the military, our culture has been set back for the benefit of others. We have been severely wronged and harmed by Earthians.

Earth should compensate us for societal imbalances Earth has caused. Confirmatory success has only benefited our upper-class, those who can strongly compete with Earth applicants and/or are well-off in Vesta's economy. This leaves us with a weak economy indeed.

Why do you think confirmatory success policies are a means to alleviate discrimination? Shouldn't it be a more positive process, such as a reward for the accomplishments made despite 80 years of oppression? According to the Alliance's definitions, it doesn't sound like people of Earth want to embrace that idea. By your logic and history, in fact, it sounds like the idea behind confirmatory success is that individuals have been discriminated against and therefore should be given jobs. But don't we all have something to gain from an individual who is capable and who has succeeded despite having faced many odds and ample discrimination?

Maybe your idea is to promote diversity. Shouldn't preference be given on the basis of an individual talent and not hair color or planetary origin? Given our minority status, it is offensive that confirmatory success categorizes and assumes that we all think and act alike.

Cultural anemia is a disease that must be dealt with through decisive action; confirmatory success only forces Earth into discrimination and segregation mentalities. Believing you have solved an endless problem by creating a new one only intensifies the issue. You will not find the means to an end by using this 'temporary remedy' to address social injustice; rather, you will come to realize that you have created a new unbalanced playing field for all life-kind.

Chancellor Gaurudo Mousen

Every day when I leave my house, I make sure my possessions are arranged in an orderly manner so that in the event that I die, my relatives won't think I lived like a slob.

THE NEW WORLD

JASON KNEW HE HAD TO remain calm and professional, despite the fact he was only 12 years old. He stood next to the bed of General Reeves, who lay silent with his eyes closed. The General's chest moved slowly as he took in his last breaths of air.

Everyone knew what to expect; they'd feared it from the beginning. Jason had been chosen as the leader of Generation Next (as the elders had called it), so he took it upon himself to take charge in such a dire situation.

He reached out and placed his hand gently on the General's shoulder. A group of children, none older than 10, crowded at the windows of the hospital-like room. A hundred more sat patiently in the Starship's center room and waited to hear the grim news.

General Reeves died in three days. The children performed a small service before shooting his body into space. No longer under the command of General Reeves and having lost all adults who had once been in charge of the ship, the Starship Frontier was now entirely inhabited by children. They had always had an elder to look to for guidance and stories about their old world, but suddenly they were all alone: They were a new generation traveling to a new world without any knowledge of what they had left. They only had curiosity for the new world they would reach in 60 years.

Jason was the only member of Generation Next to have been born on Earth. Being only a year old at the time Starship Frontier had launched, he had no memory of humanity's homeland. Everyone else, all 122 children aboard, had been born on the same ship that was to deliver them to a new world of hope and promise. For the last 11 years, Starship Frontier had been traveling on a 71-year course to reach the solar system containing Sirius, one of the brightest stars visible from Earth.

In desperate need to escape the Worlds War and a planet beset with famine, disease, overpopulation, and unbearable pollution, a group of individuals had developed The Frontier Society to combat social problems in order to protect the future of their children. As the years passed, the society had grown in parallel to the increasing problems on Earth.

After losing half of their members to an alien flu, however, the society decided to combine their resources and flee to the promising, neutral planet of Tolu Mesa orbiting Sirius. They wanted their children to live in a world without war and poverty, a world filled with color and healthy flora. On March 12, 2267, the Starship Frontier had broken free from Earth's atmosphere with 207 adults and one infant aboard.

Jason's earliest memory was the day he had been introduced to ice cream. He had been no older than four, sitting at his work-table in his family's unit, when his ailing mother sat down next to him. She had trouble carrying the light bowl, but because she knew he would like the treat, she made sure to deliver it herself.

Jason didn't remember much about his parents; they only existed as distant, muffled visions. But his first experience with ice cream had always remained sharp in his memory. A scarce commodity on the Starship, ice cream was strictly rationed. The Starship's initial supply of soybeans and odeo and maerr flower seeds was modest and the greenhouse had limited room for non-essential foods.

The majority of the children had been born two years after launch, making Jason the oldest of Generation Next by three years. His mother, who died before his fifth birthday, lived on through his vague memories: when she had scolded him for not acting like an adult in front of all the children, when she had given him his last hugs and smiles on her death bed, when she had introduced him to ice cream.

Since then, he, like all of the children, had been given a small bowl of ice cream every three months. Some of the children gobbled it down as quickly as possible while others savored every small bite. The anticipation of receiving ice cream again stayed with him until the next happy day arrived.

It had been seven days since General Reeves' body had been jettisoned into space. Jason maintained the same routine that everyone had experienced throughout their lives; having done nothing else, he had no means to think or act differently.

Every day, Jason checked the navigation computer to cross-check the system's analysis of Sirius and any unexpected objects (debris, asteroids, or other ships) that might have been be in their path. Nothing surprising ever happened. Should a problem arise, however, Starship would automatically correct its course to avoid a collision.

For the next two months, Jason became immersed in logs left behind by the elders that spoke of the glorious new world ahead of them and the reasons they had left their home planet. He studied the health and daily system functions in detail to ensure that his title as leader was justified. His purpose as leader was not to make decisions, he knew, but to monitor the perfect system. He held no position of power or creative command.

One of his many responsibilities was to check systems and maintain the ship's automatic functions. He became so absorbed in his daily routine that he overlooked the day that was once so important to him: ice cream day.

One of the girls lightly tapped Jason on the shoulder one afternoon as he was studying the last chapter of the health manual. He turned, surprised—no one had ever needed anything from him before.

"Jason?" the girl said. "Today is ice cream day and we want ice cream."

Jason was excited. Ice cream day was not an automatic function of the ship, but rather one that would require action on his part.

Two hours later, the children sat in the vicinity of the center room and its adjacent hallways, all enjoying their small cups of ice cream. Jason found that he was not as excited as he usually was. Even though he loved ice cream and it had been three months since his last bowl, he was emotionless. What was there to be excited about? Having ice cream every three months?

After reading through the safety modules and a majority of the logs the elders had left, Jason had begun to realize just how imprisoned his life and the life of every child on the ship was. He had never questioned his daily routine before, but now, understanding the life that had existed on Earth and what living on a planet was like, Jason felt that his existence didn't serve a purpose; he was merely a living transportation device to help transfer humanity to another planet. By the time they reached Tolu Mesa, he would be 72 years old, hardly an age to start a new life…should he live that long.

Jason stood and walked to the center of the room. No one seemed to notice.

"How would all of you like to have ice cream every Friday?" Jason yelled out.

The room became silent. Everyone was clearly going into a state of shock as they slowly realized that since they ran the ship, they could call the shots. Their system didn't need to stay the way it was—control was in their hands.

"I propose," Jason continued, speaking loudly enough for everyone to hear, "that we have ice cream after dinner every Friday for the remainder of our journey on this ship. There's no telling if we will still crave it in 10 years, and there is no telling we won't be able to produce it at a quick rate in the future."

The children remained silent. No one had ever been called upon to make his or her own decision before, and agreeing to this proposal felt like disobeying orders.

Instead of waiting for the children to support his idea, Jason decided to reverse the proposal. "How many of you object to receiving ice cream every Friday?" he shouted.

No one responded. Hundreds of little faces ranging from four years old to 11 years old gazed at him. Not one word.

"Then it is settled," Jason continued. "We shall start this new tradition tomorrow." The children immediately turned their faces back into their bowls of ice cream, many with wide grins.

Jason took a seat in an open space on the floor in the corner and hoped he could enjoy his ice cream and not have to worry about catching up on modules or logs for the next hour. His relief was short-lived.

A small boy followed him to his resting spot and didn't hesitate to disturb him. "My name is Mack," the little boy said as he sat down next to Jason.

"I know who you are, Mack. Where is your bowl of ice cream?" Jason asked.

"I ate it already, sir," Mack answered. "I have a question for you. What is Earth like?"

"I was only on Earth for the first year of my life," Jason said bluntly. "I don't remember anything about it. My first memory is up here with you guys."

"But you've read all those books. What's Earth like?" Mack persisted.

"It's a dying world. Poverty everywhere, depleted resources, heavy pollution, crime, famine. It's not a place where you'd want to live."

Jason took his last spoonful of ice cream and savored its richness.

"I wish I could at least see it." Mack mumbled.

Jason had never wished that before, not with having heard all the horrible stories the elders had told him. There was no reason to ponder visiting Earth. He may have lived there for year, but he had no recollection of the experience. Everything that he knew about the planet had been through his parent's perspective.

His brow furrowed in thought. Then again, would life any-where else be just as problematic as it would be on Earth? Would he really be better off living the majority or even the entirety of his life on a spaceship?

"Home," he said suddenly.

Mack looked puzzled. "What?"

"Earth is our home and we're only 10 years away from it," Jason continued. "Why live our entire life on a spaceship when we can go back home right now? What's the point of dying on this ship to escape something we may not hate and may even enjoy?"

Jason quickly stood and marched to the center of the room. "Attention everyone!" Jason yelled.

All of the children stopped their chatter immediately.

Jason continued. "I've decided to turn us around and head back home to Earth. There is no point in running away from something we don't know anything about. We should give ourselves the opportunity to live a full life without restrictions and imprisonment.

"Our current course has us landing on Tolu Mesa in 60 years. If our ship survives that long, many of us will die before we land. And those of us lucky to survive will just be alive long enough to grasp the concept of living in a new environment.

"There are no guarantees that Tolu Mesa is as luxurious as we believe it to be; likewise, Earth may not be as hazardous as we have been told. The conditions are favorable for life on Tolu Mesa, true, but it may also be barren. There is no point in wasting our lives while we wait for something to happen. We should take some initiative and control our own destiny."

The following day, Jason served everyone a bowl of ice cream. All the children were excited to get it, as always. Jason again took center stage and presented his plan to travel back to Earth on a 10-year timetable as opposed to landing on Tolu Mesa in 60 years.

No one responded to his plan, no one challenged it, and no one bothered to present any alternatives. Ten years after its departure, Starship Frontier changed its course and headed back to the world from whence it came.

In 2228, Earth passed measures to reform its government. Problems with health, nationality (regional or planetary), and education were the popular topics. Below is a sample of the information given to citizens informing them of their future voting privileges.

Registration for Earthian citizenship voting privileges requires both of the following:
1. Being over the age of 16 Earth years.
2. Having been born beneath the Earth's ozone layer or having been a legal citizen for five Earth years.

Citizens receive 10 votes per election once they've registered. Below are terms by which each individual's 10 votes are affected after reaching the age of 25 Earth years:

+1 point   Having been a legal Earthian for over 30 Earth years
+1 point   Having received a degree from a secondary higher education institution
+1 point   Having received a degree from a triary higher education institution
+1 point   Having completed 1,000 to 1,999 registered community service hours
+2 points   Having completed 2,000 to 2,999 registered community service hours
+3 points   Having completed 3,000 or more registered community service hours

−1 point   Having been convicted of 1 class C crime
−3 points   Having been convicted of 2 class C crimes
−6 points   Having been convicted of 3 or more class C crimes
−6 points   Having been convicted of any class D or higher crime
−5 points   Not having a lower education degree
−3 points   Not fitting the Preservation Society's standards of fitness based on your height and species/nationality
−2 points   Having purchased over 100 cartons of HorJub (nico-mierathane) products

If a citizen receives a "0" or "negative" rating, that citizen will not be allowed to vote.

Precautions

THE SECRET TO SARAH WRETT'S success is not that she was born with talent or connections or inherited fortunes. No, she just knows how to get things done. She has stated many times that distractions are your worst enemy.

"If you want to succeed in life," she says, "you have to focus on goals that will help you succeed. Anything else will only work against your cause."

People often ask her how to make their fortunes, live like queens or kings, and ultimately be happy. She hates this. Ms. Wrett does give professional advice, but she will not dispense random tips, especially to people on the street. Not everyone is the same, she points out, and if everyone attempted to succeed with the same goals, there would be no way to differentiate between the rich and successful and the working class and the poor.

"Don't work," Sarah often says in her motivational speeches. "Instead, let work be done *for* you. Reach a stepping stone in your life where people are willing to work for you and in your place, people who are willing to make smaller and smaller wages, leaving you with more of the profit. If you're not the one at the top, you are a slave to your employers—you'll work the majority of your life for their cause."

Rarely will Sarah give lectures or make public appearances. She does the bare necessary minimum to keep her image alive in the public mind and to maintain her celebrity status. The way she sees it, public appearances and motivational speeches only take precious time away from her true aspiration: success.

"Most people don't know what happiness is," she says, "They work eight hours a day and come home. For what? What is the point? Why let your job run your life? How are you supposed to enjoy what you have at home when you are only there as a means to take an extended break from work? I don't understand the concept of non-asset thinking."

Sarah made her riches in college, dropping out during her junior year to manufacture a line of jewelry aimed at early teens. Selling cheap plastic accessories didn't cost her much and the demand for it was extraordinary. She soon owned a company with over 200 employees. When she earned her first million, she invested in real estate, renting out her homes and letting the tenants pay off her mortgages and propel her into further riches. She sold her properties once the houses were paid off for $6.4 million in profit. Not long after that, she started her brand, *Sarah Wrett*, and became known as one of the most powerful businesswomen in the world.

"Why do work for others and help make them rich? It's ridiculous. Start your own business and have people work for you; that's what I did. Every employee who's working for you is another individual working their tail off to make you rich. That's what I'm doing now—all of you just paid $120 to come see me. I bank $80 for every head in this room. And that's how you become rich."

Maintaining one's wealth, she has always claimed, is a business game. "Some companies move their facilities to Mexico and some lay off 80% of their workforce, but I am an opportunist. I see my options and I act accordingly. I don't want to live in Mexico!

"Your business is your spouse. You have to be married to it. My job, my employees, my line; they are all the family I need. When you have something running this smoothly, when everyone in the world knows your name and your net worth is over $1 billion, you know you have reached success."

Critical reviews of her books and coverage of her numerous Teleportvision appearances indicate that while Ms. Wrett may know how to make money, she has no idea of how to achieve happiness.

"These comments are ludicrous," she responds. "In the first place, I'm very successful and have gobs of money. Secondly, if I were unhappy, why would I continue doing what I am doing? I can afford anything anyone can buy, but I limit myself; if I lavish my surroundings with pointless gadgets and fancy homes, I wouldn't have any motivation to get any work done.

"I may never marry or have kids," she admits, "but I don't have time for that. I'd be too distracted from getting work done. If people can have a family life and enjoy what their line of work is, too, great, let them eat cake. But if you are asking me if my idea of a good time is spending a year of my life fat and motionless and then the following 10 years drowning in kids crying, screaming, and constantly needing my attention, I don't need it. I don't want it. I don't crave it.

"I know how to keep my mind on work. It's simple: Know your goals and know what it will take to achieve them. You really don't need motivation, per se, but you do need to limit your obstructions. Don't take vacations, don't consume, and surely don't revel in biologically-driven urges to waste time trying to impress members of the interested sex.

"Put yourself in an environment where you will achieve. Put yourself in a place that will help you be recognized, where others will not only want to work under you but also do your work for you, during which time you work on expanding your name and growing your business. Friends, lovers, children, and purchased liabilities are only obstacles toward controlling your true happiness."

How long before routine becomes imprisonment?

A LETTER TO VESTA

Chancellor Gaurudo Mousen
3326 N. 15B
Ovalarium
South Krate
Vesta

Intergalactic Planetary Governance Alliance
265 S. 24th St. Central
Milwaukee, WI W-0187
Eastern Sace 2A
Earth

November 07, 2353

Dear Chancellor Mousen,

We deeply apologize for any perceived grievance you may have experienced as a result of the Confirmatory Success Initiative in Earth's hiring policies. Please keep in mind that the purpose of Confirmatory

Success is to create a program of opportunity; it is not a program of discrimination.

Our mission to ensure equal opportunities has allowed the people of Vesta and other underrepresented groups to gain access to fifth-level education institutions and professional jobs on Earth. If you were to look at our hiring data, you will see that the majority of cases in which an Earthian is not hired is because of a lack of qualifications rather than any factors having to do with the Confirmatory Success program. Many life forms, in fact, would not be where they are today without the benefit of this program. It has made the Interplanetary System more aware of ethnicities, distinguishing characteristics, and planetary origins; as a result, equality is enhanced, not denied.

We at the Alliance understand that certain groups were wronged historically. As a result of this, they are owed compensation or restitution. Discrimination is still present in today's society and Confirmatory Success is needed to eliminate such discrimination. It is needed to create a truly distributive fair society. Please accept my apologies for the lateness of my reply. Your letter was sent to an address that became inactive 30 years ago. Chicago no longer exists—it was destroyed in the Worlds War of 2267.

Thank you for your concern,

Jack Chamberland
IPGA Secretary

Here I am. Or better said, here I *all* am. Five clones of myself and I are about to play some three-on-three basketball. Who will win? How in the world are we going to decide who starts with the ball if we will all act exactly the same?

ABANDONED

OB, CHERYL, AND ADAM, the three surviving members of
the EARTH521 Liberty Explorer, approached an abandoned
building in hopes of finding clues concerning the planet they had
crashed on five days ago. Food rations would soon be depleted, they
knew, and they desperately needed to find signs of life. Luckily,
they believed the planet upon which they found themselves was
within the eastern Ghardi Galaxy. That meant that if the planet
was inhabited by intelligent life, those lifeforms would probably
speak either Dehl- or Jerhy-based languages, which the explorers
could speak. They hoped that the old building would contain
signs of civilization or keys to their survival.

The three walked in to find a single large, open room. Pipes traveled along the ceiling and walls; floor faucets laid in tumbled heaps, surrounded by red stains. There was no question that it was blood.

Giant unidentifiable bones lay on the floor. Some were full skeletons and were chained at the joints, some lay in single, barren pieces. Along the far wall, a large metal rack held large stabbing weapons in place: ones with large blades and others with thin, long, jagged spears.

This was surely not the sign of civilization they were looking for; rather, it was remnants of a barbaric culture, one that was obviously still struggling to advance beyond violence and the desire for torture.

The three explorers walked around the room looking for something specific that could guide them to a nearby city (abandoned or not). They didn't find anything. It appeared that whatever species had created the horrific scene had quickly come and gone.

They stepped outside and noticed faint symbols that had once boldly identified the entrance. The foreign characters looked strangely familiar...

"'House of fine meats'," Cheryl said into the silence. The others stood in mute shock.

"Come on," she said, "let's keep walking."

Dave leaned over and slapped the snooze button on his alarm clock. He felt lousy waking up so early even though he woke up at the same time every day. He closed his eyes and allowed soothing relaxation to take over his body, a faint smile on his lips.

The alarm sounded again and Dave slapped the snooze button another time. He looked at the clock and realized he had to get up.

A loud patrol car could be heard driving slowly up the street.

"Attention citizens," a voice echoed out, "For the past 28,800 days, the IPGA has made an error in calculating time on Earth. They accidentally inserted an additional three seconds into each day.

"That means that as of today, the government is 24 hours ahead of schedule. To compensate for the error and fix our schedules, we will resume all routine functions in 24 hours. Please continue sleeping, and sorry for the inconvenience."

Dave turned off his alarm clock and went back to sleep.

FLYING CARS

JESSICA McLYLA DIDN'T EARN her fortune through decades of hard work; instead, her parents merely provided her with everything she ever needed or wanted. And seeing as she didn't even have to wait until their demise to reach her riches, she's been living in luxury for years. It's been nothing but opulence for this 25-year-old trust fund baby. She has been able to buy anything she's ever wanted; any desire she's ever had could be satisfied with a simple purchase.

Recently, she'd realized what money *couldn't* buy. It dawned on her that she was missing so many things: products she'd never sampled, places she'd never visited, and scents she'd never smelled. Why? Because of time. Over the years, historical monuments had been demolished, famous presidents and celebrities had been killed, famous chocolates and fragrances had been discontinued, and wonderful animals like the dodo, quagga, tarpan, and the bos taurus had gone extinct. All because of time.

Jessica bought *Story of Life*'s first ticket available to the public for a return trip back in time. (*Story of Life* was the first return time travel corporation.) The ticket cost the equivalent of a three-year salary. Jessica would be a pioneer; she would travel back in time and return to the present.

Jessica's driver opened the back door to her personal limo. A second later, her stylish, designer heels touched the sidewalk. They clicked against the pavement and attracted more attention than usual to herself as she raced up the steps that led into *Story of Life*.

A mob of photographers and gawkers surrounded her with cameras and microphones, but she wasn't interested in talking to them. It was precisely because she adored the attention that ignoring them was the boundary of her love—her great passion was her ability to deny their interest. For now, however, she needed to escape the madness of the press and begin her travels.

Although Jessica was already a celebrity because of her fortune and time in the spotlight, she was going to be able to thank her voyage into a new frontier, time tourism, to immortalize her name. She threw *Story of Life*'s front doors open with a wide grin and leapt inside. Finally, she was in the spotlight for something she had decided to do and not as the result of other people's decisions!

A handsome young man walked around the corner into the waiting room as she sat and filed her fingernails. He wore a traditional white doctor's robe and held a clipboard in his hand.

"I'm Dr. White," he said as he approached Jessica. She held out her hand for him to shake. "If you'll come right this way, we'll go over your trip and safety precautions."

Jessica stood and followed Dr. White down the hall and into a small, barren room. It held no artwork or shelves, just an outdated fold-out table and a chair in the center of the room.

"Please take a seat, Ms. McLyla," Dr. White said.

Jessica took a seat and Dr. White unclipped papers from the board.

"You're in for an exciting trip," he said with a smile. "Now, as you know, you will have a guide traveling with you. This is strictly because of the risks involved with time travel and for minimum security supervision. Nearly all safety, security, and alteration liabilities will be your responsibility. Of course, you already know that, because you thoroughly read through our manual."

Dr. White smiled and Jessica gave out a chuckle. She reached into her purse and pulled out a stack of papers several inches thick and placed it onto the table. "Most of it," she said. "But I can assure you that you have all 72 of my signatures." She pushed the documents over to Dr. White, who began flipping through them.

Jessica watched Dr. White's eyes for any signs of reluctance. She had not read any of the documents. If her 72 required signatures had not been indicated by a highlighted X, in fact, she would have never been able to find them all. Not surprising considering that she had never had to think freely during her entire 25 years of existence.

Dr. White finished flipping through Jessica's manual. "Excellent," he said, and pushed the documents to the side. "Now, let's talk about your destinations. It is important to remember the most important safety precautions when dealing with Old-Time New York City," he began.

Jessica rolled her eyes slightly but caught herself before he could notice. She wasn't at all interested in Dr. White's safety speech—she was about to embark on the opportunity of a lifetime! She was about to travel back to Old-Time New York City where she could eat steak, drink chocolate, and shop for rare jewelry. It was going to be an extraordinary four nights and five days back in time.

Dr. White stopped talking; Jessica was at a loss what to say. He opened his eyes wider as if he expected a response.

"I know it's important," Jessica said with a smile.

"Good," he replied. "Now let's review one last detail." He looked up with a smile. "The most important detail that we have discussed many times must be said one last time."

Knowing exactly what he was talking about, Jessica quickly interrupted him. "Nothing comes back that wasn't brought back and everything brought back must come back."

Dr. White grinned widely. "Great. Great. So, when was the last time you ate and what was it?"

"I had a glass of water this morning and two pieces of toast last night before I went to bed."

Dr. White stood up and walked toward the door. "A nurse will be in shortly to dress you. You won't be wearing anything except one of our gowns with some historic money and a credit card."

He paused as he opened the door. "Any last questions for me?"

Jessica looked up and smiled. "No, I think I'm fine."

"Great," he replied, "I'll see you in the transport room." He gently shut the door behind him.

Three hours later, Jessica was ready to go. She'd been stripped naked, she'd gone through a chemical shower, she'd been fitted with a proper gown, injected with what they referred to as travel serum, and given $500 in historic dollars (HSTD) and a credit card. Because of the international inline credit crack disaster, *Story of Life* was able to create a VISA check card that would allow Jessica to charge up to $5,000HSTD, about 100 Dalds, during her short trip. That amount also included cash withdrawals. The value of HSTD and the process/concept of physical money had all been clearly explained to her earlier, along with historic slang terms, body gestures, and cultural norms.

Jessica lay on the electronic stretcher, ready to be slowly inserted into a tube filled with wires and moving parts. Dr. White approached her with a clipboard. "How do you feel, Jessica?"

She looked up half-lidded and said, "I'm doing well."

Dr. White rested his hand on Jessica's shoulder. "Now," he said. "It can be easy to panic once you are in the tube. It's a small space, there are moving gears at every angle, and the serum will make you feel like you are going to the bathroom and sitting in a hot tub at the same time."

Jessica smiled, "I can't wait."

Dr. White looked over at his clipboard. "One last bit of information: When and how are you returning?"

Jessica rolled her eyes and in a monotone replied, "Five days after my arrival. Between 118 and 120 hours, I need to strip myself of any assets and make sure I am wearing the *Story of Life* gown and nothing else. I need to be in an enclosed room or area to ensure that no one witnesses my disappearance."

"Very good," Dr. White said with a smile. His grin quickly changed into a serious grimace. "Whatever you do," he said, "will alter the future in ways you can't even begin to imagine. Whether it's your own destiny, the future, or our present, carelessness will be noticed. It may be tempting to smuggle items back with you, but even the slightest action can create a domino effect with colossal consequences."

Jessica felt insulted. Was he accusing her of something she hadn't done? Why would he assume such a thing and why say it now? Even without having read the manual, that subject had been covered thoroughly.

Dr. White gave her a cold, warning look before walking away.

Jessica jerked up and found herself in a small room—so small that she couldn't lie down if she tried. She was crammed into the corner with her knees pressed against her face.

When she looked up, blinking, she saw a mirror, a small sitting panel, and a door. Jessica stood, reached for the metal doorknob, and turned it. The wall opened up.

A well-dressed woman stood blocking what would be her first glimpse of Old-Time New York City. The stranger smiled and immediately pushed clothes into Jessica's chest. "Here, try these on," the woman said. "Your money is in the side pocket of the pants along with your credit card. These are the clothes you supposedly came into this store with, so you don't need to pay for them."

Jessica felt the need to talk, to ask this woman who she was and what was going on, but the woman was talking much too fast for Jessica to interject. "You must return to this changing room in order to travel back," the woman continued. "This is where your gown will be waiting." She paused.

"We will be watching you, Ms. McLyla. Watching you all the time. You won't know who we are or where we are; you can't escape us nor trick us, so don't even try. Have a wonderful vacation and welcome to Old-Time New York City." The woman smiled and closed the door in Jessica's face.

Jessica turned around, still holding the pile of clothes, and looked at herself in the mirror. For the first time, she noticed that she looked and felt unhappy. She stood with a frown and red eyes, about to cry.

She couldn't help it—she dropped the clothes and held her hands to her face, sobbing. She had never thought about secret, undercover security agents. How on Earth was she going to smuggle jewels and riches from the past back to her time in the present with them around? What value would her trip have if she would have nothing to show for it afterwards? No possessions to parade around to her friends back home? How could she enjoy a vacation knowing that when it was over she would have no material goods from it?

She looked up into the mirror and gazed into her bloodshot eyes. 'Don't worry about this just yet,' she thought. 'Get dressed, walk around, and see the sights first. Find some chocolate to drink and then contemplate your plan.' A small smile crept across Jessica's face as she began to sort through the pile of clothes.

Seeing downtown Old-Time New York City was an experience Jessica never could have anticipated. Of course, she'd seen photos and historical documents, but the real thing was unlike anything she had imagined! Everything seemed so archaic and horribly outdated. Buildings were obviously constructed from the inside out, they looked as if they could fall over at any second, and streets were plagued with cracks and potholes. It was all so foreign and intriguing.

She gazed in horrified awe at clunky old-fashioned automobiles emitting gasses, poorly-constructed cement and brick buildings, and constricted streets. The worst thing was that there was no sense of open travel. She walked aimlessly, mostly staring at the cityscape above her and occasionally bumping into a pedestrian who reacted with poor manners.

Soon, she found a drink store and stepped inside. She cautiously looked around to see if anyone noticed that she did not belong there and pondered what to order from the large list of unknown beverages. She knew what she was looking at must be coffee drinks, but the names and styles were all abstract to her. She just wanted some chocolate.

"Can I help you?" the young man behind the counter asked.

"Um, yes," she replied, "I'm not familiar with this menu. Do you sell any chocolate that I can drink?"

The young man smiled and replied, "Yes, we have iced chocolate and hot chocolate."

Jessica perked up with excitement. "I'll have the largest-size cup of hot chocolate, please."

Taking a sip of the hot chocolate was indescribable. Simply put, it was the most amazing thing she had ever had in her entire life. She savored every second of every sip. 'Now,' she thought, 'I need to figure out a way to bring things back with me.'

Jessica sat at a table in front of a window overlooking a busy street in Old-Time New York and pondered matters. What about eating small items of jewelry moments before returning to the present? That would allow her to smuggle ample amounts of treasures without detection, but still, that method might prove difficult if a security administrator witnessed her doing it. They might be watching her every move. Surely she could find time alone to swallow anything she would want, but how would she disguise purchasing unnecessary items?

Jessica cupped her hot chocolate with both hands. 'Such a wonderful thing, this hot chocolate,' she thought. She took another sip and slowly swallowed. How could she enjoy her trip if everything would just be a memory afterwards? How could she enjoy what laid ahead if every action would only serve as a temporary, static image until it completely faded away with time?

Jessica drank the last bit of chocolate from her large cup, closing her eyes and thoroughly savoring the rich flavor and creamy texture. 'If only I'd done some research and more planning in advance, I'd know what to do,' she thought. 'What difference does it make if I bring back one lousy ring? One insignificant little ring? Maybe there was something about that in one of the clauses in that manual. Maybe it mentioned everything I needed to know about security. What if they replace everything that I un-do back here? What if they have the right to kill me should things get out of line?'

Jessica exited the drink store, turned, and aimlessly walked down the busy sidewalk. Who could be following her? How many people could be watching her every move? What type of vacation was this turning into? One simple infraction of the time travel regulations could cost her an early return...or, quite possibly, an early end to it all.

Jessica returned to the clothing store 118 hours after her arrival in Old-Time New York City and found the woman who had originally greeted her.

"Right this way," the woman said.

Jessica followed her to the back of the store and through an unmarked door. She found herself in a small room containing nothing more than a bench and a coat hanger. Jessica's original gown hung on the hanger.

"Undress," the woman said. Jessica didn't feel the need to question the command; she'd had a feeling something like this would happen. She still hesitated a little, though—the past 118 hours had been both a vacation and challenge for her, and she hated to think of her time in the past ending.

She'd also been tormented about how she could bring something back with her, something to remember her vacation, something to boast to her friends about, something to make her a true celebrity. Finally, she had devised a plan.

Jessica had made a friend at a local coffee shop. From there, with her large sums of money, she'd paid her newly-found friend to purchase a camera in order to document her travels and sightseeing over the last few days. Her request had been simple: "Stay out of my way, get close but don't draw suspicion, and take as many pictures as you possibly can."

Just hours before returning to the clothing store, Jessica had made one last rendezvous: She'd handed her secret friend $2,000HSTD in cash and received a small plastic chip containing thousands of images. Jessica then walked into a nearby restaurant to enjoy her last meal of the past and then carefully swallowed her vacation souvenir.

Jessica stood completely naked in front of a woman who could easily decide her fate for the worse should she fail some kind of test. But it wouldn't happen because of the extra precautions Jessica had taken.

The woman smiled. "Please put on your gown."

Jessica stepped back into the small changing room and the woman shut the door behind her. She took a seat and waited, having no idea what to expect next. Soon, she became tired and drowsy, and she fell asleep.

Jessica awoke to find herself on an electronic stretcher with Dr. White standing next to her.

"Have a good trip?" he asked.

Jessica sat up and smiled. "It was wonderful!" She was more excited than she'd expected to be, plus she didn't feel any pain or nausea.

"You're all set to change and head on home whenever you feel up to it, Jessica," Dr. White said.

Jessica smiled again and rose from the stretcher. A nurse escorted her out of the transport room into a private dressing room where her original clothes lay.

As Jessica changed, she couldn't help thinking about the many pictures she had brought back with her. So many stories and curiosities of the past now belonged to her. They weren't a fading memory—they were tangible, material goods that she owned and would be able to share.

Jessica walked into the main room of *Story of Life*, where the receptionist greeted her kindly. "Did you have a fun trip?" the woman asked.

"It was wonderful," Jessica said, "so wonderful that I can't even explain how wonderful it was."

"Would you like me to call your driver to come pick you up?"

"That would be wonderful," Jessica said. "Thank you, I'll wait outside." She walked to the door and left with a bounce in her step.

Once outside, Jessica leaned against the rails of the narrow balcony that stood hundreds of stories above the ground. Flying cars whizzed by her; the stiff breeze gave her quite the chill.

She gazed out at the view of the surrounding skyscrapers that were thousands and thousands of stories tall, then leaned over the railing and gazed downward at the many layers of traffic and lights.

She felt great to be back, safe and sound. Everything was once again as it had been.

Sigma211:	Greetings
Sigmo211:	Aloha
Sigma211:	I couldn't help but notice your name, what educational software were you brought up on?
Sigmo211:	Historical Database
Sigma211:	Wow, me too!
Sigmo211:	Wow!
Sigma211:	What music do you have installed in your featured playlist?
Sigmo211:	Opus 2, their new album
Sigma211:	Wow, me too!
Sigmo211:	Wow!
Sigma211:	You seem like a really cool person
Sigmo211:	Yeah, you too!
Sigma211:	I think that since we have identical historical databases, our personalities should match if not be identical
Sigmo211:	I know, I think we could really understand each other
Sigma211:	Want to meet for lunch tomorrow?
Sigmo211:	Want to meet for lunch tomorrow?
Sigma211:	haha
Sigmo211:	haha
Sigma211:	wow
Sigmo211:	wow
Sigma211:	Max's @ 1?
Sigmo211:	Sounds great!
Sigma211:	See you there!
Sigmo211:	See you there!
Sigma211:	bye!
Sigmo211:	bye!

1912

M s. Jacobs sat peacefully in her reclining seat with her eyes shut. The hum of the train and the soothing rocking were making the trip as comfortable as possible. Only two others occupied this particular car; the mid-day train out of the city never housed much of a crowd.

It had been a stressful two weeks for Ms. Jacobs. Although she was successful in her corporate role as Vice President of Human Relations, her parent company was in the middle of a corporate takeover, which made her worry about her job security.

It had all been a blur ever since Spaver, Inc. had hit the jackpot with the rise of wireless, self-operating, signal-power electronics. Ten years ago, that technology was up-and-coming; now, it was everywhere. So popular in fact, that copycat firms were flourishing and the name Spaver, Inc. would soon become a name of the past (along with Ms. Jacobs). It's unfortunate that those who are successful are sometimes punished for their deeds.

The train jerked to a stop, causing Ms. Jacobs's head to bash into the seat in front of her. Pain radiated through her forehead.

"Thiensville!" shouted the stubby attendant as he strode through the car. "Thiensville, this stop!"

Ms. Jacobs stood up, only half-balanced, and walked down the length of the car. She stumbled while trying to walk in a straight line. A bright ray of sunlight struck her as she turned the corner of the car to exit.

She gave a gasp of discomfort and raised her free hand to shade her eyes from the sun. She stepped carefully to regain her balance; she didn't want to have an embarrassing trip or fall while exiting the train.

Her heels sank into the fresh grass. It was peaceful here, she thought, aside from the blinding sun. Birds chirped somewhere overhead.

Ms. Jacobs looked to her left and then to her right. No one else had exited the train. She looked down at her feet and contemplated her quickly-sinking heels.

Behind her, the train started to move, and at the exact moment she realized that she couldn't do anything about it, Ms. Jacobs knew she exited at the wrong stop. She could only sigh and watch the last car race into the distance.

"Great," she said aloud, still holding her bruised forehead with one hand and blocking the sun from her eyes with the other. She noticed what was most likely a train station: a small wooden building nearby with a low, wide platform that ran along the tracks.

She took one quick step forward, sank deeper into the ground, and fell. She lay motionless, not knowing how to proceed. She would need to stand up and walk onward, obviously, but doing so would surely result in falling again. She waited to build up enough strength, then thrust herself upright into a sitting position.

The sky above looked brighter and clearer than usual—it was a brilliant blue expanse with pure white clouds streaming across it. How strange to see the sky without its usual smog or aircraft-fume trails.

Ms. Jacobs took a deep breath and noticed how fresh the air was. And the birdsong! She'd never heard such lyricism before.

Suddenly, Ms. Jacobs began to feel a cold, unpleasant feeling in her hips. The moisture from the soil was slowly soaking into her clothes. It was time to stand up. She pressed both her hands deep into the wet earth and lifted herself up. Slowly, and without losing her shoes, she walked to the station.

Ms. Jacobs gave a sigh of relief as she stepped onto the wooden platform of the station. She tilted her head down to take a look at herself. Her feet and hands were covered in mud, and her skirt and waist were soaked. Not good. Her pounding headache, too, was getting increasingly worse.

The station was empty, although there was a sales window on the other end of the large room. Surely, someone would be inside to assist her.

Ms. Jacobs staggered across the platform to find the counter vacant. A sign was stapled to the post towering over the desk. "Thiensville to Milwaukee," it read in bold, black letters. "Every weekend, coming June 1913."

She stood, trying to grasp the meaning of the flyer. The ink was printed on uneven, off-white paper. No color, just black-and-white basic text. 1913? Was this a code for existing train lines?

Surely a date hundreds of years in the past served no purpose. Was it a prank?

Ms. Jacobs looked around, hoping to find someone nearby. Just then, a loud cough echoed across the platform. She followed the noise and eventually found her way to an entrance.

Ms. Jacobs walked into the station's small waiting room to find that everything was made of wood—well-crafted, to be sure, but extremely dated.

An elderly woman was curled up on one of the many benches. Ms. Jacobs gave a sigh of relief and approached her.

"Excuse me?" she asked, in a hopeful, light voice.

The elderly woman slowly turned her head and opened her droopy eyes.

Ms. Jacobs continued. "I just got off the wrong stop, and I usually don't travel during the day. Would you happen to know when the next train to Chains III will be coming?"

The elderly woman stared back without blinking.

Ms. Jacobs repeated herself. "Do you know when the next northbound train will arrive?"

Again, no response. But what kind of response would an elderly woman dressed in sheets have to give? Ms. Jacobs retreated.

Behind the back of the wooden station, Ms. Jacobs found a dirt path winding through the high grasses. There didn't seem to be any other marked trails, so she took it.

She made her way through a lightly-forested area and came out into an opening filled with people and market stands. As she made her way to the nearest booth, she noticed how everyone was dressed. It was unlike anything she had ever seen before, and seeing as everyone was wearing plain, subtle colors, she was surely going to stand out from the group with her designer suit and muddy heels.

"Good afternoon, miss!" a cheerful voice shouted.

Ms. Jacobs turned to see a teenage boy carrying a load of small animal skins over his shoulder with a long stick and string.

"You don't look like you are from around here," he said.

Ms. Jacobs gazed at the boy's dirty face and well-beaten clothes. "I think I'm lost, actually. Where exactly am I?"

The boy smiled. "You are in Thiensville, Wisconsin, ma'am!"

Ms. Jacobs shook her head, bewildered. "I'm not familiar with Wisconsin, young man," she replied.

"Well!" the boy exclaimed, "Wisconsin's economy is based on farming—dairy farming, specifically. But many of us are miners and lumberjacks. Our train system will be completed some time next year and will connect us to Milwaukee and the large-scale industrial jobs that are rapidly growing there. We all believe that once our train system is in place, Wisconsin's population will rapidly increase by 1920."

"1920?" Ms. Jacobs repeated, still confused. "What year is it now?"

The young boy smiled again. "1912, ma'am." He turned and kept on going through the market stands.

She wandered from person to person and heard stories from everyone about themselves and their town: how the town worked as a community, what they did to assist their families, how the barter system functioned. It was fascinating for Ms. Jacobs to experience how excited everyone seemed to be despite living in what was to her prehistoric times. Every member of the community was putting in a hard day's work, she soon realized. One elderly woman sat on a short bench in front of her house with a textured board and a bucket of water, bartering her laundry services for collecting goods. Other people were trading produce in exchange for eggs, furs, knitting, fabrics, and household goods.

Ms. Jacobs was taken aback by the overall filth. Everyone's clothes were dirty and full of stains, rips, and tears. Dust was being continuously kicked up into the air and had settled on everything, especially everyone's hair. The fact that they lacked sound building materials such as cement and tile could be seen in their muddy, uneven walkways and poorly-built structures.

Ms. Jacobs walked to a porch of a nearby building and took a seat.

"Taking a rest, are ya?" came a woman's voice from behind her.

Ms. Jacobs turned around to see a 50-year-old woman standing behind her. She was wearing a ragged, dirty dress and held a broom in one hand. "Well you just sit tight, dear, I can work around you," the woman said as she began sweeping the porch.

"How do you get out of here?" Ms. Jacobs asked.

The woman, looking confused, kept sweeping. "Here? I'm not sure what you mean. You mean Thiensville?"

"Yes. How do you leave Thiensville?"

The woman stopped sweeping. "Why would I want to leave? Everything I've got and need is right here. When the train opens up, I might take a day to travel and experience a train and see the big city, but I've got too much to do around here." The woman smiled, made a few last passes with her broom, and walked back inside.

Ms. Jacobs sat and stared at her hands, not knowing what to think. How could she have traveled here? She had never heard of Thiensville during her many commutes on that particular rail line and route, yet the conductor had clearly announced "Thiensville" and she chose to exit.

She sighed. Regardless of the reasoning or logical explanation (or lack of them), she was stuck in the year 1912. She did her best not to have a mental breakdown—she'd save that for later, when there would be no one around to bother.

A little girl walked up to Ms. Jacobs, holding a fur in one hand. She stopped in front of her as if Ms. Jacobs was blocking her way into the house.

"Why do you get to wear that?" the little girl asked in a complaining whine.

Ms. Jacobs was confused. "What do you mean, little girl?"

The small girl looked down and kicked the dirt lightly. "I don't know," she said.

"Eleanor!" came a voice from the porch. "Come inside and get ready for supper."

The little girl ducked her head and walked up the steps and into the house.

Ms. Jacobs turned to see the same woman who'd swept around her. "How have you been during the last five minutes?" she asked.

The woman gave a loud chuckle. "Yeah, right. Don't get me started." She grabbed the broom and started sweeping the porch again.

"Why are you sweeping again?" asked Ms. Jacobs, noticing that the woman's smile looked forced.

The woman's arms swayed back and forth as she swept. The broom, thought Ms. Jacobs, was probably just knocking back and forth whatever dirt might still possibly remain. "Oh," the woman replied eventually, "you know how dirty this porch gets."

Ms. Jacobs noticed Eleanor in the distance, rolling around the floor of the main room like any small child would. The two of them made eye contact and Eleanor stopped and giggled, then extended her arm slightly.

Ms. Jacobs didn't know what to make of the girl's gesture—she didn't seem to be pointing at herself or anything outside. Her arm moved to the side again, and her short, stubby hand pointed to an electrical outlet on the wall, inches off the ground.

Eleanor's loud, cackling laugh made the woman stop her sweeping. "What on Earth do you think you are doing?" she asked. She propped the broom up against the building, walked inside, and shut the door behind her.

Ms. Jacobs sat dumbfounded, listening to the muffled yelling coming from inside the house, yelling that was eclipsed by another noise that drew her attention. She turned to see a woman approaching her. Unlike everyone else she'd seen, this woman was wearing a business suit.

Suddenly, everything became clear; the approaching woman was Rosemary, her business colleague.

Rosemary took a seat next to her on the porch. "Do you like it here?" she asked.

Ms. Jacobs smiled, realizing that she simply hadn't been able to recognize her surroundings. "You know," she replied, "it's more convincing than I could ever give you credit for. This goes beyond any current mindset or knowledge of the past—you could convince anyone that they traveled back in time."

Ms. Jacobs was able to keep her outlandish experience to herself. Fatigue and a bump on the head can go a long way; for Ms. Jacobs, it caused her to overlook the reality of being in an old-time village and instead convinced her that she had traveled back in time.

Is it ever rational to deduce that you've traveled back in time hundreds of years? Maybe a simple, more rational explanation would be more sufficient.

"Where are the BANANAS!?" an elderly man shouted in the produce section of a grocery store. Shoppers quietly turned to look at the old man as he waved his arms about and shook his head back and forth in annoyance.

"No BANANAS? What's going on here??" he raved on.

An employee quickly approached the man. "I'm sorry, sir, but we are out of bananas. We should have more by 6 a.m. tomorrow," he said patiently but firmly.

The old man furrowed his brow and dipped his chin toward his chest. "Goddamn it, how can you not have bananas? This is a disgrace. You should be ashamed of yourself!"

Frozen in Time

MARY AWOKE SUNDAY MORNING and headed downstairs. But something odd had happened that morning: She hadn't found her husband, Mark, next to her when she had woken up. They had both gone to bed at midnight, and he always slept in later than she did.

Mary was entertaining the thought that he might have awakened early to fix the kitchen counter since it was on top of their to-do list. She stepped down the last bit of stair and headed toward the kitchen.

It was not only spotless, it was brand new! The counter had been completely re-done, the stove and refrigerator were brand-new stainless steel appliances, and the floor had gone from being flimsy floorboard to being large, 17" tiles. The job must have taken a crew of 20 to complete this in such a short time...and it had been done so quietly that she hadn't awakened. How had anyone managed to replace tiles and a counter while removing and replacing appliances?

"Honey?" she called out loudly.

No response. She walked through the house in her tank top and bright pink pajama pants.

"Mark?" she repeated as she crossed from room to room. There was no sign of her husband.

Mary entered the Teleportvision room and noticed that the Sunday paper was lying on the coffee table. Not knowing where her husband was or what to expect next, she decided to sit, relax, and read the newspaper that he obviously must have brought inside that morning.

She sorted through the entertainment, arts, and main sections, and then the ads, making piles on the floor as she went.

Something else was different: The newspapers didn't make a sound when they landed. She looked down and noticed thick, bright carpet; one she'd never seen before, covering the entire floor.

Just then, the front door opened.

"Mark?" she called out, turning around and looking toward the kitchen. Footsteps echoed and grew louder and louder as they approached.

Mark walked in, wearing baggy pants, a sweater, oversized sunglasses, and a baseball cap. He stopped at the entrance to the room and stared at Mary.

She couldn't help but laugh. "Why in God's name are you wearing that?"

Mark just stood and looked at her.

Confused, Mary began wondering if this was really her husband.

Mark slowly walked around the coffee table to take a seat on the opposite side of the couch, leaving the middle cushion open. "Mary," he said in a low voice, "I have a problem."

Mary still felt confused. "You sound funny. Are you getting a cold?"

"No," he responded, "I need to tell you something, and it's important you believe what I tell you."

Mary shook her head slightly. "Wait a sec, honey, first tell me who made all these improvements in the kitchen."

Mark didn't respond.

"How did you install new carpeting?" Mary persisted. "Did you do this all overnight?"

Mark continued his solemn stare. "I have something to tell you."

Mary gazed back at her husband in shock. He'd never sounded this serious before. "What is it?" she asked.

In answer, Mark slowly grasped the bill of his cap and pulled it off, unleashing long, grey hair. He pulled off his sunglasses to reveal wrinkles, sunken eyes, and long, twisty, grey eyebrows.

Mary gasped. Her 33-year-old husband suddenly looked like he was a 65-year-old man! The two gazed wordlessly at each other for an instant before Mark looked down.

Mary's mind swam with questions. "What happened to you?" she whispered. She leaned toward him and reached out to touch his face, lightly stroking his cheeks and brushing her fingers through his hair. "Is this real?" she asked.

Mark continued to stare at the floor. "Honey," he began, slowly and painfully, "I am somewhere between 60 and 68 years old."

Mary, stunned, said nothing.

He looked Mary in the eyes. "Are you familiar with *Story of Life?*" he asked.

Mary sank back into the couch. "The return time travel corporation?" she asked.

"Yes," Mark replied. "One of my clients works there and gave me a unique gift for helping him—a device that has the ability to slow down time.

"I only accepted it because it was a gift. The unit sat on my desk for weeks and I refused to try it. Such power can create corruption, I thought. I didn't want to become greedy or use it for ill means.

"One day, though, I noticed a bulge sticking out of the lower back of a customer's jacket. He wasn't my client, but I'd heard some twisted things about him. That's when my curiosity kicked in. I pushed the button on the device, and everything stopped. People stopped moving and everything went completely silent. It was just me and a hundred frozen people—it was surreal.

"I stood up slowly, ever so carefully, not knowing what I was dealing with. But later I learned that time hadn't sped up for me—everything else had slowed down.

"It took me some time to adjust to my new altered reality, but eventually, I made my way over to my customer with the bulging jacket. I lifted the backside of it. Sure enough, I saw a pistol lodged into his pants.

"Lifting his coat had been like moving a frozen, wet towel in the sense that his jacket molded to wherever I placed it. Very, very strange...I removed the gun, walked out the door, and into the street.

"I was astonished to see a silent downtown: There were hundreds of cars and pedestrians, and they were all silent and motionless. Not wanting anyone to find the gun, I threw it down the sewer, went back inside to my desk, and pressed the button again. Immediately, everything went back to normal."

Mark stopped to gaze at his Mary.

She was clinging to his every word. Her lips were quivering and her eyes were filled with tears; she wanted to reach out and grasp her husband's hand, but she couldn't read his body language. Had he chosen to sit away from her because he had more horrifying news to tell her?

"What happened next?" she asked.

"I didn't use the device again for several weeks," he continued, looking at the floor again, "but my mind was swelling with ideas and adventures that I could live out if I could stop time. Just think of the possibilities. I could travel anywhere I wanted, finish all of my paperwork, and tie up life's loose ends in the blink of an eye.

"I started using the device. Instead of working out at Lex's, I'd take an hour off from time to time during my workday to enjoy a long run in suspended time. Nothing is more peaceful than jogging in the city when you are the only thing moving.

"Then I started using it before you got home to finish my work so that I could spend more time with you. But the more hours I spent locked in time, the more sleep I needed; after all, I was awake throughout it all, and I was aging.

"I lost track of how often I was using the device; often, I'd sleep the entire time I activated it just to catch up with reality. I had nothing but good intentions…and when we had our fight over the kitchen counter, I decided I would use it just one last time. One last time to complete one last task…and then I'd destroy it. I had come to the realization that I must have aged at least six months with my initial addiction."

Mary interrupted, tears running down her face. "Why didn't you tell me, honey? What have you been doing for 30 years?" She could barely speak through her tears.

After an awkward pause, Mark slowly continued. "I knew it would be difficult to tell you about what I'd done. Such a selfish thing. I tried holding the device behind my back, holding on to your hand, and pressing the button, but it would only work for me. That's why I thought I would destroy it so that I'd never have to explain it and it would never be an issue again.

"Last night—at least, last night for you—I decided to take a week or two off work and re-do the kitchen. It was a stupid idea, but I wanted it to be done. I wanted to surprise you. And I figured that if it was my last trip, I could afford a couple of weeks.

"Not having moved heavy items during a state of time-lapse, I miscalculated and had an accident—I broke my arm. It was put into a cast at the hospital that night, and I decided to stay locked in slow-time until both the kitchen was done and my arm was healed. I was so ashamed of what I did, I thought I could afford a few more weeks to patch up my mistakes.

"It took me longer than expected, but I was nearly finished with the kitchen. Because of my broken arm, though, I was slower and often clumsier. I should have taken better precautions..." He paused, then continued with a shaking voice. "I broke the device; the new fridge crushed half of it, and it stopped working. I was trapped."

Mark began to tear up and had to stop. He covered his face with his hands and began gasping for air.

Mary slid over to the middle cushion of the couch and softly placed her hand on Mark's shoulder as he did his best to continue. "It took me years to teach myself how to build another device. I must have read every book in existence on time devices. Years of loneliness, years of regret, years of nothing but searching for one goal: how I could unlock myself from my time prison.

"I thought my release would never come; I kept thinking I would die and never see you awake again. I can't tell you how many days I just stared at you in your sleep. Holding you, wishing I could talk to you one more time."

He lifted his head and looked at her with tear-filled eyes. "I thought I had lost you! I couldn't find the answers anywhere I looked. I nearly gave up after 25 years of trying, but I had to teach myself. I had to create my own inventions based on what I'd read. I don't know what mistakes I kept making, but finally, having tried over and over again, I was able to find my way back home."

Mary sat motionless, too upset to ever cry. "What have you done, Mark? What have you done? Why didn't you tell me?"

She leaned forward and gave her aged husband a hug. They clung to each other tightly.

After an eternity, Mark slowly shifted away from her. "I have a favor to ask you," he said.

Mary looked on with wide eyes as Mark reached into his pocket and pulled out a small black device with a white button in the middle of it.

"This is my invention," he said, "I don't want to destroy it. I want you to, but I want you to do something first. I want you to explore the world. I want you to try exotic new foods, see far-away places, read all the books you've never had time to read.

"But do it responsibly, not like me. Take two-week vacations and come back to me for a week, or a month…a year, it doesn't matter. This is a blessing as much as it is a curse. It is the most magical and devastating thing that has happened to me.

"Catch up on time with me, Mary. Take advantage of this unique opportunity and catch up to my age. Will you?"

Mark took his wife's wrist and slowly slid the device into her hand.

I saw the look on his face. Even though he had a stop sign, he had no intention of stopping; it didn't matter that he was legally obligated to stop at the corner. I could tell that he was careless, but I kept on pedaling on my bike. I might be dead now, but at least I was right.

RESEARCH METHODS

D R. PATRICK NERVOUSLY WALKED, hoping to remain unnoticed. He was well aware that being 65 years old and having a thick, white beard and glasses meant that he would stand out.

A couple appeared in front of him and crossed his path, causing him to jump back and drop his notebook. He leaned over quickly to pick it up with shaking fingers.

It was clear that he was too anxious to go exploring. Dr. Patrick had just arrived to a time hundreds of years in the past to study commonalities among cultures sharing linear paths. He'd known it was a one-way ticket when he signed up with *From a Distance*, but that hadn't bothered him. He was determined to explore far-flung societies and learn about unknown cultures. Doing so had always been his profession as well as his passion.

He strongly believed that the ability to connect to other cultures, both from a personal and analytical standpoint, provided a more accurate perception of others. Comparing and contrasting a variety of ideas tends to eliminate bias and bring positive attributes to light, he knew. By better understanding differences in our society, we can enhance knowledge of ourselves. Dr. Patrick had booked his one-way vacation to expand his admiration of the world and gain a better appreciation of humanity's roots.

When he was a young man, the Worlds War of 2267 had greatly influenced Dr. Patrick's aspirations. His life had been radically changed when his home was blown to pieces on his 10th birthday. It was sheer luck that his life hadn't ended then. If he hadn't disobeyed his parents' request to stay home for dinner that fateful night, he would have been killed along with them. But instead, he'd survived and grew up without a family, knowing that his home and loved ones had been selected by a Threftaaj warrior ship for destruction despite not having any connection to the Alliance or the popular rebellion or even to any local governments.

Hundreds of homes had been targeted every day at random across the globe in an ongoing counterattack on the Alliance. Those events had made the young Dr. Patrick question how life worked. If quantum physics is right, he'd thought, then randomness does not exist. Events only look random to us because we cannot make predictions or know precise details of our history. Our limited knowledge hinders our capability to perceive how scenarios will play out.

The idea that his family had been killed and that his home had been destroyed based on a random order for destruction from the Threftaaj baffled Dr. Patrick's young mind. What had accounted for this random selection? Surely something could explain the selective action that had resulted in such violent attacks.

By the time he was 18, Dr. Patrick had already graduated from a third-level educational institution. Over the next six years, he completed his last two degrees and, through his copious books and articles, began to reshape how the native cultures of Europa were viewed and understood.

But now Dr. Patrick stood in a panic and desperately wished that he wouldn't seem out of the ordinary. He spotted a bench across the road that was clearly reserved for the pedestrians who thronged the streets. Carefully, hoping not to draw attention to himself, he began walking toward the bench. No mistakes, no trips, no bumps…he safely took a seat.

Now, finally, he could relax and make his initial observations of the historic, primitive culture he found himself in. Did the Earthians even refer to themselves as such yet?

Dr. Patrick opened his notebook and took out his pen. This was the moment he had been anticipating for the last 15 years. He was going to be able to look up, bask in the glow of the local culture, and begin his new research.

A large road sign caught Dr. Patrick's attention. *MAIN ST., U.S.A.*, it said. Clearly, he was in the center of the town. 'This must be its most prized area,' he thought. 'A clean, shiny place where citizens socialized and visited.' Dr. Patrick had studied Old English and was able to understand signs.

The buildings across the street were colorfully decorated with stripes and looked like they were very tall, although Dr. Patrick thought their supposed height was most likely due to exaggerated facades that had been placed atop one-story establishments. *Early 1900s*, he wrote in his notebook as an initial observation. He'd use that date as a basis to compare future findings.

No cars or any other type of vehicles roamed the streets, and only an abandoned set of train tracks lay where the citizens walked. Luckily, however, the large crowd of people allowed Dr. Patrick to assess many different cultural norms.

One of the first things he immediately noticed was the high percentage of children compared to adults. 'Surely, in the early 1900s,' he thought, 'traveling with youth younger than 10 years in age seemed like it would be uncommon,' but seeing so many young people made him reassess the matter.

He decided this area must be a very popular one. If it weren't, it would not be kept in such pristine condition, have a variety of shops, be flooded with people, or be so popular with children. While scribbling down notes on the differences in fashion and dress, a small boy approached Dr. Patrick and tapped him on the shoulder. "Who are you, mister?"

While Dr. Patrick was well educated in Old English, he had very little training with pronunciation and slang. He hesitantly replied as best he could.

"Maaay numm Patrick," he said slowly.

The small boy's excited grin disappeared. He took a step back.

Dr. Patrick felt a moment of panic. Did this boy suspect that he was from a highly evolved civilization? The unknown often produced fear and hostility in early cultures, Dr. Patrick knew, which meant that he had many reasons for concern. But surely he didn't have to worry so much when talking to such a young person. The boy didn't run away. He continued to stare at Dr. Patrick with his eyes wide open.

A woman, most likely the boy's mother, grabbed the boy by the arm and dragged him away. Dr. Patrick couldn't make out everything she said, but it was something about bothering aliens.

He gave out a soft chuckle. Knowing that extraterrestrial civilization contact hadn't happened yet, he found her admonishments amusing.

Dr. Patrick sat and watched the crowds walk by. He cherished every possible moment, analyzing this historical moment in time, taking notes about every observation as the hours passed. He was ecstatic about his findings, which were far greater and more diverse than he had expected, thanks to the fact that Main St. USA was obviously a historical and modern landmark and provided almost everything the citizenry would need—a post office, a candy store, several restaurants, street vendors, a trade center.

Even royalty, or officials, of some sort seemed to be present. They occasionally walked past Dr. Patrick and greeted the citizens, who in turn were very enthusiastic to meet and greet them. It was likely, Dr. Patrick decided, that most citizens were willing to travel long distances for the rare chance to meet them.

But what Dr. Patrick found most interesting was the dress of the citizens. Most were wearing what appeared to be below-casual attire; meanwhile, the royalty was fashionably dressed. Some of them were oddly dressed in large decorative suits. Perhaps they were mimicking large beasts of the time or whatever gods they worshipped. The differences in dress could be a result of a barrier between classes, Dr. Patrick decided, or even a possible requirement or law. The royalty never acted like the citizens. They seemed to merely mingle and greet. He didn't notice any of them eating, sitting, or resting. It was as if they were there solely to serve the lower class. Even the children seemed to know who they were and acted more excited in their presence than they did with their elders.

The streetlights began to flicker as the sun started to set. Sparkles and tiny bulbs lined the sides and storefronts. It was a beautiful sight for Dr. Patrick, who had never seen anything so magical. No matter what he did or didn't discover, he knew, he was finally living out his dream and experiencing a different culture and way of life.

With nighttime falling, the streets became even busier. Dr. Patrick kept sitting on his bench, enthralled at what he was witnessing. There didn't seem to be any government or law enforcement, and everyone had smiles on their faces. No incidents or arguments occurred while he sat and watched. All he saw were joyous faces, couples holding hands, and excited children who laughed as they skipped and jumped around their elders. He had truly struck gold in history, he thought. He'd found a unique civilization that was filled with life, love, and openness, a civilization that didn't exhibit any signs of crime or poverty.

It wasn't much longer until Dr. Patrick realized everyone was walking in the same direction. He wasn't worried. Everyone was still smiling and holding hands, but surely there had to be a reason why everyone was moving en mass. Curious, he decided to walk with the crowd and see what was happening.

He found it quite surprising that he was being pushed and bumped after having walked 20 yards. Based on what he'd observed earlier, that kind of disrespectful behavior seemed very peculiar.

Dr. Patrick and everyone else were approaching a large, black gate that was being guarded by uniformed officials. Was it a prison? he wondered. Was everyone so happy to be out and about because it was their only free time each day? Each week? Each year?

He looked around and saw that the youth were still happy. Many of them were waving small electronics that lit up in a variety of colors as they swung them around. Others wore small black hats with plastic half-circles sticking out from the sides. As he got closer to the gate, Dr. Patrick was directed to an individual exit and forced to walk through a turnstile that monitored his entrance (or exit?).

Hundreds of citizens were walking straight from the gate into a large, multi-acre area filled with transportation vehicles. It struck him that he was observing the temporary closure of the royal land, most likely for the night. A land filled with so many honorable people that thousands of vehicles were necessary to transport the populace. What a prestigious honor it was to explore such a land. Were only a select few permitted to visit each day?

Dr. Patrick took out his notebook again and struggled to jot down any final thoughts. As the crowd waned, Dr. Patrick looked up and noticed an elaborate sign that read *The Magic Kingdom*.

His jaw dropped, then came back up as his lips curved into a wide grin. 'Of all places,' he thought. 'Of all places, I couldn't ask for a better location or better moment in time. I've been placed in the middle of a royal, magic fortress.'

Soccer is strictly a team-effort sport. Some child athletes are at a disadvantage while growing up and adapting to how the game is played. They are discriminated against for being different, whether their difference is one of weight, height, or popularity. Because of this, they learn the faults of their teammates and can see what improvements are needed from their outside vantage point, but they're never given a chance to fully participate in the game.

FLYING PIGS

THE ROOTS AND TRADITIONS of the Seaforth family date back to 1898, when their ancestors took their first steps onto American soil. As the story goes, the first ones off the ship were Slevin and Meriel, a strong, loving couple, and their son Breck, who was nearly eight months old at the time.

Their touching story begins with hardship. During the long voyage across the Atlantic, Breck fell ill. No one on board knew quite what to think. Some said he had pneumonia; some said he was suffering from brain damage. Others had entirely different ideas. It was not until the family came ashore and was able to seek help that they discovered Breck had a case of pertussis, better known then as whooping cough.

Neither the doctor nor the parents expected Breck to survive. "I'll see pigs fly the day Breck is back to 100% health," Slevin said. Nonetheless, Breck continued to hold on for weeks after having arrived in America.

No one knew quite what to make of it. How could a child with such a deadly disease survive? And yet, he didn't just survive. He prevailed.

Throughout adolescence, Breck was healthy and succeeded in both athletics and academics. In high school, he graduated at the top of his class and was a statewide sports hero because of his contributions to the state rugby football team. In fact, they won the championship.

In 1919, Breck made history by inventing the concept of metered mail, which he developed and sold to the United States government for a large sum of money. With capital to invest, Breck started the Ohio Bell Telephone Company, which soon became the dominant phone service across the state of Ohio. His patriotism also led him to invest in Ford, an all-American company; in return, Ford's stock rose and made Breck a millionaire in 1924.

Soon afterwards, Breck became very involved in the fight for American Indians and gained national attention as the voice of common America. This fight was soon won in June of 1924, when Congress declared American Indians to be United States citizens. With millions of dollars and several companies under his belt, Breck turned his goals toward helping humanity. He stepped out of the spotlight and into the realm of nonprofit organizations so that he could put his creativity, imagination, and capital toward social advancement.

Although he was a non-materialist and believed in sharing his wealth, Breck had a penchant for collecting ceramic figures and rare memorabilia depicting flying pigs. Throughout his childhood,

Breck had cherished a small sculpture his father had given him on his 10th birthday. The sculpture was a pig with wings; it symbolized a time of vulnerability and hope. Ever since Breck had gotten the sculpture, he had yearned to collect anything and everything he came across that resembled a flying pig. To him, they represented his parents' struggle for freedom, their love of life, and their love for their one and only child. Flying pigs meant independence; somehow, they encouraged him to strive to always find happiness and hope. Because of Breck's work with humanitarian causes and internationally recognized organizations, the flying pig became a symbol of hope, of faith in humankind, and of the Seaforth family itself.

Breck Seaforth died in November of 1963. Humanity lost a great hero. It was a sad and yet joyous day across the planet. As the years passed by, the symbol of the flying pig was kept alive by Breck's descendants.

In 2341, something terrible happened. A man by the name of Allun Edmund (although he could never be officially identified) started a worldwide revolution on Earth. He developed a following and was able to encourage youth culture to actively participate in their government's activities. He took on the flying pig as his symbol.

Fortunately, Allun's true aspirations soon became public. By then, though, he and his "War Pig" brigade had declared war on multiple government agencies across the globe, demanding the extermination of all Jasperian people. Because so many individuals had been brainwashed into thinking their War Pig actions were making the world a better place, it took Earth seven years to rid itself of the terrible Pig army. Within the War Pig brigade, there were two main units—the Ground Running Pigs and The Flying Pigs. Each had their own flag, commanders, and separate agendas, purpose, and followers. Once the Pig War was over, surviving followers developed their own organizations to bring down various governments and to harass Jasperian individuals and communities.

By the time the Pig War began, descendants of the Breck Seaforth family were scattered across the planet. Most of them still carried the flying pig as a symbol of their family pride. For them, although the pig had originated hundreds of years before they'd been born, it was still a symbol of hope and perseverance. Unfortunately, with the negative connotation the pig held for the rest of the world, the Seaforth families were seen as outcasts and terrorists upon sacred soil.

By the end of the war, of the 46 Seaforth families, two had been brutally murdered, 30 had their houses burned to the ground, and the remaining 14 had been forced to move to Mars to escape continual harassment and threats.

Everything the Seaforth family valued in its traditions was represented by the flying pig. Their spirits and traditions would not remain free, they knew, if what they held true went against the cultural norms of their society. Would the flying pig icon ever again be treasured for what it had originally represented—positive energy, belief in charity, and the future of mankind? Or would it always be attached to its current meaning of hatred? No one could say. Reality is based on perception. The meaning of any given symbol is only valid when it's observed.

Cold fusion changed the world in a way unlike anyone had ever imagined, and with unforeseen consequences: Widespread panic immediately followed the discovery. Everyone worried that hundreds of millions of people would lose their jobs, and in fact they did. But surprisingly, the overall outcome was not a negative one. With new technologies, worldwide supplies of food and water dramatically increased, and hunger nearly ceased to exist. Those who did still have jobs quit, for there was no reason to work when food and water were so plentiful and inexpensive. The concept of money lost its traditional value and the world soon became one large socialist state.

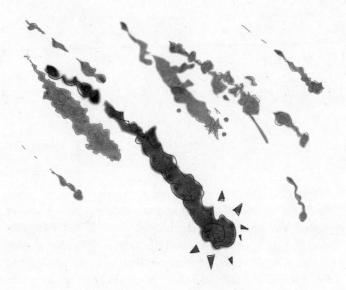

THE BERSERKED

A CROWD WAS GATHERED in front of the local electronics shop, where all Teleportvisions had been tuned in to the anticipated address by the Press Secretary of the United States. It was time to end the rumors and educate humanity about the occurrences on Earth over the past 14 months. The crowd hardly minded the light rain; their concern lay with what had become of their country. They waited with apprehension, knowing that something had gone terribly wrong.

Flashes filled the screens and 4D holographic panels and the crowd grew silent. Lane Backus, the Press Secretary, walked behind a podium and immediately began to speak.

"Fourteen months ago, an unknown object entered our atmosphere and deposited what we believe to have been 67 devices onto our planet. These devices, ARTS, or artificials, were intelligent substances, but not life forms. Although scientists will disagree with the definition of 'life,' we have concluded that these ARTS were not made up of cells and therefore were not life forms as we know them. Each device landed separately, thousands of miles apart, on every continent and in every ocean."

Lane took a deep breath and continued. "Few ARTS survived because few were lucky enough to have had access to perfect breeding grounds. Those that came to rest on land in a vegetation-rich environment *did* survive, however.

"We have recovered and studied approximately 30 of the 67 ARTS that landed in inhospitable regions. We found that they possess higher intelligence than we do and also have the ability to reproduce, constructing replications, when housed in the appropriate surroundings. What they lack are cells. Cells are the key ingredient that make us unique and human. ARTS started out small, but they soon gathered enough materials to create and reproduce taller, stronger, and more resilient offspring. It didn't take long for them to be capable of destroying human life, which they began to do a week after their landing. After two weeks, they had increased their numbers to 643 units and were already in their third generation."

Lane paused, giving himself time to prepare for what he needed to say next. "Many theories have been circulating as to the purpose of the ARTS and why they landed here on Earth. Conspiracy groups have said that ARTS are police mechanisms built by other civilizations to control potential threats in the solar system, automatically deploying themselves at the right time to regulate life on our planet. Others think that the IPGA created

ARTS; in the meantime, religious zealots believe they are messengers from God. According to what we have learned on the ARTS in the past 14 months, we have concluded that they landed on Earth in a desperate attempt to escape their native environment. We cannot guess what part of the solar system they are from or by what means they escape, but they've certainly found their way to Earth and have made this their new home.

"Twelve million people were slaughtered by the ARTS in the first month. Six million were slaughtered in the second, four million in the third. There have been no reported deaths in the last three weeks. We estimate that the slaughtering of humans is now over; the ARTS have now adapted to our culture and environment. We believe they are in their 60th generation here on Earth. Since their fifth month here, however, we have not been able to trace their whereabouts, partially because they've become less mechanical and more life-like.

"June 7th was the last time we captured and examined an ART, and that's when some startling discoveries were made. The ART was lighter in weight and had taken on a more humanistic appearance, including a skin made up of cells. It appears that their intelligence and rapid reproduction has evolved into a semi-human formation. In the last nine months, in other words, the ARTS have slowly become undetectable. There is no determining their identity, their mindsets, or their overall intentions now that they have assimilated into out culture.

"In the 19th century, we thought the American Indians were not human. In the 20th century, we thought blacks weren't human. In the 21st century, we thought Jasperians weren't human. And now, as we enter a new chapter in our history, we deem these ARTS as not being human. In time, we may come to think that the ARTS are human as well. But what is best for us? For life?

Considering that we don't have the ability, intelligence, or power to transform their agenda, which very well may have changed and evolved along with their physical design, it may be best to adapt to their presence and learn to appreciate them as quickly as possible."

Don't give that bum money. There is a reason he is there, and he is learning what lies behind that reason. He won't reap any benefits from a hand-out.

SELECTED SHORTS

KEVIN CABSONITE WAS A decent guy. Honest, law-abiding, and relaxed, he never stood out. Cabs was a nickname given to him in the sixth grade that had stuck with him. He had no unusual talents that distinguished him from others, nor did he have any unusually bad habits. His biggest accomplishment was his family; there was nothing Cabs cherished more than his loving wife and two children.

In his seemingly conflict-free life, Cabs finally did run into a problem, one that began during a vacation in Egypt. He was standing in a local marketplace, locally called a *souk*, in Aswan, one of the many cities he and his family were visiting on their way to Cairo. Beads hung from every possible nook and cranny, and the booths were divided by cloths and rugs draped over ropes.

The swarm of people made it difficult to stop and admire artwork and antiques without causing a traffic jam. That was a shame because the *souk* was filled with local merchants displaying a variety of goods—hibiscus flowers, teas, colorful fabrics, metal serving ware, decorative arrangements, and almost anything else imaginable. In lieu of the variety of items for sale, Cabs found himself standing in front of a small stand where the merchant was selling shorts.

As much as the slick designs and delicate fabrics intrigued Cabs, he was astonished to see shorts at all. Although popular in America, he hadn't seen anyone wearing them anywhere in Africa, let alone in the middle of Egypt.

Some of the elegant shorts had incredibly vivid colors; others featured dark, sleek embroidery work. He decided he must buy a pair. Unlike tasting various candy bars and sampling pastries and culinary delights, a pair of shorts would stay with him forever. Little did he know that this day would become the most memorable day in his entire life.

Cabs stared at the selection of shorts, wondering what each color and pattern might represent. He was drawn to the trendy-looking purple pair with swirled embroidery…but then again, it was purple. Cabs wanted to understand the artistry and the culture of the place he was visiting. Since he only spoke a few words of Arabic, finding out what he needed to know might prove difficult. After spending some time gazing at his options, Cabs narrowed the selection—the purple pair, a brown pair with rugged pockets, and a black pair, which would be an ideal style to match a nice summer shirt.

Cabs caught the attention of the merchant, who was sitting patiently under a small tent supported by rope attached to the

back of a camel. The merchant slowly rose and made his way over
to Cabs, giving him a harsh look. The stare on his face made
Cabs very nervous, and he thought it would be best to pull out
his translation card.

As he stuttered and panicked, trying to find the words he
needed, the merchant's stern, but somewhat charming, voice
overrode his anxiety. "Aye spake Anlgeash, you know."

Cabs looked up from his card in relicf, smiled, and quickly
stuffed the card back into his pants.

The man continued in his slow, deep-voiced way. "Can aye
intest you in somting?"

"Yes," Cabs replied. "I'd like to buy a pair of these, but I can't
decide which one I want."

The man smiled back. "Vell, this is a vary impartant chaice
you mast make now," he said.

Cabs looked at his three choices again—purple, black, and
brown, and then eliminated the black ones. Too dark, he decided.

"Naught know which pair?" the man asked.

Cabs gave out a sigh. "I don't know which pair to get, the
purple or the brown."

The man smiled again, this time with great amusement. "Thare
es mach difference in thos two calars, my friend. Tell me, good
sir, what do you want more of in your lifetime?"

Cabs chuckled nervously. He hadn't realized that his aura or
personal moods would determine his souvenirs. "More of?" Cabs
pondered aloud. "Well, that's hard to say...hmmm.... Time. Is that
a good answer?" When he didn't receive an immediate response,
he paused, then heedlessly continued. "Yeah, I'd say I want more
time to spend with my kids and wife."

The man gazed deeply into Cabs' eyes without saying a word.
His smile had vanished, and his brow was slightly furrowed. "You

mast gaht the lavandar." Without waiting for confirmation, the man turned around and slowly walked to the rack of shorts, carefully selecting the purple pair and handing it to Cabs.

"Tha spirit of this is a wonder of tyme. You must make three wishes in arder to utilize fully."

Cabs smiled as he took out his wallet. "Three wishes, eh?" Cabs reached into his wallet and handed the man 200 Egyptian pounds, knowing that would be more than enough. "Time," he said. "That's my wish."

He turned to walk away but was stopped in his tracks by the man's voice. "That is a formless wish, sir, and I need three of them."

Cabs turned around again. "Three wishes? Okay, you got it." Cabs paused to think about what he might choose. "To be the smartest man alive," he finally said. "To be famous, in a powerful type of way, and to leave an everlasting memory with as many people as I can." He stood still, waiting for approval and wondering if there would be any further questions.

"Tank you, sir," the man said, smiling once again. Cabs kept standing, waiting to see if the strange man might say anything else, but there was nothing. It was time to go.

Just as he took his first step, the man started up once again. "I find it quite notewathy you did not wish for anything atha than personal glorification, good sir." Cabs didn't bother turning around. He had had enough and needed to return to his family.

Cabs awoke in a pool of sweat, feeling like he was burning alive. He sat up and looked around. He had just fallen asleep in a park in Abydos with his wife and kids, yet he now lay in the middle of the desert. He was surrounded by sand, sand, and more sand for miles around. Nothing but sand.

The hot, glaring sun beat down on him as painful heat waves pounded against his forehead and roasted his skin. He squinted in an effort to make something out of the flat horizon line. He just needed to see something in the distance; the last thing he wanted to do was walk in the wrong direction. If he did that, he could be dead in an hour.

Cabs walked toward what he thought was a dot on the horizon line; he hoped it would prove to be some type of shelter. Rivers of sweat poured down his arms and dripped from the tips of his fingers. His head began to feel light, and he would have liked nothing more than to lie down and go to sleep. But he knew better than that. The second he laid down, he would never wake up.

After hours of walking through a seemingly-endless desert, he reached the dot in the horizon line and happily discovered that it was a large tropical tree. He was shocked to find three men dressed in simple cloth tied together by their wrists and bound to it. They sat silently, each trying to capture some of the shade.

As Cabs approached them, they watched him with their fiery eyes and didn't say a word. Cabs didn't bother trying to speak; whatever was going on here, he didn't want to become involved.

A loud, deep voice caused Cabs to jump: "QUAL!"

He turned to see an angry man holding a whip. He was dressed in a long suede jacket that was covered in hooks and bells. It was a pretty ridiculous outfit for the desert, or anywhere for that matter.

"Como HA!" the man yelled. Cabs could do nothing but stand still, terrified. The racial and societal power implications of the situation had just occurred to Cabs—the crazed uniformed man was white and the three men tied beneath the tree were black.

Cabs felt a great pain in his stomach. He pressed his right hand against his belly as fresh blood flowed onto his hand. He had been whipped.

Without warning, the man whipped him again, this time on his leg.

Cabs fell onto the hot, sandy ground and couldn't help but let out a scream. "Stop!" Cabs curled miserably, feeling sharp pains in his stomach, his leg, and now his entire left side from the fiery sand.

"English?" the man asked, this time in a milder, slower tone.

Cabs squinted up at the man. "I speak English, yes," he said.

The man chuckled, reached down, and grabbed Cabs by his arm, forcefully lifting him to his feet. "Why here?" the man demanded.

Cabs spoke with great caution. "I think I'm lost. Where are we?"

The man chuckled again and replied, "This is the Kingdom of the Kongo." He bent to untie the three men from the tree. Cabs felt a spark of hope, which was instantly banished when he realized the man with the whip was just rebinding the three men more tightly.

'Kongo?' Cabs thought.

Upon close examination of the man with the whip, Cabs noticed he had a large knife or possibly even a sword fastened to his waist. This man was obviously not a person to challenge.

His jacket had patches and markings on the sides and back, including some sort of shield on his left arm. It had a red border with yellow crowns within it, in turn bordered by blue rectangles and topped with a royal crown. All other markings on the jacket were in a foreign language Cabs couldn't decipher.

Cabs watched the man untie one of the three men. The two who remained closed their eyes and bowed their heads. The freed man tried to run, but it was too late. The white man grabbed his neck, unsheathed his sword, and began chopping at the free man's leg, who quickly fell to the ground, screaming in agony. His attacker struck his neck, and with several solid blows, the man's body went limp, and the head fell, rolling over several times as it came to rest on the scorching sand.

Blood was everywhere—soaked into the sand, splattered all over the two remaining men, on Cabs, and covering the crazed man.

"I only have supplies for four men, my friend," the man said. "Because you're here now, I had to kill one. Why let one go when I can teach these two what punishment is before the long journey begins?"

Horrified, Cabs didn't say a word, not then or during the hours that followed walking in the blazing sun. Just when he thought it was all over, that he would pass out and surely die, Cabs noticed an ocean in the distance. He soon felt a constant, far-off breeze that began to cool him.

The four of them found a trail along the coast that led them to a small village with large docks jutting into the ocean. Cabs wanted to part company then, but if he was going to survive the nightmare he found himself in, he felt there was no choice but to tag along. He had no idea where he was nor what his next supply of food or water would be.

The village proved to be small relief for Cabs's confusion and discomfort. Not only did most people not speak English, but he found that the situation was worse than he expected. Hundreds of terrified-looking black men, women, and children were tied up along rows and rows of posts with metal chains. The crazed man chained his two men to a post and brought Cabs to a nearby cabin and continued on his way.

Cabs was greeted by two men dressed in similar garb to the crazed man. They greeted Cabs in a language he couldn't recognize. Cabs hesitated.

"I'm sorry, I speak English. Do either of you?" he asked.

One of the men smiled. "Aye. English!" he raised his hand to shake. "Come in!"

The cabin was unlike anything Cabs had ever seen. His first observation was the complete lack of electricity—no air conditioning, no lights, no clocks, no fans, and it was hot as hell. There were, however, unlit torches on each side of the room, each capped with a metal disc to prevent fires. A large painting of the same red-and-blue coat of arms that Cabs had seen on the crazed man's jacket was hung on the wall of the cabin. It dominated the room.

The door opened again. Cabs was greeted with a smile by a new man dressed in similar attire but with more colorful markings on his sleeve.

"Hello! I'm General Adalberto Benedict, at your service," he said as he held out his hand. His words were very clear and his manner very direct.

Cabs shook the general's hand. "My pleasure." He paused, then plunged ahead with the questions that had been racing through his mind ever since he'd woken up in this strange place. "I seem to be at a loss for an explanation as to how I got here, General. My last recollection is that I was in Egypt."

The general gave a blank stare in return. "You were exploring villages? Eejipt, you say? We honor your devotion to our trade endeavors with the New World. How did you end up so far south? I've never seen an Englishman here before. How can we be of service to you?"

Cabs stuttered again, trying to come up with something to say. "What can you do for me?" he finally asked.

The general cleared his throat. "We have a shipment going out tomorrow that's headed to the New World. I'd be glad to grant you the option to leave on it, should you want. I must warn you, though, that if you choose to travel to the New World, you will be subjected to a long voyage, and you may not arrive until mid-1721."

Shocked, Cabs stood still. He looked down at his shorts and wondered. It wasn't until three days after buying them that he'd finally worn them—that's when he'd fallen asleep in the park. Then what? Had he traveled across Africa and woken up nearly 400 years in the past?

"Sir," the general broke into his thoughts. "Do you know where you would like to go?"

"I'll go to America," Cabs replied, mostly for lack of an alternative plan.

"You'll go where?" the general asked, clearly confused.

"Ah, uh, the New World. I'll sail with the shipment that's going to the New World tomorrow."

"Very well. I'm sorry you were subjected to what looks like a rough journey. Please join us for dinner tonight. You'll be on your way first thing in the morning."

It may have taken fewer than three months to sail the Atlantic, but those three months were by far the worst three months of Cabs's life. Living and being forced to work on a slave trade ship was a hell beyond anything he could have imagined. The conditions for the Africans were terrible, to say the least. Men, women, and children were all crammed into spaces just large enough to barely sustain life. The stench was unbearable. There must have been at least 500 people stowed away in the lower deck of the ship, all chained to posts, without enough space to lie down. Some refused to eat, ensuring a slow but certain death. Others struggled for survival but were still thrown overboard with weights when food supplies diminished and bad weather delayed the ship's arrival in port. As often as he could, Cabs snuck food down to whomever he could. He may not have helped any in the long run, but he knew he was making a difference for the time being.

Spending months aboard the slave ship gave Cabs time to plan his future. By now, he had burned his lavender shorts, never wanting any 'favors' from them ever again. He had been given proper attire by the Portuguese, and without a shower or shave on board, he blended in with the despicable crew.

Cabs became convinced that he'd been placed in the 1700s for the sake of his personal growth, as well as his first wish to become the smartest man alive. He could continue to age and possibly die before 1800, but then again, perhaps his aging would be postponed until he'd caught up with his 'present' life.

Existing before his known past would likely provide many difficulties. Considering that his entire family as well as his wife and her relatives had grown up in Boston, he knew it would be in his best interest not to interfere with the timeline of events. He would have to travel as far west as possible and have the most minimal effect on the world in order to prevent altering the fate of his wife and kids.

Cabs arrived in Virginia in late March of 1721. With no money to his name and everyone a stranger, Cabs was limited in his mobility. He knew, though, that he had to escape the East as soon as possible in order to maintain the integrity of his future timeline. That meant he couldn't stay in Boston or New York; nothing east of the Mississippi would be safe, he decided. He made his first major error when he asked travelers if they were headed to Chicago. Considering that Chicago didn't exist in 1721, it was an unwise inquiry that he hoped wouldn't change the course of time.

After three days of living off food scraps, Cabs stumbled upon a family that was headed west, moving to what he believed to be St. Louis to join their cousins who'd left the year before. The family didn't call it St. Louis—instead, they said they were traveling to the city of Louisiana, they told him, and based on their descriptions, Cabs felt it would be a wise choice to join them.

He secured a spot in the wagon in exchange for labor along the way. The six-month trek was anything but pleasant; though better than the slave ship, it was now he who felt almost like a prisoner. They poked along across rugged terrain, jolting and heaving and always worried about how they'd secure their next meal. Setting up camp and taking it down every day was difficult, as was dealing with mosquitoes, sunburn, and strong winds.

There were three kids in the family. The youngest, Sarah, died in the second month. Whatever her illness, they all had it, as she was the youngest and weakest, and it hit her the hardest. She endured intense stomach pains before she began vomiting. Hours later she turned blue; eventually, she stopped moaning in pain. Within another hour, she was dead. Cabs dug a grave, and the family held a short service in memory of the little girl.

The voyage to St. Louis ended just as winter was beginning. By then, the family had become wary of Cabs's excellent health: He never fell victim to as much as a common cold, and although he'd been bitten by mosquitoes, the bites never bothered him. Any cut or bruise he'd gotten had healed within a matter of hours, a fact that he'd tried to keep to himself. This proved rather difficult when spending all day every day close to the family for nearly six months. It was clear to him that he had an advanced immunity that would most likely allow him to survive until 2144, the year he still thought of as his 'present.'

He realized that if he wanted to survive and live with his family once again, he was going to have to limit how much people knew about him. That, and he'd have to avoid accidents. While cuts, bruises, illnesses, and mosquito bites healed quickly, things like having limbs cut off, drowning, being shot, or hung would most likely be irreversible.

Upon arriving in St. Louis, Cabs thanked the family once again for their generosity and then went in search of the city's center. Cabs knew he couldn't take a job with any notoriety or celebrity status attached to it, for his known presence would surely initiate a new timeline of events. He couldn't even take a job that would mean interacting with the public in any sort of way—no waiting tables, no bartending, no simple gigs repairing shoes. He would have to stay underground and do his best to remain unnoticed until the time was right to move east. That wouldn't be until after 2102, when his wife would be born.

Ten years passed as Cabs worked as the janitor of the local general store. He tried to seek better wages and more stimulating work, but having to compete with slavery, his options were severely limited. The years passed without any excitement or noteworthy events, and the majority of Cabs's time was spent reading anything he could get his hands on. His fear of altering his present outweighed any desire to move.

Decades passed, and Cabs began to hear about the emergence of other cities west of the Mississippi. His beard and ability to change professions could only go so far to conceal his identity.

Cabs knew he had to travel before it was too late. He was able to hitch a ride with a group of willing travelers and move on.

During that journey, Cabs planned the future of his travels. With the nation expanding and more and more cities cropping up, he was no longer forced to settle in any city longer than he preferred. The year was 1811, and although Cabs's recollection of United States history was limited, he made his list of things to do west of the Mississippi that couldn't possibly alter time—prepare for the Great Depression; attend a Buster Keaton film; photograph the controversial second alien landing in Roswell, New Mexico in 2097; see Elvis, the Beatles, and the Rolling Stones.

Aside from those landmarks, though, he drew a blank. All the things of substance that he wanted to do would surely alter too many people's lives—stop Hitler, invent world-changing technologies, write epic movies and songs, prevent cigarettes from becoming a cultural staple, promote civil and women's rights. Any involvement in or help advancing the historical timeline would surely go against everything he wanted to preserve.

Once personal computers and the Internet were available, having a positive impact might be easier, but until then, Cabs resolved to take advantage of literature, films, and travel to see all that he could outside of the eastern United States.

After Cabs left St. Louis, he arrived in Los Angeles. There, he lived for 10 years before becoming a nomad, traveling with anyone who would take him along and going everywhere he possibly could. He worked every type of lowbrow job. Over the centuries, he traveled to hundreds of American cities and towns and explored much of Canada; then, as more time passed, he saved his money and began traveling around the world. Cabs made sure that he only flew when it was absolutely necessary, and even then he flew strictly on standby. Creating fake visas and IDs was not a problem for a man who had seen everything and been nearly everywhere during the past several hundred years.

Cabs began having trouble finding excitement in life. Traveling, reading, exploring, and working numerous meaningless jobs took a toll after so many years.

The year 2100 came. Cabs decided that once the year of his and his wife's birthday approached, it would be safe to live in New York for the remaining 44 years. With each advancing year, Cabs was able to identify his graduation from high school, his time spent at college, and his relationship with his wife, including when they had their first date, bought their first house, and had their first child.

The date grew closer and closer to 2144. Cabs had limited ideas about how he was supposed to replace his former self with his current self. His best hope was to rendezvous with his family in Egypt, not planning to interfere unless dimensional paths failed to merge after the fateful evening he fell asleep in Abydos. He kept a close eye on his family and kept as much of a distance as he could, given the fact that he hadn't seen his wife and kids for nearly 400 years.

On the morning of November 18, Cabs awoke with a terrible headache. He was soaked in a pool of his own sweat and felt like he was burning alive. He sat up and found himself outdoors and in broad daylight. The heat was overwhelming, but that was the least of his concerns. When he tried to stand up, the pounding in his head made him topple back onto the ground.

Unexpectedly, a soothing, familiar voice filled his ears. "I told you not to fall asleep. The shadows shifted, and now you're burned."

Cabs opened his eyes to see Linda, his wife, standing over him and smiling. All his pain immediately vanished, and tears began pouring down his face. He reached out and hugged her lower legs as tightly as he could. "Oh, Linda!" he cried. "I missed you so much!"

Linda knelt down and looked in her husband's eyes, confused. "What's wrong?"

Tears continued to stream down Cabs's face. "I can't really explain it, but it's so good to see you."

Linda, obviously shocked at her husband's display of affection, paused for a moment, then said, "You're dehydrated enough without those tears. I didn't know a little bit of extra sunshine could do this to you." She lifted a water bottle to Cabs's face, and he drank.

"I went somewhere, Linda," Cabs said. "I can't tell you all at once; it won't make any sense. But you have to believe that I went somewhere."

Linda didn't argue; she'd never had a reason to doubt her husband despite the fact that this time she knew well and good that he had been sleeping under the same tree for the past hour. Cabs did not want his wife to doubt his sanity during those final two weeks of vacation in Egypt, so he planned to reveal his travels after they had returned to Boston.

As the plane touched down at Boston-Logan International, Cabs leaned over to Linda and whispered, "We are taking a day trip to New York tomorrow."

"Why?" said Linda, clearly surprised. "We just left New York an hour ago."

"No," Cabs said confidently. "This is different. I saw something during my vision under that tree, and the only way I can explain everything to you is by going to New York."

Back home, Cabs made his wife even more curious when he grabbed two empty suitcases to bring on their trip.

"What are those for?" Linda asked, as Cabs loaded them into their car.

"They're for the return flight. We are going to have much more to bring back."

Cabs refrained from telling Linda anything about the specifics of his adventures since 1720 on the western coast of Africa. Only once did she ask where they were going in New York, and his reply was, "My home for the last 44 years."

With their children in a babysitter's care back home, the two safely landed in New York and took a taxi to a large apartment building in Queens.

When the taxi stopped at the address, Linda looked up at the surrounding buildings in confusion. "Is this it?"

"Yes," Cabs replied, smiling. The two walked into the lobby of the nearest building, an upscale apartment complex with two security guards at the front desk.

Cabs was greeted kindly by the guards. "Well, hello, Steven! We haven't seen you in weeks," said one of the guards, giving him a friendly smile.

Cabs leaned forward and said softly, "I locked my keys in my room. Could you let me in?"

"Anything for you, Steven," the guard cheerfully responded.

She walked to the elevator, followed by both Cabs and Linda, the latter of whom was giving her husband a very puzzled look.

The three exited to the 18th floor, and the guard opened the door to 1802. "Have a great day!" she said as she walked away.

Cabs pushed the door fully open.

"What is this?" Linda asked, as if she was interrogating a murder suspect.

In reply, Cabs lifted his arm and ushered her into the large open room. Linda took a few hesitant steps. Cabs followed and shut the door behind them.

"Please sit," Cabs said, motioning for her to sit on the couch. She did, but she was obviously very tense about the entire situation.

"What is this, and who are you supposed to be here?"

Cabs stood across the room from Linda, smiling slightly, knowing that it would be nearly impossible to convince his wife in a matter of seconds. "That vision I had, under that tree in Abydos?"

"Yes…"

"Well, it was more than a vision; somehow, I traveled back to 1720 and have spent the last 400-plus years traveling around the world." He rushed on before his wife could interrupt. "I didn't age, I didn't fall ill, and I made sure I didn't alter our present lives. I didn't socialize more than I needed to, and I didn't influence individuals or the public in any way."

Linda didn't respond. She stared at her husband, wanting to believe him but feeling that he was lost in his own reality…although that theory still didn't explain the apartment and his alternate identity. "Whose apartment is this, and who is Steven?" she asked very slowly and calmly, despite being on the verge of tears.

Cabs took a few steps toward her and sat down in a chair to face her. "I moved to New York in 2100." Cabs paused to let that bizarre information soak in. "I've been living in this apartment for 10 years. I've had to constantly move because I don't age. Because of this, I had to constantly hide my identity and create false names everywhere I went."

Linda burst into tears. Cabs let her cry, hoping she would eventually accept what must have sounded utterly preposterous.

After watching his wife sob for minutes on end without any signs of calming down, Cabs stood and raised his voice. "I ate an ice cream cone the first day it was introduced at the St. Louis World's fair in 1904. I speak Russian, Spanish, German, French, Italian, Swedish, Romanian, Mandarin, Japanese, Hindi and Portuguese. I've met Marilyn Monroe, Elvis, Abraham Lincoln, Stravinsky, Salvador Dali, Buster Keaton, James Dean, you name it. I've been everywhere, and I've done nearly everything. I know it all, and I'm sick of it."

Cabs turned to the bookshelf behind him, which was almost as tall and wide as the wall, filled with albums, binders and storage bins. He reached out and grabbed a thick envelope and dropped it on the coffee table in front of Linda, spilling out an array of photographs. She stopped sobbing and picked up a few photos. The first showed Cabs standing next to Abraham Lincoln. The second showed him in front of the rubble that had been the Berlin Wall.

"What is this?" she asked, as if they were crayon drawings.

"I took those," Cabs answered. "Well, I had people take them. I was very fortunate with Lincoln because back then cameras didn't have split-second apertures, so I—"

Linda cut him off. "These are pictures, Cabs!" she yelled. "They're obviously fake!" She broke into sobs again.

Cabs let her be a second time. He walked back to his bookshelf and took out a small box. Kneeling in front of the TV set, he reached inside the box, lifted out a disc, and inserted it into a nearby TV. "Can you watch this, please?" he asked softly.

Linda, still sobbing, looked at the screen, which was displaying the front of a house from an off angle, as if it were shot in secret. After realizing that the house was the one she'd grown up in which had been demolished in 2134, Linda immediately stopped her crying and gazed on in amazement.

"That's my house!" she exclaimed.

Cabs smiled. "You know that dent in your Dad's BMW that your entire family blamed on me? The reason they warned you to never marry me? Your brother Billy did it. I've got it on tape." The TV showed a black BMW slowly pulling into the driveway and striking the side of the garage. A young man, not Cabs, stepped out of the car and walked around, assessing the damage.

Cabs turned the TV off, walked back to his bookshelf, and took down a large box. He carried it over to Linda and sat next to her, then proceeded to show her some items in the box—a certificate of ownership of 7,000 acres in Colorado, a bank statement of $52 million, and several unlabeled discs.

"What is all this?" Linda sniffled.

"I've collected some insurance for the future during my last 400 years. We are proud owners of an exquisite ranch in Colorado. I bought the original URL links for hundreds of products and companies so that I could sell them back at sky-high prices. And I have original footage of important moments in American history that haven't been seen before, events like the JFK assassination, the first Beatles concert, and a revealing interview with Malia Ann Obama after her presidency.

I've got hundreds of videos that the world needs to see. High resolution photographs of extinct animals, paintings by famous artists I rescued before they would have been destroyed by the artist.

I know more about history than any history book. I didn't just read thousands and thousands of books. Over 400 years, I lived them.

Now come on, we need to pack, see a few people, and catch the red-eye flight back home in 10 hours."

"Where are we going, and who are we meeting?" Linda asked, still shaken.

Cabs stood and walked back to his bookshelf. He tapped large boxes on the bottom shelf with his foot. "You see these? These are all manuscripts of my travels and adventures. Right here, I've got the truth behind the abolishment of slavery, the end of the Civil War, and the terrorist truce of 2067, and why America has become the worst offender against citizenship-free rights."

He walked back to Linda and held her hand. "I spent the last 44 years figuring out a way to organize my life so that I could meet you again and how I could influence this world for the better while providing the best future for you and our children."

Cabs and Linda met with a book publisher whom they knew through a close friend. It didn't take much convincing to realize that what Cabs had written was not only educationally and culturally important, it was also a ticking time bomb of a bestseller, ready to explode.

Explode it did, as did the next one. The two books became instant hits, providing new historical photographs and giving specific examples of the birth of corporate profit incentives and growth. The second book was purposely published 10 months before the public release of Cabs's new JFK assassination tape. Reviewers gave him high praise, and Cabs became a celebrity within a single year. The $52 million he had saved proved small compared to what he was earning now.

A new cultural movement emphasizing dramatic change in government began in colleges and amongst youth culture. It didn't just happen in America; it swelled in a number of other industrialized nations as well. Cabs founded CFAD (Citizens for Freedom and Democracy), a worldwide group that supported complete democracy rather than 'represented democracy,' as he called it. The group took action against local officials as well as top politicians and representatives.

Five years after the release of his first book, Cabs and CFAD had a worldwide influence. Billions of people became aware of what their respective territory governments were doing and started playing a more active role in redefining them. At the same time, though, tens of millions of others were upset about what Cabs stood for and had created in society; they insisted he did nothing but spread rebellion and distrust against governments and the established way of life.

Following a 40-day global tour promoting CFAD, Cabs returned home. He'd just passed the torch of the presidency to his successor at a well-attended benefit dinner. With his books published, his videos made public, and his worldwide group having achieved a self-governing status, Cabs was ready to relax and enjoy his family and the world around him.

He wasn't welcomed with open arms, however. "We have a problem," Linda snapped the moment Cabs entered the house. "Our youngest daughter, who, may I remind you, is now 13, is going through absolute hell. Do you have any respect for your children? You just go about—"

Cabs cut her off as soon as he could, for it seemed as if she was about to go on forever. "What happened?"

"She can't go anywhere!" Linda nearly screamed. "In your triumphant 400-year experience, you were so careful that you didn't alter the life you once knew before your trip to Africa. Can I ask you what is so familiar about it now? Did you not think about what it would do to you and your family? Did you not care to preserve the future we were heading toward?" Linda paused and stared at her husband in disgust. "The media hounds us every day. The kids can't enjoy their childhood without being ridiculed by other kids who are jealous of what we have. Your own children are as famous as movie stars and are showing up on the covers of all the sleazy tabloids!"

"And you," she went on relentlessly. "The kids see you portrayed in a negative light everywhere they go. How can they not be confused about who you really are? We're prisoners in our own home because we can't step outside without having five bodyguards around us. I hope you are happy with this life you have chosen, because I'm not!"

Linda stormed up the stairs and into the bedroom, slamming the door behind her. Cabs, still holding a bag and coat over his arm, carefully placed them on the ground. He felt a bit dazed. He walked slowly through the house. The sound of cartoons playing on the TV droned on in the background.

The doorbell rang. Cabs looked up to the ceiling, waiting to hear his wife's footsteps cross the hallway as she headed toward the stairs, but they didn't. The doorbell rang again.

Cabs walked back through the house and opened the door to see Jason Kreite, one of his former junior aides at CFAD, smiling and holding a package for him.

"Don't you have a new president to advise?" Cabs asked a bit sarcastically.

"You left the dinner before I could give you this package," Jason said.

Cabs reached for the box and noted it was from his publisher in New York. Then came an odd-sounding click.

A sharp, burst of gunfire sounded, and Cabs fell, package and all.

Rumors began circulating hours after the shooting, and the incident hit the news the following day. CFAD planned an international funeral tour for the loss of such an historic man. They dressed him in a suit and placed his body in a clear, sealed, silicone casket, one that would be proper for viewing but would still protect and preserve his body.

Thousands upon thousands of citizens came to pay their respects. New York was the first city. From there, Cabs's body was to be flown to London, Berlin, Paris, and Moscow, returning to Boston for his burial. Because of unforeseen conditions that occurred while the casket was in transit between Berlin and Paris, though, heat and humidity rose inside the casket, causing Cabs's body to expand and burst while in Paris in front of thousands of live mourners and over a billion viewers at home, leaving an everlasting memory for all who were watching.

A busy street is filled with pedestrians and moving vehicles. On every block, groups of individuals jaywalk to save seconds getting to and from work. A speeding car violently turns a corner and is just feet away from a tall man wearing a suit. A woman jumps from the sidewalk and tackles him, pushing him out of the way of the speeding car, which continues down the street at a dangerous speed.

The man looks up at the woman and thanks her. She smiles and continues on her way down the sidewalk.

The man runs up to her and grips her shoulder from behind. She turns. He looks her in the eyes and asks, "Why did you do this? Why did you risk your life for mine?"

The woman smiles and places her hand on the man's. "You are an Earthian. You have so much more power and influence than I do. You are more important that I am."

AMNESIA

JACK HUNCHED OVER AWKWARDLY, clutching his torn clothing. The last few hours had been nauseating and confusing to say the least; he had no idea who he'd once been or might still be. All he could do was gasp for air and vomit his current troubles onto the hot desert soil beneath him. He looked down and saw the shimmering ruby blood that was slowly trickling off his boot and soaking into the arid soil.

Jack's mind was blank: Where was he? What did he look like? He thought long and hard as he continued his walk down a desolate desert highway, but even when a vague recollection of his appearance did flash into his mind, it didn't trigger any memories or a sense of familiarity with his surroundings.

All around him was barren desert. Brown shrubs and thorny loose twigs were the only vegetation he could see. Since he had no memory of his existence, though, was he walking back to whence he'd come?

A lone building along the vacant highway proved to be nothing but a mere shack with its front wall torn apart and the objects within it scattered about. By the looks of it, he found when he stepped inside, it appeared to have been a diner that had been destroyed by a powerful force. Jack maneuvered through the rubble and walked inside to find a long counter flanked by remnants of chairs and tables. A rusted fan hung from the corner ceiling, slowly turning with some faint echo of electrical current. There was no other movement.

Even given the disarray and disorder, though, something seemed out of place. The fan was the only item that appeared to conduct electricity; there was no fridge to keep drinks cold, no fryers or stoves or ovens to cook food. There wasn't even space to store ice—there were just old wooden counters, tables, and chairs. Jack's step faltered again when he noticed an array of hammers and oversized cutting tools hanging on the wall.

A slight crackling sound stopped Jack in his tracks. He whirled around to see an elderly man across the room pointing a rifle at him. The barrel of the rifle swung to over the right and exploded with the sound of a shot.

In a panic, Jack turned to see a man outside the building fall to his knees and then crawl out of view. "Can never take your mind off 'em," the old man murmured as he walked out through the missing front wall and disappeared around the corner. Immediately, two additional gunshots echoed, followed by silence.

Jack hesitated before he stepped through the missing wall and made his way to the corner of the building. At least one body, he knew, lay out of sight. He cautiously lifted his boots high with each step, trying not to cause any noise, but being silent was difficult—the ground was made up of loose rocks that had a tendency to knock against each other with each step.

Jack peered around the corner, only exposing his head to gain a quick view before pulling back to safety. There were two bodies on the ground, both face down and motionless. Jack rounded the building and approached them.

The old man lay on his stomach with his rifle in one hand. Jack walked to the second body and carefully rolled it over with his foot. The man's front side was riddled in bullets, and his one-piece, single-color outfit was ripped to shreds. A small river of blood had formed underneath his body, trickling down a slight slope to form a small red pool. Jack noticed that the unfortunate man at his feet was seemingly wearing the same shredded attire he was.

A slow, deep voice startled him. "You have to be careful." The man's voice was barely a whisper. "They all look like us. They know how to take down our ships, but their blood tells us apart. Our—" the man stopped and went limp.

Jack turned toward the old man. He rolled the body over with one foot, exposing the old man's chest. It was covered in dark green liquid.

A howling scream split the sky, followed by two large objects that looked and flew like jagged lightning. Jack ran into the street behind the diner and watched, confused, as a crowd carrying guns, pitchforks, and long wooden sticks formed an angry circle under the two spacecrafts that were hovering above them.

A burst of brilliant white light shot out from one of the ships and struck the crowd. Half of the people scattered; the other half fell to the ground, motionless. Jack looked down at his torn one-piece outfit, then at the body of the man who had spoken to him.

A dreadful crash sounded behind Jack. He spun back to face the street again. One of the ships had fallen. The other was already far off along the horizon.

The people who were still standing gathered together and began to head in Jack's direction. He would have to act quickly and learn how to adapt.

The halls of Eaton middle school echoed with the announcements that occurred every morning at 9:12 a.m.

"¿Dónde están mis conejos?" the principal would announce in a tearful panic. "¿Dónde están mis conejos?"

His voice became desperate. Whatever he was talking about, it was clear he was in distress. Unfortunately, Principal Derpstein, the manager and leader of the school, had been giving the same announcement every day for years. Students sat at their desks and rolled their eyes, wondering what was wrong. They waited for the announcements to cease, but they never did.

One Last Meal

THE ANDERSON FAMILY SAT ON the cold cement floor, huddled around a small radio in their basement. The single light bulb lighting the room slowly swayed back and forth. Explosions and loud crashes boomed in the distance; everyone could feel small vibrations underneath their cold legs.

A scratchy voice over the radio spoke. "The president has declared a state of emergency. Our visitors from another world are hostile, repeat, hostile, and have taken no interest in communication. We urge you to seek shelter, preferably in basements and other belowground structures. Do not trust the enemy. We can't—"

The radio filled with static. The father, a young, clean-shaven man, reached over and turned the dial off. "Well, we still have power for now," he said in a calm manner. "I suggest we make something to eat while we can; we haven't had anything all day. Things don't look good. Who knows what they want with us and what their purpose is. Let's at least enjoy a meal. Anything that you want and we have, I'll make for dinner."

The father looked at his wife and two children. "Cecilia, what would you like?"

Cecilia, a six-year-old girl whose cheeks had turned bright pink from crying, looked up at her father. She was still in tears. "Can I have a bacon sandwich?"

Her father smiled and replied, "A bacon sandwich? Are you sure you will like it? You've never had one before."

Cecilia nodded her head yes.

"Brian, how about you?" the father asked.

Brian, a 17-year-old young man with some acne splotched across his face, sat in silence for a moment, his arms and hands visibly trembling. Finally, he looked up and answered, "I want ribs, ribs loaded with the rest of the barbeque sauce we've got."

"You got it," his father said immediately. He then turned to his wife. "Honey, what would you like?"

Nervous and upset, she stared at the floor, unsure of what to say. "I'm not that hungry, but I could go—"

Suddenly, an extraordinary series of noises broke out—they sounded like weapons being fired, buildings collapsing, and explosions.

The family sat motionless.

"Sausages, please," the mother quietly replied.

"Good choice," said the father. "I think I'll have a little bit of all of what you're having."

Can you imagine a world in which technology compensates for laziness and incompetence?

A Familiar Face of Death

JEFF GARBY TURNED THE CORNER to his street and drove through his familiar neighborhood with a wide grin on his face. Illegal act? Maybe, but Jeff was finally home now and ready to continue his life. For years, he'd been contemplating how to better himself and clear his conscience of his involvement in the Eberton estate sale.

Every year for the past 10 years, Jeff had feared that his unintentional participation would come back to hurt him in some way—being charged fines, losing his license or his job, possibly even being imprisoned. The only way he could think to change his situation was to completely erase what he'd done.

Fortunately, his actions had been minimal, so minimal that altering them wouldn't affect the course of time. There were just two complications, really: He'd be breaking two laws, one when he returned to the present and one when he altered the past. Nonetheless, Jeff knew it was the right thing to do. Not only was this best for him, it was best for his family. Best for his employers, too, in that their names wouldn't be connected with his actions, and best for the criminals—that way, they'd have fewer accomplices.

Ten years ago, Jeff and his family had moved to Chicago as a result of a job transfer and promotion. In the early stages of learning the ropes of metropolitan real estate, Jeff had unknowingly become involved with the Iceland Mafia. With their launderings and other illegal deeds, the Mafia needed a licensed real estate agent to sign off on several properties, someone who'd be legally responsible should their properties turn sour.

It wasn't until months after the deal that Jeff realized the extent of his involvement. Signatures were collected from Mafia members that cleared them of all responsibility for their illegal activities as well as their ownership of thousands of square meters of office space; both would later be used against Jeff. At any moment in time, those papers could be dug up and used against him, he knew, destroying his life, family, and everything else he'd worked to achieve.

At least erasing his name from the papers would be easy. Jeff traveled back 10 years using a return ticket with *Story of Life*. After having scrutinized their bylaws and precautions, he was able to secure the perfect trip: one that would leave everything in the timestream exactly the same, with the exception of the omission of his name on the incriminating documents. No one would see him, no one would be affected by his being there, and the present would remain unchanged. Not even the smallest butterfly would be harmed.

And the plan went off without a hitch. Jeff snuck his way into the conference room where his priego and members of the Iceland Mafia had signed the documents and exited, leaving the papers unsupervised for the next hour.

Jeff stepped out of a nearby cabinet, removed the two papers with his signature, and replaced them with blank sheets. He then left the building without having made the slightest alteration to the timestream.

His return to the present was equally satisfying, because nothing had changed at all. No one from *Story of Life* interrogated him as to what he'd seen/done in the past. (On the application, he'd said he was traveling back to view his father's funeral, which had conveniently happened at the same time.)

Jeff pulled into his driveway and turned off his car. He reached into his pocket and pulled out the two sheets of paper with his signature on them. Sighing with relief, he put the papers in the glove compartment. Everything was perfect now…it felt like a tremendous weight had been lifted from his chest.

Jeff raced to the front door, leaping over every other step on his porch. A split second before swinging the front door open, something halted him in his tracks: Through the small window on the door, Jeff saw his five-year-old daughter giggling with delight, gnawing on a large cookie as she sat on her father's lap.

"Oh, no," Jeff slowly gasped out loud. Here he was, staring into his own house at himself. He quickly took a step to the side so that no one would see him through the window. How could this have possibly happened? His plan had been perfect and was carried out with the utmost care.

But the problem had nothing to do with his plan or its effectiveness—Jeff hadn't returned to his known present. Instead, Jeff had traveled to the future of the time he'd traveled back to, which in turn had given birth to another version of himself.

Jeff raced back into the car and grabbed his sunglasses and cap. He quickly put them on and ran back to the door. He rang the bell.

His priego came to the door. "Yes?" his alternate self asked as he opened the door.

Jeff shocked his priego by taking off his sunglasses. "I'm from the future," Jeff stated. "We've got a problem."

Jeff's alternate self looked completely startled, but Jeff didn't have time for small talk. "We've got to get this taken care of immediately—it will only take 10 minutes or so. Come with me." Jeff turned and got back into his car.

Two minutes later, his priego left the house and sat in the passenger seat. "This explains why my car was missing this morning," he said. "I reported it stolen... So, what's happening? How far from the future are you? You don't appear to be much older."

Jeff started the car and drove off. "I'm hardly from the future. Seconds, if anything. You know the Eberton sale?"

"Yeah," said Jeff's alternative self. "You mean the one that I made when we first moved here? I remember receiving the completion documents for that, and my name wasn't anywhere to be found on them. Where are we going?"

Jeff raced down the freeway. "I traveled back in time and omitted our name from those documents. The Eberton deal was affiliated with the Iceland Mafia. Had your name been on it, we would be irrefutably affiliated with illegal activities. But that's all fixed now, aside from the problem of me being sent back to the wrong dimension or time.

"The papers I took are in the glove compartment. Take them out. They need to be destroyed." Jeff exited the freeway and entered the preservation wildland area, driving past any buildings or signs of life.

"What are we doing here?" his priego asked.

"We need to destroy these documents," Jeff answered, "and if that doesn't do anything, we'll go back to *Story of Life* and get our lives sorted out. Jeff pulled over to the side of the road and popped the trunk open.

The forest muffled all noises except for the symphony of crickets and moonbugs, singing and chirping from their various hiding places. Far away from any main road or building, the only light source was the beam of light coming from the car's headlight.

Jeff fished through the trunk and found what he was looking for. "Would you like to do the honors?" he asked, holding up the papers and lighter.

His alternate self smiled and took the papers in one hand and the lighter in the other, stepped away from the car, and lit the papers. As the flame approached his fingers, he dropped the papers and finished watching them char and curl into a thin, black crisp. "So, are you supposed to disappear or something now?"

Silence. The priego looked up to see that Jeff had vanished. He heard rustling behind him and turned to see Jeff holding a tree branch as thick as his thighs. Before the priego could say anything, Jeff swung the branch and cracked it against his priego's head.

The heavy blow immediately knocked the priego's body to the ground. Jeff raised the club again over the all-too-familiar body and smashed it down upon the motionless head. Three more cracks to the face satisfied Jeff; surely, the priego was dead.

Jeff dragged the body into the bushes and out of sight from the road. The body would be eaten by the wild beasts in the woods before anyone would ever notice it. And should the body be discovered and identified, it would an exact DNA match. Concern would be for his life and well-being—murder charges would be irrelevant.

Jeff returned to his car and cleaned himself off. He was positive that his family wouldn't suspect that anything unusual had happened. Once he'd finished wiping off the last of the bloodstains, Jeff started his car and drove back to continue his now-perfect life.

103 million people died in the Worlds War of 2267. Harry, who was in a fighting unit in H67.3, beat the odds and survived. Soon after the war ended, however, he developed OCD and overdosed on drugs when he forgot when he'd last taken his medication. But he was one of the lucky ones. He survived the war.

THE PRESERVATION SOCIETY

HEALTH CARE, DISEASE CONTROL, and illness reversal have all been strong personal, political, and moral issues pressed forward by both individuals and communities. On Earth, as costs for these concerns escalated, citizens complained and demanded a socialistic style of governing health preservation.

In 2203, Earth found a new love for science and government. Vaccines were developed for all diseases, whether they were of indigenous or alien origin. Super-pills cured nearly all colds, fevers, and small aches and pains. The generation that followed had virtually no need for physicians—the number of doctors waned until only emergency personnel and spiritual advisors remained.

The Preservation Society became the largest supplier of these life-changing vitamins and drugs; overnight, the society became a success and a monopoly. No one questioned how it achieved such magical results. As the years passed, the Preservation Society grew. One corporate office became four, then five, and then ultimately 27. Once every citizen became a member of the society, it was logical for the government to own and control the entire operation. No one bothered to think of anything other than peace and prosperity for all Earthian kind.

Fifty years later, the Preservation Society lost its public support because the health of the citizenry had improved so much that the purpose of the organization was questioned. A strong opposition force claimed it was wasting government funds—no one was sick and no one needed to see doctors, detractors said.

The public lost its desire to fund a government organization that individuals couldn't directly relate with in terms of its momentous accomplishments and current necessity. Citizens were in impeccable health, and the majority believed that the Preservation Society served no purpose. Why should anyone support something that offers no benefits and might not even exist?

They look like us, act like us, and behave like us. So why are they killing us?

WEATHER CHANNELS

I wish I could go into details about the matter of Earth's first global catastrophe, but seeing as the Preservation Society and social extremists would surely have me killed if I talked about the specifics of what happened, you'll have to excuse my vagueness.

The problems that led to the catastrophe crept in so gradually that few expected anything momentous to happen. After all, the use of fossil fuels was a thing of the past, CFCs no longer existed, and the future seemed brighter than ever. So who could possibly have thought that we were headed for something terrible? (Although improving slightly from a horrific state doesn't equate to prosperity.) Luckily, scientists in New Finland were developing an artificial weather machine that would regulate temperatures, storm fronts, and rates of condensation in every country of the world.

This weather machine, named Phoenix 1.0, was merely a prototype, and as such, it had a variety of kinks. With the recent weather complications across the globe, however, there was no choice but to put Phoenix in action in an effort to try to neutralize the conditions that plagued our atmosphere. It went without a hitch; soon, it had replaced all naturally-occurring weather conditions. The machine was such a success, in fact, that it was soon considered to be mankind's best invention.

Because everything was controlled, the New Finland scientists could eliminate hurricanes and tornadoes, supply constant rain, and ensure the best weather for presidential and royalty outdoor occasions. Farmers no longer had to worry about their crops because all farming regions were given the perfect amount of rain and sunshine; produce flourished. The once-halfway-melted icecaps reformed into their natural states.

Everything was perfect...but perfection had its price. Although there was no concern over the future state of humanity, complaints about the Phoenix 1.0 grew in number. Athletes, ranging from those in professional teams to those in youth leagues, were forced to change their schedules or face playing in the planned rain. The scheduling of activities to avoid predictable heat, rain, and winds soon conflicted with the needs of businesses, clubs, and organizations. Crime rates soared during heavy rains; predictable weather allowed criminals to plan ahead and seek the best conditions to escape detection. Hollywood movie studios began offering large sums of money for abnormal weather conditions during shoots, altering the weather schedules and angering the masses who had slowly become accustomed to their new way of life.

Billions of people were forced to tune into their local, geographically-determined weather channel so that they would know how to organize their needs and daily habits. Growing outrage about the rich and powerful receiving preferential treatment was unavoidable. After the Phoenix had been in service for 11 years, the CEO of O.D.E. Corporation, the creator of and administration behind the Phoenix, made a historic statement:

"Thank you. Over 20 years ago, O.D.E. Corporation of New Finland established project Phoenix, a weather response system (WRS) designed to combat the ever-changing atmosphere and increasingly-harmful weather conditions on Earth. Eleven years ago, after the events of [description omitted], we became a vulnerable planet in desperate need of a solution. We implemented the Phoenix 1.0 much sooner than we'd anticipated, but we didn't have a choice.

"On [date omitted], Phoenix 1.0 became fully and flawlessly functional—in fact, it went beyond our expectations in fulfilling the Earth's needs. Crops flourished, hunger disappeared, and weather forecasting became an exact science. But shortly thereafter, we, as a species, rejected this notion of perfection. We were used to our old systematic way of life, the one that nearly caused our global extinction. Knowing the future climatic conditions and then working around that carefully-planned weather schedule was not appreciated by the majority of the population.

"We at O.D.E. have fought the growing opposition, but there is only so much we can say or do; we understand what the majority of us want and need. Therefore, starting a year from today on [date omitted], the Phoenix 1.0 will become fully randomized as Earth used to be during its natural era. We will no longer ration and plan around famine regions, croplands, global events, and possible future catastrophes: Phoenix 1.0 will operate on its own schedule of unpredictability. No longer will we have the misfortune of knowing what lies ahead."

Craig sat down with Foerrius, an explorer from the Cyrieric galaxy. Foerrius was asking too many inappropriate questions, and Craig thought it was best that he talk with him privately to avoid further disconcerting looks from the group.

"Foerrius," Craig began, "Men and women of the human race go through a process of getting to know each other before they engage in legal relationships and procreate."

Foerrius looked puzzled. "I don't understand this concept of pre-marriage."

Craig paused, not knowing how to explain. "We date first, which leads to romance, which leads to marriage."

Foerrius stared at Craig blankly, a confused look on his grey, silky face. "If the dating process takes such a long time, then why do you divorce so often?"

Craig raised his hands and shook his head. "I don't know. We get bored."

Double

KEVIN WAS A BUSINESSMAN and he was good at it. Not necessarily the business part, but he knew how to live the lifestyle. It's the kind of life with large profits and low liabilities—perfect for Kevin, who always wanted to do as little as possible to succeed.

Unfortunately for Kevin, despite the fact that he always had the ideas, the mindset and the motivation of a businessman, luck hadn't caught up with him. That may have been because he stuck to what he believed to be the core philosophy of business: Do as little as you can while impeding others…and make record profits in the process.

Kevin moved from job to job, never enjoying the work that each one required of him. He quit each position with perfect timing; if he had stayed just one more day, he surely would have been fired.

He was a complex guy, yet at the age of 44, still had the brashness of a young hooligan. Work bored him, so he didn't do it very often. Why work hard when you can lie, cheat and steal instead? As long you don't get caught, no one is aware of what you've done. Appearance is everything, a fact that Kevin had come to appreciate and exploit. He was in shape, always well-groomed and was a stylish dresser. He knew how to attract positive attention; consequently, people were drawn to him.

His manufactured magnetism was what made it possible for him to secure a time-travel trip through *From a Distance*. Ever since the local office had opened, it had been nearly impossible to book a trip...but not for Kevin. He had found a loophole by means of the *honorable research intentions* clause. That *clause* allowed people who were pursuing an educational mission to jump to the top of the waiting list. The truth of the matter was that Kevin wanted to travel three years into the past to take advantage of his present knowledge to secure riches, popularity, and success. Of course, he knew he had to make up a credible proposal worth studying in order to secure an immediate trip back in time.

He knew exactly where he'd start. He wanted to witness one of the most important inventions mankind had ever devised: electric power. During his application phase, he argued that human civilization couldn't have advanced without electricity. When we gave birth to electric power, he said, mankind became intelligent. What miraculous wonders would lie ahead if our ability to control electricity had happened a half century earlier?

Kevin proposed to travel back to 1745 in order to mediate a feud between William Watson and Benjamin Franklin in the hopes that the discovery of electricity would occur 50 years earlier. His argument was that, although Alessandro Volta had created the first electric battery in 1800, William Watson may have beaten Volta to the punch if not for Franklin's meddling.

The waiting list to travel with *From a Distance* was eight years, but because of the strength of the application, Kevin was able to secure a departure date just four months after applying. He was faced with two dilemmas: First, he was scheduled to travel more than 300 years back in time, not three; and second, he had been notified that he was selected for a rare return mission, which didn't interest him. Although *From a Distance*'s official stance was to ban return travels, it often discreetly allowed them for educational advancement trips by scheduling the scholar-travelers to return 24 hours before they'd left. The theory was that the time traveler would return before the initial departure, thereby eliminating any changes that may have been made in the past…yet the traveler would bear all knowledge gained during his or her trip. It was a theory that wasn't widely accepted. Other scientists believed that, by traveling back in time and then forward again, a traveler creates his own dimension and therefore would never interact with the time commonly perceived as 'present.' Once Kevin realized the limitations of *From a Distance*, he started to look for a way around them.

With its lack of rules and regulations, the time travel black market was an obvious place to start. There had always been rumors that the black market had developed the necessary technology to override any trip restrictions. No one knew exactly how this was done—all details were confidential and were carried out after putting the traveler to sleep. Many people believed that black market agencies implanted a microchip in the palm of their traveler's left hand that monitored time and returned them to their known present after 72 hours. This widespread belief resulted in numerous cases of clients removing their left hands upon arriving at their destination.

Kevin pulled his black-market strings and arranged to meet with a man by the name of Scole. That was how, at 5:00 on a Sunday morning, he wound up standing at the corner of an abandoned intersection. Once home to a thriving commercial enterprise, this area had lately become a desolate morass of prostitution and debauchery.

Kevin stood nervously, having already transferred a month's worth of earnings into an online holding account. After what seemed like an eternity, a short, stubby man in a top hat and long trench coat approached him.

"Are you Kevin?" asked the man in a low, raspy voice.

Kevin kept his calm—he didn't want to act overly nervous and scare the man away.

"Yes," he replied.

The man held out his right hand. "You put payment through Meekow?"

Kevin raised his hand and gave the man a firm shake. "Yes, I did."

Without any warning, a sharp pain shot through Kevin's hand and spread upward into his wrist and lower arm. The man didn't seem to notice. He was squeezing tightly and not letting go and Kevin was too breathless from the pain to utter anything.

Seconds later, the man dropped his hand. Kevin gave a sigh of relief as the pain immediately ceased.

The man just stared at Kevin. Kevin felt a new feeling run through him; this time it was a jolt of fear. What would happen next?

"Our transaction is complete," the man said. "A microfiber has been implanted into your right arm that will redirect your travels once *From a Distance* sets your course. Should I be unable to access your payment, I'll make sure that you get sent back far enough to ensure death by an Albertosaurus."

The man turned and walked away. Kevin's black market exchange had taken less than a minute.

The following Friday, Kevin sat patiently in the reception room of *From a Distance.* He had expected news reporters to hound him, hassling him about his intentions for time travel, but no one had shown up. Then again, that made sense—any media had been bad news for the emerging time traveling business ever since the memory losses, decapitations, and other deaths reported from less scrupulous agencies. *From a Distance* had obviously learned how to keep things under wraps.

Kevin began to doubt his transaction with Scole. What if the plan didn't work and he really was sent back to 1745? What if he wasn't able to return? It would be a harsh existence and certainly no electricity. What a terrible waste of the remainder of his life! Living conditions would be so primitive that he wouldn't be able to use his current knowledge to advance his social standing. Any 'invention' he could conceive from the modern era would be so far outside the realm of anyone's understanding that he might be deemed insane. He would be an outsider with no knowledge of the world, forcing him to resort to petty crimes for survival. He might even have to rob locals on the streets just to get by.

A tall man in a white one-piece outfit interrupted Kevin's unhappy thoughts.

"We are ready for you," the man said in a soothing voice.

Kevin stood and followed him through a set of double doors that opened the instant the man pressed his right hand against the bare wall. They walked down a long corridor that stretched as far as Kevin could see. There were no doors.

Kevin wondered what was going to happen. Would he be incapacitated so that he wouldn't be able to leak the secret process of time travel to the public? Would they possibly test him for black market interventions?

After walking for what seemed like an eternity, the man stopped. For the first time in his life, Kevin heard complete silence. No humming, no static, no rustling. Nothing.

After only a few seconds of the silence, Kevin's mind began to play games with him. He had to be hearing *something*; after all, a person can't experience *nothing*. The blind may see nothing, but they experience blackness.

A sharp ringing pierced Kevin's mind, followed by a slight pulsing sensation. The man turned to face Kevin and smiled. "Are you ready for the adventure of your life?"

Kevin simply smiled back. The man once again reached out and placed his hand against the bare wall next to him. A blue light shot out from the wall and began shaping a perfect square around his hand. Nearly blinded, Kevin had to look away, shielding his eyes with his hands.

When he lowered his hands, he was sitting on a city bus bench at the familiar corner of Fourth and Ninth. Everything appeared to be just another normal day in 2055. Everything, that is, except for Kevin's right hand, which burned as if he'd just pulled it out of a fire.

He grimaced, but to his relief both his hand and arm appeared to be in good condition despite the inexplicable pain. Although it was difficult, he forced himself to ignore it—he had to find out what year it was.

He rose from the bench and headed toward a local newsstand. He grabbed a paper and was relieved to see the date: December 14, 2052. His eyes briefly closed in relief. Perfect! His plan had worked. The pain in his arm was even starting to subside.

Now that he knew the date, Kevin could begin to implement his plan to gain success and wealth. All he had to do was find his priego.

After a short walk across town, Kevin reached his old apartment building from 2052. Without a key, entry was going to be difficult. He spent a moment pondering the idea of jumping up to the fire escape stairwell, but quickly dropped that idea. He wasn't going to sneak into the building where he *lived*.

He slowly approached the building. Luckily, an elderly woman was slowly exiting. Kevin hurried to the door and held it for her.

"Ma'am," he said, barely able to contain his excitement at not having had to sneak inside.

"Such a nice young man," the old woman said. "Thank you."

Kevin ducked inside. Five floors up, and he would be proposing a new business plan to a three-years-younger version of himself!

As Kevin walked past the front desk, the clerk looked up in confusion. "Good to see you again, sir," the young man said hesitantly.

Kevin was disappointed. The clerk had clearly mistaken him for his priego, which meant that his three-years-prior self must have just stepped out. "Forgot a few things, that's all," Kevin replied with a smile. He gave a slight wave as he walked toward the elevator.

Upon reaching the fifth floor, Kevin made his way toward his apartment. Fortunately, he had the foresight to stash a copy of his door key inside a crack in the hallway wall. He fished it out.

From what he'd learned over the past few weeks, Kevin knew he'd have to be very careful when he introduced himself to his priego. In 2052, time travel was not yet available to the masses and he knew his sudden appearance would surely provoke alarm. The best way to approach the situation, Kevin thought, would be to write a note and appear soon afterwards. The worst case scenario, aside from not introducing himself correctly, would be giving his priego the wrong idea before the ideal moment in time. A break-in would certainly qualify as a bad idea—he had to be careful, careful, careful.

Kevin walked to his door and squinted into the peephole. He couldn't see anything, of course, but he could tell that no lights were on. He knelt down and rested the side of his head on the floor so that he could look under the door. Still no light. Kevin stood, inserted the key and pushed the door open with the utmost care.

As soon as he saw the dinner table full of dirty dishes and the cheap electronics, Kevin knew something was horribly wrong. Nothing looked familiar, especially not the crazed face of the man staring at him, the man who held a large frying pan in his hand.

Before he knew what had happened, the pan hit the side of Kevin's head and knocked him facedown on the floor. The blow from the pan was followed by a swift kick to his ribs. He was down for good, Kevin realized, and felt an expanding terror. There was no use in trying to get up.

He could hear the man's deep breathing as he maneuvered to deliver a sharp kick to Kevin's kidneys.

Kevin's mind was teetering; he struggled to breathe. Whoever this man was, he had to get away from him.

Just as Kevin felt a burst of energy, enough to get himself to his feet, he came face-to-face with his attacker again. Instead of fighting his way out, Kevin had no choice but to race into the bedroom and slam the door shut. He locked it with his hands shaking, breathing heavily and leaning against the doorjamb for support.

The door shook with the man's violent pounding; his profanity was piercing Kevin's ears. Kevin managed to stumble to the window, open it, and push himself onto the fire escape staircase, which he ran down unsteadily.

Kevin limped into the nearest coffee shop. He slid into a seat, put his elbows on the table to steady himself, and dropped his throbbing head into his hands. Pain permeated his gut with every breath. He looked at his right arm. Something was definitely wrong. What dimension had he been sent to? This was not a simple trip of three years into the past.

He slowly leaned forward and pressed his forehead against the cold table. His mind raced even as his pulse finally began to slow. If something in the time-stream had changed and his priego was no longer living at his apartment, how would he be able to track him down? Surely, his virtual identity would not be the same; he wouldn't be able to log into any of his priego's accounts. And if his priego wasn't exactly as he had been three years ago, even if Kevin did find his previous self, he would probably have a completely different personality. His younger self might even object to his proposal. So much for his future riches and glory.

Kevin remained hunched over the table, hoping and waiting for some kind of epiphany. Then it struck him—it was *December* 2052, not August, which meant that he traveled back in time two years and eight months, not a full three years. Kevin already moved out of that apartment. He was at the wrong building! He raised his head with a giant grin, then stood and limped out of the coffee shop.

By the time he arrived at his 'current' apartment building and went through the front lobby, Kevin's step had lightened and his pain had diminished in light of his renewed anticipation. It was a relief to be able to take the familiar key from his pocket to unlock his door.

Inside, everything was as it should be. He walked through every room to make sure his priego wasn't present, nor anyone else for that matter, and sat down at the kitchen table with pen and paper in hand. Seeing a note written in his own handwriting would surely reassure his priego.

Kevin,

I have traveled back in time to speak w/ you regarding an important matter. You may be familiar with the Aires project. During the years that separate us, it developed into commercial time travel. I took the opportunity to travel back in time three years to meet you. I didn't want to startle you with my presence until you'd had a chance to understand the circumstances. We have some exciting possibilities to work on together. I'll return at 8pm tonight.

Kevin made sure to include his signature cartoon, something he had done ever since he was a kid. He left the note on the kitchen table and walked out of the apartment.

It was almost 5:00 p.m. If his memory served him right, his prior self wouldn't be returning to the apartment until 6:00 or 7:00; he had plenty of time. He walked across the street and entered his usual pub. He found an empty seat at the bar and settled back to watch an old soccer game that he couldn't remember if he'd seen before.

When it was almost 8:00 p.m., Kevin made his way back to the familiar hallway. He stood at the end of it, looking at his apartment door, and felt a twinge of nervousness. Surely his priego would be waiting with anticipation, yet Kevin still hesitated before walking down the hall and knocking on the door.

It didn't take long for his prior self to open it. As soon as their eyes met, Kevin knew that his priego didn't have any fears or even doubts about their interaction. The two stared, inspecting each other with curiosity. Nothing appeared out of the ordinary; they looked to be the same age and were wearing similar clothes.

Kevin's priego opened the door wider and welcomed him inside. He followed himself, a bit bemused, and took a seat at the kitchen table. His priego sat across and gazed at him, a bit askance.

"Is there something wrong?" Kevin asked.

"No," his priego replied, "I'm just curious why you came to see me. Am I about to do something terrible or something completely idiotic?"

"No, not by any means," Kevin replied.

"But are you stuck here?" his priego persisted. "Are you able to return to your time?"

It was then that Kevin realized he would not be able to tell the entire truth. As he'd come to know in business, you can't trust anyone, not even yourself. Aside from becoming his own partner, he would be mirroring his priego as he lived his new life in their common time. He couldn't divulge too many details too soon.

"Yes," Kevin said, "I can return."

"Then what's wrong?" his priego repeated, leaning forward. "Something must have gone wrong, or I'm about to do something wrong for you to find it necessary to travel through time."

The conversation had only begun, but already Kevin was uncomfortable with the direction it was headed. His prior self didn't seem to be seeing an opportunity for advancement and education. Kevin had to quickly make his intentions clear.

He leaned forward as well. "I have a business proposition for you," he said. "I want us to work together. Together, we can accomplish something powerful."

His priego didn't say anything but his expression conveyed doubt.

Kevin pushed on. "With the knowledge that I have, I can make correct decisions when it comes to your career. I know the mistakes I—you—made and the opportunities I missed. Together, we can steer clear of those mistakes and be incredibly successful."

His prior self was deep in thought—no smile, no initial hint of excitement. He simply sat and stared at Kevin.

Kevin didn't know why his words weren't music to his priego's ears. "Well? What are you thinking?" he finally blurted out.

His priego *hmm*-ed and began to speak. "Well, sure, what you're saying makes sense, but does this mean that everything I do in the next three years is going to be a complete failure?"

Kevin couldn't believe what he was hearing. He was offering the chance of a lifetime to his own flesh and blood, but his own self was too consumed by the possibility of future failure to take himself seriously. What a joke.

"What are you talking about?" Kevin couldn't help sounding a bit harsh. "Nothing terrible is going to happen; you'll just continue with your life. You won't have any great successes or failures. You'll stay exactly where you are, just trying to work your way up."

His priego still seemed to have his doubts—he looked entirely unenthusiastic. "It's just sad that I have to accept that I failed at something I haven't even done yet," his prior self said. "Can't you just give me some pointers to help me fix things?"

Kevin sighed. "I could," he said, "but that wouldn't even begin to compare to what we could accomplish working together."

This time, his priego responded quickly. He sounded defensive. "I don't understand why you want to relive the last three years. Don't you just want to tell me what to do differently and then go back and reap the benefits alone in your own time? Why do we have to share everything?"

Kevin was taken aback. Not once had he thought he would have to explain his actions. It was as if he was pitching a business proposal to someone he had never met. "Listen," Kevin said, on the verge of losing his patience, "it's not that simple. Besides, there are many advantages to both of us if we pass ourselves off as one person. But never mind the details of that." He waved a hand in the air, trying to dismiss his priego's doubts. "I want to talk about how we can take over Might-Tech by redefining your mission and your role there."

His priego still looked cynical. "What's wrong with Might-Tech?" he asked. "This is a shoo-in! I don't believe it's going to fail. It can't."

"It doesn't fail," Kevin said hastily. "The problem is that it doesn't succeed, either. You think you're guaranteed millions even if it doesn't go through, but you don't realize that Might-Tech will be hit with a corporate catastrophe."

His prior self's eyes widened. "What? What on Earth could happen to ruin the company?"

Kevin rubbed his eyes, suddenly feeling tired. "An internal terrorist attack is going to kill 6,436 people next year," he said flatly. "You won't be near it, but your precious Might-Tech corporation will be destroyed in one of many explosions, and so will all your research and with it the money you've invested. The terrorists will ruin it all."

His priego's shocked expression matched his pale face. "Internal terrorists? Over 6,000 people? What happens after that?"

Kevin sighed. "Internal terrorists are what we've come to call American-born terrorists who want to aid others in committing attacks against us. As far as the explosions go, no one really knows for sure what happened…or at least the public will never be given an answer. Some say military personnel used our own weapons against us; others theorize that foreign allies united against us. No one really knows. But that's all beside the point! The point is, we have to team up to make sure that no matter what else happens, we still end up on top."

His prior self leaned back in the chair. Obviously, there were still many questions on his mind. Kevin knew that three years earlier, his Might-Tech stock was healthy; there was seemingly no chance it would fail to earn him at least several million dollars. Unless, of course, the entire company, with all of its subsidiaries was destroyed, a scenario too unbelievable for his priego to even imagine.

Kevin realized that he had found himself in a situation he hadn't anticipated. He assumed, incorrectly, that his priego would enthusiastically go along with any plan he brought forth. The priego knew Kevin too well. Why should he be trusted? How could Kevin prove he wasn't a failure in his own time and that it was more than a catastrophe that led him to travel back in time? How could he convince his prior self that he wasn't simply trying to take over his past life while reaping the benefits of his future knowledge?

Kevin sat across from himself, speechless, contemplating what to say next. Each man was a mirror image of the other, faces filled with curiosity, fear and doubt. As they sat, each had the same thought: Was he looking into the face of a friend or an enemy?

I'm trying to prove a point. When I think of it I'll let you know.

ONE FOR ALL

JARED WOKE UP ONE MORNING to find that his dream had come true. Everyone on Earth had been transformed into an exact likeness of himself. Not just one person had become his replica; everyone had. That meant that he wouldn't have to deal with stupid people any more, and there wouldn't be people who didn't care about others...and there wouldn't be ignorant people running around, either.

Jared popped his morning bagel into his hi-wave toaster and turned on the Teleportvision to get the morning news. Sure enough, there he was, the morning anchor host. What a fortunate turn of events! Not only did he look great, but there weren't any pointless news stories. No talk about what non-important, non-accomplishing 'celebrities' had done (or hadn't done) the previous day. This was real news, not the death-and-fear report. The Jared anchor talked about universal problems, world advances, and the trade status of the IPGA.

It was a great morning—worthwhile news, no loud noises coming from the apartment next to him, and no loud banging coming from outside at six in the morning to ruin his sleep. Jared dressed, brushed his teeth, and headed to work.

The morning commute was an even better surprise. He was used to bumper-to-bumper traffic all the way to the office and could only hope that he'd get up to 20 kilometers an hour on the freeway. But today, Jared was able to drive a constant 30 kph to work. All the drivers didn't dilly-dally in traffic, not even for a second, and they didn't cut from lane to lane, either. No right turns from middle lanes, no sudden stopping to gawk at something on the other side of the road, no driving under the speed limit. Hundreds and hundreds of compact, fuel-efficient cars, without a single SUV or large vehicle on the road. What a beautiful sight!

Jared actually got to work early for a change. Tomorrow, he realized, he'd be able to linger at his apartment for another 20 minutes before getting on the road. He was greeted kindly by himself (the receptionist in the lobby), and everyone in the elevator seemed happy to be sharing the small space.

He exited at his floor, entered room 521A, and gazed at the beauty of the cubicles, all perfectly aligned and without clutter. Everyone's cubicle was neat and orderly. Best of all, there was no constant noise, just quiet, cheerful, and peaceful employees hard at work.

Jared took a seat at his desk and turned on his computer. Ah, the beauty of it all. The entire world had gone Jared. No more misinformative, non-intelligent, or pointlessly uncreative programs on Teleportvision. No more gossip magazines (or any gossip-filled news, for that matter), and no more crime. Poverty, drugs, war, ignorance, intolerance, and inconsistency would be things of the past.

Jared stood up and took another look around the office. Everyone was handsome and just as neat and clean as he was. Of course they would be; they were all Jared.

He sat back down at his desk and opened the mid-May report on his computer and found something particularly shocking—an error message.

"Restart your computer," popped up on his screen. Jared stared; he'd never gotten a message like that before. What was the problem? He was just opening a file.

He restarted his computer and waited impatiently for it to reboot. The process took much longer than usual. "Damn," he murmured.

A head quickly popped up from behind the cubicle wall. "What seems to be the matter, J?" his duplicate asked.

"My computer told me to restart, which it never does, and now it's taking forever to reboot," Jared complained.

The man looked back at him with a deadpan expression. "You serious?" the man asked. "Well, hey, read the manual, and see if you can improve it." The man disappeared behind the cubicle.

Jared gazed back at the screen, which still seemed to be stuck. 'Read the manual?' he thought. He pawed through his desk, looking for anything that would prove helpful, and eventually found the drawer full of thick paperbound books.

He debated which manual to examine first. The five of them were spread out on Jared's desk with each edge lined up exactly with the next one. 'Computer Manual,' one read, then 'Open

Resources,' 'Wasted Resources,' 'Misguided Resources,' and 'Daily Routine.'

What information could these manuals possibly contain? Jared impulsively grabbed the 'Misguided Resources' manual and opened it to the first page: 'Misguided Resources, edition 48.3.4, published January 21, 2243.' That was followed by the publishing dates of the 25 most recent updates, each one dated within four months of the next.

Jared skipped over a few pages and found a detailed paragraph explaining the increasing amount of homelessness in society and the number of less-than-desirable current jobs. 'More of us are resorting to living on the streets at the same rate that the demand for our less-privileged jobs is increasing. Some of us have been lucky enough to land a creative position or an organizational/administration job, but others have not been as fortunate. People have no interest in pursuing work in construction, janitorial services, or anything that involves filth.'

Jared looked down at his overflowing trash can. Surely someone should have emptied it by now. He peeked his head around to his other self working in the cubicle next to him. "Hey, where is the janitor to take out my trash?"

The man burst out laughing. "Good one." He wiped his eyes and continued working.

Jared looked back at his computer, which was still trying to reboot. "How long has it been since we last had a janitor in this office?" Jared asked.

The man stopped typing at his computer. "The last janitor?" he began slowly. "That must have been…two years ago? Forget what his wage was, but his daily responsibilities sure beat ours. If only one of us was willing to be the janitor, it would all work out!

But the job would have to come with a damn high salary for any of us to be willing to resort to janitorial work."

Jared slouched back down in his seat and decided to take a look at the computer manual to try and understand why his computer was refusing to boot up. As he paged through the specs in the manual, to his surprise, he found that because everyone possessed the same enthusiasm and level of intelligence when it came to computer design and microprocessing, no extraordinary advances in technology had been made. In fact, the manual asked that all citizens thoroughly read through it in an attempt to spark much-needed new ideas.

"We all think alike and we are all the same," he read, "but by reading and understanding the contents of this manual, we can evolve as a species rather than individually." Jared was baffled at the amount of non-computer information in the manual. Instead of explaining how to *use* the computer, it explained how the computer worked. Repair, cleaning, and maintenance services would be impossible because that kind of expertise apparently no longer existed.

Jared closed the book after having read a mere four pages (out of 824). Looking back at his desk, he noticed that he hadn't looked inside the 'Open Resources,' 'Wasted Resources,' or 'Daily Routine' manuals. Considering that each was nearly as thick as the others and having already grown tired of the little he had already read, Jared decided not to continue reading.

Work was not an option at the moment since his computer was still struggling, so he stood and walked toward the door.

"Where you off to?" a familiar voice asked. Jared turned around to find his next-cubicle-over duplicate peering over at him.

"Computer is still loading, so I'm going for a walk," Jared replied.

He exited the building and walked down the street. It was much more pleasant than it had been the day before. No car horns sounded, and there were twice as many public vehicles on the streets. The air was cleaner, and it seemed like there was more blue sky above and green trees surrounding him. Everything around him was functioning like an orderly machine, and everyone he saw looked exactly like him—properly groomed and tidy. What bliss.

It occurred to him when he was walking past a grocery store— Yoo-Hoo Galactic, his favorite drink that was a rarity in any store. If the manager, the owner, and all the employees were duplicates of himself, surely the drink would be in stock and readily available.

Jared rushed into the store and hurried toward the drink aisle. Sure enough, it was there, bright and shiny in its yellow packaging, standing prouder than any other drink in sight.

Jared was just grabbing a large bottle when he heard "Hey!" coming from right next to him.

He jumped, not expecting anyone to be so close. He turned to find another ones of his doubles standing just a foot away. "Yes?" Jared asked.

"I'm low on cash today. Can you buy me one of those?" Jared couldn't believe what he was hearing! Just *buy* it for him? Why would the man think he would do that?

Jared paused. "Uhhhhhh…" he stalled.

The man stared at him. "Is there a problem? I don't need 50 of them, just one."

Jared still couldn't believe what he was hearing. "You have a credit card, right?"

"Well, yeah, but I'm not gonna use it for one drink." He turned, grabbed a drink, and started walking toward the front of the store. "Come on!" the man said, waving his arm for Jared to follow.

The man kept walking, but Jared didn't move an inch. Was the man joking? He sidled over to another aisle, then snuck up to the front check-out lanes.

The man turned around and walked back into the drink aisle, obviously looking for him. Jared whipped out his wallet and quickly paid for his own drink, then quickly snatched his change. He was heading for the door when he heard the voice again. "Hey! HEY!"

This time, the man was angry. "What are you doing?" he yelled, as he jogged to catch up with Jared. He stopped him in the middle of the sidewalk.

"What do you want?" Jared asked impatiently.

The man didn't seem to be in a mood for games. "I just wanted a simple thing. One simple lousy drink. You can't even do that for me? I mean, I AM you, for crying out loud. Thanks for your continued support in making this a better place!"

The man finished his short tirade, spit into Jared's face, and walked away.

Outside an antique store, Bobby rubbed a lamp with the utmost concern. Seconds later, a beautiful female genie emerged from the spout and floated next to him.

"You have three wishes," she said.

A lover of animals, Bobby said, "My first wish is to be able to transform into any animal that I want."

The genie raised her hands and clapped them together. "Granted," she said.

Bobby smiled, closed his eyes, and tilted his head back ever so slightly. His body began to quiver and melt. Suddenly, his body disappeared; his clothes fell to the ground. Movement from underneath the fallen clothes revealed a cat.

Unfortunately, along with his physical alteration, his intelligence changed, too—he was now a cat in mind as well as in body, and he no longer had any concept of who he was. Bobby ran to and fro as cats tend to do…but his antics ended abruptly when he was hit and killed by an oncoming car.

The Garbage Man

FRED LANGSTER NEVER MEANT for his life to turn out this way—sad, quiet, and alone. But he has brought it all upon himself, he believes.

Years and years ago, during his time at the academy, his goals had been like anyone else's, but there just wasn't room for everyone to get everywhere they wanted to go. Fred is not a risk-taker nor an optimist; if anything, he is a bit apathetic.

It doesn't come as a shock, then, that when former fellow classmates hear about Fred's current occupation, they nod without surprise. In their eyes, he was always destined to be a garbage man.

It's not the job that causes his underlying frustration, though, it is the lack of human interaction and appreciation for his work and himself as a person. His life of solitude has imprisoned him in an everyday job every day of the year.

But clinical depression is not something that affects Fred; he remains content with his place in society. Sure, he'd missed some opportunities (he'd once dreamt of working for the Intergalactic Planetary Governance Alliance, the desired employer of many of his academy classmates), but Fred understands that everyone can't have it all. If he were living his dream, after all, someone else would be stuck living in his shoes, disposing of other people's garbage party after party, picking up and mopping up the remnants of more important people's lives.

Things aren't looking good…in fact, things haven't looked good for 25 years, not that Fred has ever bothered to do anything about that. Desire for change has always been met with an equal level of lethargy on his part.

Fred enters the control room of the ship and collects the bags of garbage from the trash receptacles. Neither the captain nor the co-pilots greet him. It's as though he is an insignificant entity. They don't pay any attention to him at all. If he could have been at least a freelance pilot, his self-image would surely be better. Whether you call it luck, fate, or karma, garbage is where Fred Langster is meant to be. People only respond to him when they need to dispose of unwanted items.

Another day passes, and Fred's favorite time of the day approaches: dinner, relaxation, some Teleportvision, and sleep. After enjoying the first three things, he climbs his loft onto his mattress. He has no obligations for the next eight hours…bliss. He cherishes those few seconds of thought-less consciousness he has before he slips into a night of dreams.

Six hours pass, the alarm sounds with a deafening tone, and Fred awakens to begin a new day. His eyes open grudgingly; he'd rather stay in peaceful slumber.

"I'm up!" he yells. The alarm quickly shuts off. "Get me some coffee," he adds. The tall, angular machine on the opposite side of his confined space starts to rumble and steam. The coffee will be ready in three minutes, he knows.

Sitting up in his bed, he pauses and for the first time seriously contemplates how sad he has become. How long, he wonders, does it take for routine to become imprisonment? But no sense in thinking about that. It's time to get ready for work.

Spray disinfectant and rag in hand, Fred makes his early rounds on the ship. He starts by cleaning the side windows, which he believes is the most important part of his job. When customers reach a high level in society, high enough to cruise on The Chronicle, a weekly intellectual vacation cruise, they should always have a clear view of the stars. In the distance, Fred notices the green shine of the planet Jasper. It will be another three weeks before The Chronicle lands on the green planet for its two-month maintenance check. When it does, Fred will have one of his six opportunities a year to take half a day and explore this fascinating world.

As he reaches the middle of the long line of windows, Fred catches a glimpse of a couple walking toward him. The man is dressed in a well-fitted black tuxedo, and the woman is in an elegant dress that shines more brightly as she approaches the light.

Fred stops for a second to gaze at their happiness. Here is a couple that has not only found happiness and love, but has kept them alive. He can tell they're deeply in love by the way they walk so closely next to each other, hand in hand.

This ship houses humanity's greatest minds, people who have been awarded the equivalent of Nobel or Pulitzer Prizes. Only the elite of interplanetary society fly on The Chronicle, the ship that has become known as the home of tomorrow's thoughts, innovations, and dreams.

When the man notices Fred's quiet stare, he says hello.

Fred is confused. No one has ever said hello to him at random before. "Hello," he responds slowly.

The couple continues to walk on, eventually disappearing around the corner. Fred continues to wash the windows that separate him from deep space.

About the Illustrator

A NATIVE OF PUERTO RICO, ANTONIO DELEO graduated from The School of the Art Institute of Chicago, concentrating in performance and children's book illustration. He resides in San Juan, working as an illustrator and as an actor for TV, film, and radio. He is currently illustrating a series of young adult books about surgical experiments involving children and is developing a book titled *From Winter's Night: A Tale of the Snowflake*. Antonio enjoys skipping stones, growing crab apples, and coming up with different ways to sing 'Oklahoma.'